Praise for *At the Waterline*

Brian is a talent, all right. Here's a marvelous floating tribe of drifters and soul catchers, written with zest and grace at the waterline. While on board, wear a life jacket.
—Robin Cody, author of *Ricochet River* and
Voyage of a Summer Sun

At the Waterline is one of those books that hooks you on the first page but then slows down to reel you in. As the seemingly mundane events unfurl in the lives of an eccentric collection of river dwellers, Friesen's novel gradually reveals a great truth: that every life—every life—hides remarkable drama and overpowering tragedy.
—Molly Gloss, author of *The Jump-Off Creek*
and *The Hearts of Horses*

Reading Brian K. Friesen's *At the Waterline* is like witnessing a musical story performed at the piano for two hands—the baseline rhythm of river, current, wind, season, island, and boat all playing against the melodic shenanigans of the human: love, tragedy, secrets, the slow repair of a life, gruff age against brash youth, and the mysterious search for some hints of harmony through it all. Before reading the book I'd always wanted to live "on the water." Now I have.
—Kim Stafford, author of *100 Tricks Every Boy
Can Do: How My Brother Disappeared*

A quick and enjoyable read, especially for someone like myself who lived aboard for close to four decades. Friesen understands the dynamics of living on land and living afloat, and the commitment that's required when a home is not a house. "You can't stand with one foot on a dock and another on a boat for long," he writes early in the story. While his characters lead dramatic lives, it's the sensations of ordinary living aboard that captured me most:

how it feels and sounds inside a boat, the way a passing outboard engine "filled the small room with its soft hum and then faded downstream," how a passing wake takes time to reach you from across the water. The scenes of marina life ring true, from the helter-skelter arrangement of yachts, cabin cruisers, converted barges, and derelict boats, to the way people from every social and economic background—underclass to high privilege—find a balance that doesn't exist in most land-bound neighborhoods. "It doesn't matter how big or fancy your boat is," says Jack, the crusty self-appointed harbormaster. "Life on the water just isn't possible unless you're hanging on to something else"—a statement that applies as much to the people on the dock as it does to lines and cleats.

—Migael Scherer, author of *A Cruising Guide to Puget Sound* and *Sailing to Simplicity: Life Lessons Learned at Sea*

At the Waterline

At the Waterline

Stories from the Columbia River

Brian K. Friesen

Ooligan
PRESS

Portland, Oregon

At the Waterline

© 2017 Brian K. Friesen

ISBN 13: 978–1-932010–92-3

Ooligan Press
Portland State University
Post Office Box 751, Portland, Oregon 97207
503.725.9748
ooligan@ooliganpress.pdx.edu
www.ooliganpress.pdx.edu

Library of Congress Cataloging-in-Publication Data
CIP data available on request

Cover design by Andrea McDonald
Interior design by Alyssa Hanchar
Illustrations by Leigh Thomas and Riley Pittenger

William Stafford, excerpt from "Grace Abounding" from *Even in Quiet Places*. Copyright © 1996 by The Estate of William Stafford. Reprinted with the permission of The Permissions Company, Inc., on behalf of Confluence Press, www.confluencepress.com.

References to website URLs were accurate at the time of writing. Neither the author nor Ooligan Press is responsible for URLs that have changed or expired since the manuscript was prepared.

Printed in the United States of America

For Larissa, George, and Hanny-Bo

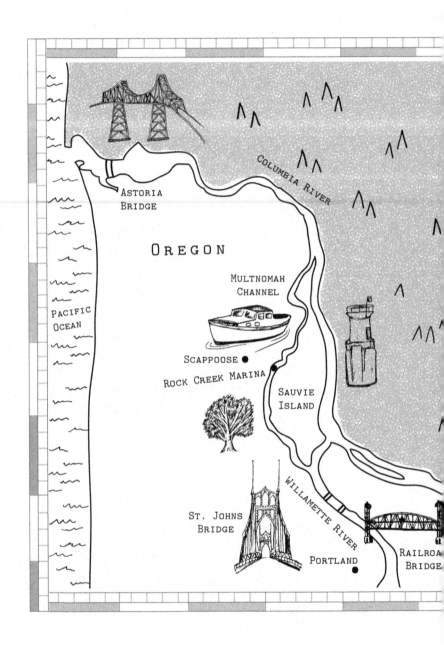

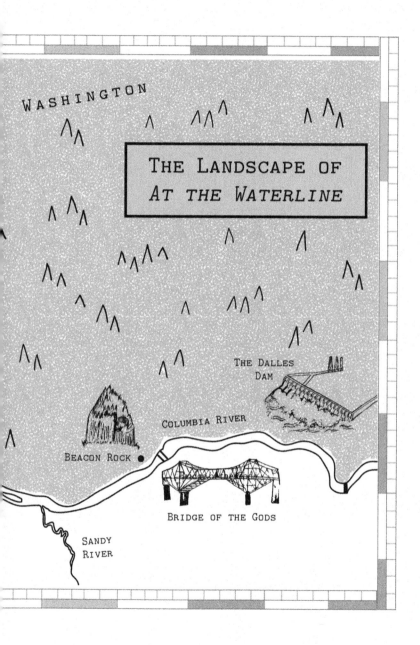

WASHINGTON

THE LANDSCAPE OF
AT THE WATERLINE

THE DALLES
DAM

COLUMBIA RIVER

BEACON ROCK •

BRIDGE OF THE GODS

SANDY
RIVER

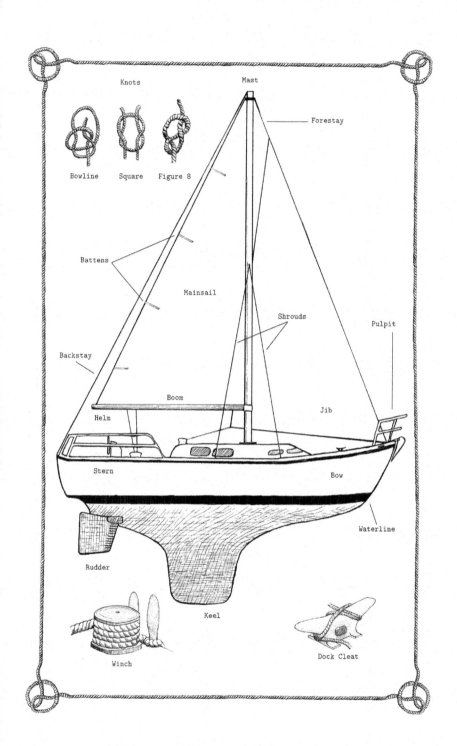

Knots

Mast

Forestay

Bowline   Square   Figure 8

Battens

Mainsail

Shrouds

Pulpit

Backstay

Boom

Jib

Helm

Stern

Bow

Waterline

Rudder

Keel

Winch

Dock Cleat

One version of the story told along the Columbia River takes place in the early 1970s. A young man in his late teens had a death wish and tried to launch off Hayden Island at a hundred miles per hour on a motorcycle, sailing over the river with the vague but supposedly calculated plan to land on a wide stack of hay bales on the Washington shore. Afternoon wind pushed him straight down into the water, where the spangles and flags dangling from his leather outfit tangled with the handlebars and pulled him to the river bottom; the current carried him far enough downstream they never found the motorcycle—or the body that had been fused to it—until, over the years, it eventually became a knotted mass of twisted metal and bones. Salmon would find shelter there. Inside the exhaust pipes. Inside the ribcage. Inside the skull. Of course, this scenario is highly unlikely: a version that emerged when "Evel" Knievel and his many impersonators were all the rage.

An older version of the story, according to local Oregonian lore, involves a train carrying a shipment of early motorized bikes and crossing the river on its way to Seattle for a showcase. A young thief, who had stolen away on the train, unstrapped one of the bikes and tried to ride it off the flatbed car as it crossed the Interstate Bridge. A gust of wind blew him off balance, and he and the motorcycle sailed over the edge. The straps from the flatbed wound into the bike's rear wheel and wrapped him tightly to the warming, spluttering machine on his way down to the water. Currents eddied in his lungs, in his ears, played in his hair. Wilder currents wore the flesh off his bones.

By the turn of the twenty-first century, the story featured a young man who had strapped his motorcycle to the shrouds of his sailboat so wherever he made landfall, he could ride into an unfamiliar sunset. Some say he committed suicide by riding off the boat deck and into the river. Others say he tried to jump the bike from his sailboat onto another nearby. They say he would have made too, if not for the wind that picks up most afternoons on the river.

Most versions of the tale carry a message about taunting the gods who made the Columbia and who still blow wind across it. The bones of the tale are always there in the telling, but details of the scene vary according to the times and trends in which they are told. One consistent theme is the foolish delinquent who defies the laws of nature and society—the adrenaline-fueled Icarus of each era, always ending in the depths as a set of bones on a bike. Judgement for transgressing boundaries. Punishment for too much passion.

The wind always finds its way through the cracks and into the story. Wind plays at the surface, flowing against the current, whipping the water into waves, creating the appearance of a river returning upstream. If you raise a sheet of canvas into the air to catch some of that wind, you'll throw yourself at the mercy of forces you cannot predict but might eventually learn to read.

Prelude

On a windy night in the late summer, Chad and his wife, Abby, were sailing up the Willamette River toward downtown Portland, where they planned to moor for the weekend on the transient docks, when Chad wrecked their sailboat and nearly killed Abby in the process.

Abby was down in the cabin talking on her cell phone to her parents in hushed tones. Chad was at the helm, steering with the tiller balanced between his knees while keeping tension on the three lines he held in his hands. The winds were strong—the port jib sheet got hung up in the bow pulpit, and the jib halyard caught on something at the top of the mast so the sail was stuck and catching too much wind at the wrong angle. The wind began to spin the boat around in circles no matter where Chad tried to point the bow. Even against the river current, the wind was pushing the vessel downwind, toward a low-hanging railroad bridge.

Abby climbed up the steps from inside the boat, struggling for balance, and called out over the rush of wind, "What the heck are you doing?"

"Abby, please, I've got to get the engine going. Can you grab the tiller?" Chad turned the key near the throttle, and the starter whirred over and over. The engine wouldn't turn. The starter was slowing down.

"Here!" shouted Chad. "Grab the tiller and swish it back and forth. We've got to get the boat moving forward in the water so we can stop spinning."

Abby nodded and grabbed the long shaft of wood that attached to the rudder.

Chad turned the key. The starter wound once, slowly, and came to a stop. He turned the key again. Nothing.

The horizon spun by. He turned his head to follow it in the dark. The railroad bridge drew nearer.

He rested a hand on Abby's shoulder and spoke into her ear. His voice was too loud and too close—she recoiled.

"Sorry," he said, and tried again, lowering his voice. "I'm going to get on the CB radio and try to get ahold of the bridge operator to tell him to raise the bridge."

"The mast is too tall, isn't it?" she asked.

Chad shook his head. "No." He rubbed her shoulder lightly. "We'll be alright." Hopping down into the cabin, he switched on the radio and rolled the volume dial up and down. He pressed the receiver button rapidly several times. No sound. He spoke into the receiver. "Burlington Northern Railroad Bridge five point one, this is the sailing vessel approaching from downstream." He let go of the receiver button. Nothing. Of course. The batteries were dead now. He'd worn them down trying to get the engine started.

Chad murmured, "Well, we're screwed."

He tried the receiver again. Maybe there was just enough power for him to be heard even though he couldn't hear anything on the line. It was stupid, he knew, but he pressed the receiver button and spoke anyway. "Railroad Bridge, if you can hear me, I'm requesting that you raise the bridge span. We're adrift, and we're fucked. Do you read me? Fucked!" Chad let the receiver drop to the cabin floor. He looked at Abby through the hatch door to see if she had maybe heard what he was saying, but she was looking toward the bow and manning the tiller. Abby wasn't too fond of cussing. The wind rippled over her light jacket and through her hair as she leaned back and forth to keep her balance.

Chad stepped up onto the deck and said, "No radio. The battery's dead."

She tilted her face toward the sky. Chad wasn't sure if she was looking up at the bridge or rolling her eyes in exasperation. Then she said, "We might as well try to signal the bridge with a flashlight."

"Wait! Yeah, there you go. That might actually work. I'll go find it. And the air horn too."

By the time he'd rummaged both out of a storage box in the cabin and climbed back up on deck, he could see the bridge's operations booth on one of the towers. A light was on in the window. Chad shook the pressurized can and pressed down several times. The air horn pierced the wind in sharp blasts. He aimed the flashlight beam at the window above and pressed the horn several more times. A dark form appeared in the window then faded from view.

A deeper horn from the bridge blared through the air and then grew silent. Orange lights came on, blinking at track level. That was when Chad saw the train rolling slowly out onto the bridge, its bright beam of light illuminating the bridge trusses. They were close enough now for Chad to see the sharp, round shadows of bolts on the bridge supports high above them. The bridge didn't rise. More horns clamored, relentless and shrill. Train brakes screeched.

But it was too late. The top of the mast struck the bridge deck. Rigging snapped, and the mast moaned and buckled backward, falling toward the cockpit where Abby stood. Chad dove headfirst through the hatch and into the belly of the boat. His arm crunched painfully on the cabin floor. Lines and rigging swished through the air outside, and the mast crashed onto the deck. When Chad pushed himself up and looked out the smashed hole of the hatch, he saw Abby. Her eyes were closed. Half her body was pinned under the mast.

Chad half-crawled, half-climbed out of the cabin with his good arm and tried lifting the mast off her with one arm. It didn't budge.

"No! No! No!" he yelled over and over. "You motherfucker! Please, God, please!"

He tried getting his good shoulder under the mast and pushing upward with his legs. He tried over and over again, facing away from Abby, trying to lift and push and lean hard and pull and lift so that he wouldn't have to look at her.

A couple hundred yards before the sailboat would have drifted into the St. Johns Bridge downstream, a large rescue boat arrived with its red lights spinning. Abby was airlifted from the middle of the river by helicopter and taken to the hospital. Another Coast Guard boat towed what was left of the *Arctic Loon* to a boatyard that would buy it from Chad for salvage.

Later, as the sun rose, Chad arrived at the hospital. The doctors made sure he could see Abby when she regained consciousness, but her parents were there and didn't want to be in the emergency room with him. They had always been reticent in Chad's presence, which he'd attributed to their stolid religiosity. Up until now—now that Abby's arm and her chest and her pelvis were all crushed. Chad lost track of how many fractures there were as the doctors listed them. He didn't know there were so many ribs in a body to be crushed.

For days after the accident, over the course of several surgeries, her parents pushed past him to hear what the surgeons had to say, nudged him out of the way to be at her side, and crowded him out of the circle of relatives that made a ring around her bed. She was asleep most of the time, but when her eyes were open, she'd only briefly meet his gaze. She spoke little, and when she did, it was to her parents.

Chad slept on a bench just outside Abby's room or pretended to sleep while her parents were there. He tried to sleep sitting up, couldn't, then tried laying on his side, balancing his broken arm in its sling to keep it from moving or sliding downward. He sat by Abby's side and held her hand and spoke to her when her parents weren't there. "It's alright," she said. "I should have been helping you more. I let you do more work than one person could do. So don't blame yourself." But of course he blamed himself.

Her parents made arrangements without him knowing. After two weeks, Abby went straight from the hospital back to living with them. With no more hospital benches or chairs to sleep on, and no home left to return to, Chad camped out in his Volvo in front of her parents' house. He would knock at the door sometimes, and sometimes Abby's mother would answer and let him in for a few minutes. Sometimes no one came to the door, even though their cars were there in the driveway. After a while, her mother began to call the police, standing in the front window with one hand on her hip, and the police would come and ask Chad to leave the area. The last time he returned and knocked on their door, Abby's father, who never once met Chad's eye after the accident, wheeled her out onto their front porch so Chad could sign papers and say goodbye. The doctors thought that she would mostly recover, with about 75 percent of her upper-body mobility. Chad never really witnessed the full extent of the damage. "The damage you've done," her mother said during that final visit. He continued to call and plead, but Abby's phone number eventually changed. It was over.

Chad's parents divorced when he was very young. He had no memory of the three of them together as a family. During grade school, Chad lived much of the time with his grandparents on his father's side of the family. He remembered his grandfather the best. During World War II his grandfather had joined the Merchant Marines rather than fighting directly in the war. Chad's father, on the other hand, hoped for a war in which to fight, so he "went all the way," as he put it, and joined the US Navy.

Grandpa read stories to Chad at bedtime, mostly maritime fiction. Using different voices for different characters, he read about Horatio Hornblower, Jack Aubrey, and young Jim Hawkins. They talked about sailing together when Chad was older. Grandpa took Chad to local Sea Scout meetings and taught him to tie dozens of knots. They climbed onto boats that were safely secured to the dock at the Coast Guard station nearby. They studied navigation rules, points of sail, and learned the difference between port and starboard, forward and aft. They practiced calling out commands for tacking, jibing, casting off, and making sail adjustments. Chad was just about to earn his knots badge when his grandfather had a stroke. It was the first of many in the few months before he passed away.

After his grandfather's death, Chad moved between his mother's house and his grandmother's, where his dad moved after Grandpa's death. During his senior year of high school, Chad's grandmother passed away—he almost didn't graduate. It became clear Chad wasn't going to follow his father's desire and join the Navy, and neither was he about to dive into college full time as his mother had hoped. That summer, his father sold the old house. Both Chad's parents moved from Oregon to different states. Chad stayed and bought a sailboat.

He used the college money his mom had saved for him to buy a used, thirty-foot, fin-keeled Cascade with the name *Arctic Loon* painted on the stern. When they were first dating, Abby visited him on the boat, docked at a marina on Hayden Island, about ten miles north of downtown Portland on the Columbia. She moved aboard after they were married.

Excited to share their life on the water with friends, Chad and Abby entertained guests. They took friends out cruising on the river, though they had little actual experience in sailing. Even on a clear day, an hour of sailing into the wind left them red in the face, deaf in both ears, and blind and itchy in both eyes. And cold. And not talking to each other. They learned what lines not to hold onto at certain times by always grabbing the wrong ones. The wind ripped lines from their hands, leaving them rope-burnt and bleeding. They took their friends out for sailing trips only to find that the wind wasn't blowing. On the rare occasion there was wind—and they thought it was a good day to die—they raised a sail or two. If friends were with them on those days, then going sailing became a lot like shouting in-comprehensible instructions in a foreign language while float-ing helplessly downstream. Lines got caught or wound up. Sails sank into the water. The engine flooded, and they drifted among other boats and barges until the pistons dried out. "Does sailing always go like this?" was a question asked more than once on the *Arctic Loon.* Abby's routine answer was "yes, but only when you are sailing with us."

After a few months, Chad and Abby were alone with each other, having run out of friends with whom to share their in-creasingly dubious adventure. It might have been a romantic ex-istence, if both of them thrived on challenges and loved living on the river, with no friends and no money but hours to spend mak-ing sense of all the lines incessantly wound into a quagmire of knots. Not to mention the hundred other things wrong with the boat and the challenge of sleeping with all the violent rocking and jostling and banging of hundreds of lines against hundreds of masts outside the main cabin. And the bugs. And the moist, moldy environment. And allergies.

Halfway through their second summer on the water, Abby slowly backed away from sailing. She stopped handling ropes and lines, even when Chad was scrambling to handle four or five of them at once. And she gravitated back toward land in subtle ways. Usually the two of them used the showers that had recently been installed on the dock while they ran their laundry in the small coin-op laun-dry room separating the men's showers from the women's. The showers were only fifty or so steps away from their boat. But Abby started showering up on land where the marina had another facil-ity next to a workout room. It took five minutes to get there. She shrugged her shoulders when Chad asked why she'd started prefer-ring that one. Her new habit of shrugging her shoulders communi-cated more than either of them were willing to say out loud.

In the fall after his divorce from Abby, Chad started college. His money had mostly been sunk into the sailboat, but there was just enough left to salvage something out of the wreck of his life. He got into student housing at a state university and waited for student loans to kick in.

He studied literature and folklore and history and writing. He talked with professors after class. He roamed far and wide in academic research. He thought maybe he could learn to write his way out of his loss and confusion and loneliness. But before and after class he had little to say to fellow students. He learned and remembered the first names of only four other students in four years. He sat alone every night at the McMenamins one block from campus and drank the coffee a friendly bartender spiked for him. He lived from quarter to quarter on student loans. He had trouble formulating plans for the future.

Four years later, in June of 2001, several officious-looking robed men whom he had never met handed him a diploma and shook his hand. He found himself unemployed and about to lose his dorm room. He was no longer a student. He was no longer anyone's husband. The four people whose names he knew moved away. He found Portland-area docks to sit on, sometimes fishing, sometimes taking on odd jobs like washing and waxing boats, cleaning storage closets at marinas, or rewiring the lights at the top of someone's mast. He dropped resumes off at a dozen marinas up and down the Columbia, earned what he could through the fall, and paid his old roommate to keep a space for him in the dorm room.

Just before campus emptied for the Thanksgiving holiday, he got a call from a marina on the Multnomah Channel. He'd gotten a job. A full-time job at Rock Creek Marina, about half an hour northwest of the Portland metro area by car. He'd work in the floating office/fuel dock as an assistant to the marina's manager, Rick. All he needed was to find somewhere close to the marina to live.

On one of his last days on campus, he drained his final cup of spiked coffee at the familiar bar and then drove, with whiskey humming in his brain, upstream along the Columbia, back to the boatyard where he had sold the *Arctic Loon*, to bid farewell to any recognizable pieces of his former home. The owner of the boatyard was relatively new and didn't remember there being a sailboat with that name anywhere on the property, but he let Chad wander through the yard to look at the old sailboat hulls.

Chad found several sailboats in a far corner of the lot, half-buried under a spray of blackberry vines. The *Loon* was there, barely recognizable apart from the mangled fiberglass of the stern. He ran his hand over the dry, faded blue hull. At the lowest point, just above where the keel curved sharply downward, was a perfectly round hole about the size of a fist. He peered at the dark hole and wondered how far it reached into the boat. Someone had intentionally bored through the hull. "What the hell?"

He found a boatyard ladder and climbed aboard. The mast, rent in two, had been lashed to the deck. The boat's name on the crushed stern pulpit appeared to read, in faded letters, "AR T OON." Chad walked the deck carefully in case there were other breaches in the hull, but the deck was surprisingly sound. Several of the thin windows had been removed, as well as the cabin doors. He stepped into the dim light of the cabin and fell all the way to the fiberglass floor below, scraping his shins on the door opening and landing on his side, crying out loud as the air rushed from his lungs. He rolled on the floor moaning for a minute until his breathing returned to normal and then checked his arms and legs. No broken bones. Some blood on his shins. Nothing too serious. He gazed up at the first few evening stars shining through the hatch. The wood stairs were gone. He pushed himself to his feet and felt his way around the cabin. All the salvageable wood had been removed: the teak stairs, the walnut wood floor, the oak chart table. The shelves and cupboards. The bulkheads were gone. All the seat cushions and foam mattresses were gone. Surprisingly, the sinks, the toilet, and most of the plumbing were still there. There were still a couple of laminate countertops and shelves. His reflection in the mirror above the bathroom sink startled him when he walked by.

The round hole in the bottom of the boat peered up at him from the foot-deep depression at the center of the cabin floor. The hole had been drilled at a low point in the bilge, and now he understood why. With the windows and the hatch doors removed, the inside cabin was exposed to frequent rains. Rather than letting the boat slowly fill with water, someone had drilled out a crude drain spout. "What a waste," he said, his voice sounding hollow and unfamiliar in the small space.

Chad rummaged through the few remaining drawers in a partially removed dresser. Among broken pencils and mildewed maps, he found the faded blue boat title. Surely they hadn't overlooked this? He saw his name still listed as the seller but the buyer line was empty. Either they hadn't bothered to transfer the title over or they hadn't even known it was there.

This was still his boat.

Abby had let him take care of the "boat stuff": the financing, the permits, and the insurance. He supposed that the boat was still sort of partly hers, in spirit if not legally or financially. Almost nothing remained of the boat that had been their home. How much of this place had Abby actually ever settled into and claimed as hers? As theirs? With his head tilted slightly, he looked around and wondered. How much had she shared his naïve boating interests and how much had she merely put up with them?

He looked at the ceiling and the holes where windows used to be. A roof that could be patched was better than the total lack of a roof. All he really needed was a tarp to tie over the deck topside, and maybe he could sleep here while he took a little more time to find an apartment.

Their tiny microwave, kitchen utensils, and dish sets—all of them wedding gifts—were gone. The gimballed stove and oven were gone, but the hundred-gallon water tank that supplied the faucets was still there. He tried the galley faucet and wasn't surprised when nothing came out. No electricity to run the electric pump in the cabinet under the sink. That made sense; he hadn't seen a power cord plugged into the outlet up on deck, and when he checked the storage lockers under the cabin benches, he saw that the boat's deep-cycle batteries were gone. That meant no lights, no heater, no power for the small fridge and freezer. He found one of the manual pump handles in a galley drawer. Maybe he could still pump water through one of the faucets that way. He screwed it into the slot beside the large galley sink and cranked the handle up and down. Water splashed into the sink in short bursts with each pump.

Chad talked to the boatyard's owner, who said Chad would be doing him a favor by getting rid of the hull for him. He agreed to tow the sailboat someplace on land close by and threw the old jack stands into the deal. After some coaxing, Rick at Rock Creek agreed to Chad's strange living accommodations. Chad had the landlocked sailboat towed to a mostly empty graveled area at the edge of the marina's parking lot.

Chad cashed his final student loan check, picked up an old wooden ladder and a few furnishings and appliances from a nearby thrift store, plus a couple hundred feet of extension cords, and he was in business. He couldn't bring himself to sleep in the forward cabin, where he and Abby used to sleep, so he settled down in the aft cabin instead. At night, his body sensed a rocking motion that wasn't there. He closed his eyes and could almost hear the water lapping against the hull.

During the day, he operated the pumps at the marina fuel dock half the time, and the other half he sat at a desk behind the register counter of the small floating store that doubled as the marina office. He worked each day fueling up boats, selling food and supplies, walking ramps and docks and floating platforms, and delivering mail to tenants. He was there to work but also to watch, to listen, to learn, and to become a student of the river.

Whatever the water touched was riparian: that moist layer of air and rich earth along the shore was an Eden for many forms of life. Some drowned in a daily flood, while those that knew how, thrived. There was something riparian too about the people who spent most of their time on the water. Those whose language and equilibrium had been dictated by the elements around them. Who'd learned to hang on in the ever-shifting swell and drift of water under their feet. Contrast and contradictions abounded for those who had learned to meander despite limited space or to be still in the midst of all that rocking. Chad wanted to belong to a place and to a people, to face some of his own failures and learn from them, to be useful, helpful, and maybe even peaceful.

Part I

One

Chad watched as the hunched elderly man tied off his skiff in front of the fuel dock and marched stiffly toward the sliding glass door. Chad had seen him float by the fuel dock on his skiff during his first couple days on the job, but the man hadn't stopped by until now. The small boat—a raft, really, made of plywood layered over more wood layered over Styrofoam—was flat and rectangular, some six feet across and ten feet long. The edges were worn, the corners slightly dinged. It was hard to tell the difference between bow and stern when it was moored unless you saw the small two-stroke outboard hanging into the water on one side or saw the stern-side door of the thin phone-booth-shaped pilothouse mounted smack dab in the middle of the deck. While piloting, the old man stood half in the pilothouse and half out in the weather. One hand gripped a thin, black steering wheel and the other rested on the throttle. His small dog, a black miniature pinscher, raced back and forth from the bow to the stern. On windy days, the water washed over the bow and the man seemed to bob along the river in an upright casket with windows.

The old man reached for the door handle. The dog wandered around the side of the building.

"Skookum, get back here, you little shit stain. You'd better stick that fucking tail between your legs. Get over here!"

He enunciated his cuss words perfectly. No slurring. The consonants he spat out struck the air like the clacking of a typewriter. He barely moved above the waist; his neck and back hunched forward so his face bent toward the ground. He turned with his feet and looked up at Chad through his eyebrows. He seemed to face everything and everyone head on.

"I'm Jack," he said. He shook Chad's hand firmly—hard enough that Chad's eyes squinted a little.

"So you're young Chad, right? Seasickness hasn't chased your guts back to the shore yet?"

Skookum came around the counter and paced at Chad's feet, sniffing. Chad told Jack that he had lived on a sailboat for a little while after high school and before buckling down and going to college, that coming to work here was kind of like coming home.

"Is that so?" Jack said.

Down near Chad's feet, Skookum backed up and growled, a small whirring sound. Jack opened the beer fridge, pulled a can of Miller Genuine Draft from the shelf, and placed it on the glass counter with a click. He told Chad to put it on the books.

"The books?"

Jack pointed underneath the till, and Chad found a piece of paper with "The Harbormaster" written across the top and a list of charges carrying down the page in two columns. Jack cracked the can open. It shivered a little in his hand.

It was late morning. Chad told Jack the weather looked pretty nice. He spoke in the habit of pleasantness and deferment. Abby had been a caregiver for a while to a number of elderly clients, before and after they were married. Having spent half their nights in the spare bedrooms of several of her clients, Chad thought he knew how to listen. The kinds of questions to ask. How to be nice.

"I don't give a flying fuck about the weather," Jack said. The corner of one eye held the smallest crease of a smile. His voice rattled but still carried great depth and heat.

"Let's get one thing straight between you and me: there is no bullshit in here." He pointed to his temple with his free hand. "You try to feed me any, you are going to be in a world of hurt, got it?"

Chad smiled. "Right, no bullshit."

"That's right. You learn quick. That's good."

"So, do you live down here?"

"What do you mean do I fucking live down here? I'm the harbormaster. I helped build this place. No bullshit, young man. You remember that."

Chad looked over to the corner of the office where his new boss, Rick, had a large, paper-strewn desk. He was gone again, leaving Chad to fend for himself with customers and tenants. Rick hadn't said anything to him about a harbormaster. He turned back to Jack who squinted one eye at him. Chad raised his eyebrows. He must've been kidding, right? Chad said, "Harbormaster, huh?"

"Damn straight. They taught you to use that fucking computer at your fancy new desk before all the important stuff, right? Well, I live in that floating cedar shack, the farthest one on the downstream side, which means I get to see every last piece of bullshit that comes floating out of this place. You remember that."

Jack took a drink. A drop of beer hung from his chin. He didn't seem to notice, or didn't care.

"I hear you just graduated. An English major."

Chad nodded. He hesitated, his mouth open, not speaking. He knew Jack was coaxing him out onto a thin plank.

"That all you got to say about it? Just bobbing your head around like it's too heavy for your scrawny pencil neck?"

"Yeah … Yes. I wanted to study history, and I tried a little creative writing, which I liked better."

Jack set the can back down on the glass with a light tap.

"Creative writing? That sounds way more important than just plain old writing. Just make sure it's not a bunch of bullshit writing, and we'll let you stay so you can sell us beer." He took another gulp. "Since no one has trained you about the important stuff on this job yet, you ought to know that me and Skookum make our rounds through the marina twice a day checking on things: once at sun-up and once at sun-down. You'll see us go by now and then."

Jack picked up the can and held it. He asked how the boss was treating Chad, how things were coming along. Chad asked which answer he wanted—the one where he said, "fine and good, and Rick is sure a swell guy," or the other. Jack smiled and opened the door.

"You'll do fine. I'll tell you what answer I don't want out of you. Don't you give me any bullshit. C'mon, Skook! Vámanos!"

Chad watched from behind the counter as the dog hopped onto the skiff and Jack unwound the dock line with his foot. The outboard sputtered to life, and they puttered away downstream.

Working at the marina offered Chad as much time out of doors as it did inside the store. He walked up and down the docks, making his rounds, checking for broken drainage pipes, frayed power lines, and boats that appeared to be taking on water. He gave tours to potential tenants and offered friendly reminders to tenants who were neglecting bills. There were half-a-dozen children who lived at the marina year-round, and Chad was told there would be even more of them during the summer. Chad had to make sure they were wearing life jackets whenever they were outside and then follow up with parents if other tenants complained about kids running up and down the docks without life jackets on. Jack came to the office to let Chad know about some of these things, but mostly he found out when tenants stopped by the fuel dock in a huff.

Every once in a while, Chad would find Jack sitting on a bench in the shade, wiping his forehead and breathing heavily. He said he had emphysema, which forced him to take long breaks when walking even short distances. You wouldn't know it to hear him talk. When he spoke, he might go on for hours if you were willing to listen. Whatever stamina his body lacked, his mind, or at least his mouth, seemed to make up the difference.

On most days, Chad's interaction with Rick, the marina owner, amounted to a "good morning" and a "see you tomorrow." When Rick was in the office, he was often on the phone arguing with customers and employees about invoices for the boatyard repair shop he owned several hundred yards downstream. Otherwise, he was up on land, visiting with investors and the owners of his bigger accounts.

Tricia, a whimsical, middle-aged Rock Creek employee, held the boat-hauling and boatyard end of the business together with her calm presence. She was the one who had seen Chad's resume and pushed to get him hired. A couple days after Chad arrived, she moved her workspace from the desk between Rick and Chad in the marina office to an office downstream at the boatyard. It soon became clear to Chad that Tricia was moving her work to get some distance between herself and Rick, who questioned her every move. The boat-repair and boat-delivery ends of the business were where he stood to gain or lose the most money.

To get hold of Tricia, Chad had to call her on one of the three landlines in the office. When he called about Jack, "the harbor-master," she said, "Oh, I forgot to tell you about him. Yes, he's got an honorary position that exists mostly in his head. And you can tell him I said so too, if you see him before I do. You can also tell him I said he has to be nice to you or I will sneak a bunch of kidney beans into Skookum's dog food." Tricia's voice always sounded as if she were rushing to get her sentences out before the words were overcome by her pervasive laughter.

"You're enjoying this from up there on land, away from everyone's beer breath, aren't you?"

"Oh, absolutely. I'm sorry I abandoned you, but I'm trying to salvage a hundred-thousand-dollar repair job this week, and it wasn't going to happen with Rick yelling at the customers I'm on the phone with. Don't worry about old Jack. His bark is way worse than his bite. He actually loves poetry and literature, even though he can't focus on small print anymore with his bad eyesight. He has quite a few stories of his own up his sleeve. Just don't back down. And don't try to pet Skookum, either. Give that a few months first."

Chad was about to ask whether it was Jack or the dog he should worry about most, but Tricia had already moved on to list some of the responsibilities that Jack and a few other tenants had in exchange for moorage, beer, or both. "Most of this is pretty unofficial. Jack lives at the marina in exchange for looking over things before and after Rick is gone for the day. Sometimes Jack makes you write down what he owes you, but he never pays. Just don't give away any cash from the till—apart from making change—and the money should balance out at the end of the week. I'll worry about that."

Chad began to understand the unofficial layer of business going on at Rock Creek Marina. There were no files for Jack in any of the employee records. Just an understanding that came from knowledge of the place and its history, knowledge Chad could only develop over time. There were no reports or files for the stories he would need to learn to be a person in the place that was Rock Creek Marina rather than an employee operating in a position there.

There's a transition you make moving from a fixed point on land to a world afloat. You can't stand with one foot on a dock and another on a boat for long without committing one way or another, unless you want to fall into the drink. In the past, on the river with Abby, the life of constant shifting had been a way to live more consciously in his own body. To live a more physically active, careful existence, with a million purposeful actions. Maintaining balance gave Chad a sense of peace, unlike his quietest, stillest moments on land. Ever since he'd crashed the boat and had to move off the water, he couldn't shake the feeling of being adrift. The more time he spent on the dock during work hours, the better he felt. He was beginning to see how the weather brought changes to the water and to the shoreline. There was always more to see and hear and smell on the water: seals chasing salmon upstream, the ripple of a snake moving across the surface of the water, the fresh scent of new rain falling on a dry shoreline.

In the eyes of those who lived on the river, Chad's official position at the marina was indeterminate at best compared to the positions of authority that Jack and some of the others held. Jack was rooted to the place. The river flowed in his bones. He was in his early eighties and had lived on the river all his life. Not just any river either. He had lived most his life on this channel that flowed out of the Willamette and into the Columbia, the waterways that surrounded and created Sauvie Island, the largest island in the state of Oregon. Jack's parents had settled on the island before the First World War, and Jack had lived there, or on the Oregon side of the channel, since he was born. He told of rowing across the channel to school in the late thirties and early forties, back when it used to get really cold. The river froze over once, he said; it was that cold. His family's was the first farm on the island to have electricity. They used to get called to the Oregon side of the Multnomah Channel to help roll dead bears or elk off the railroad tracks on the hill above the marina in the years before the state highway.

Jack had seen marinas come and go, watched them erode, watched tensions build between Native Americans and white men and fishermen and powerboaters and sailboaters. His loyalties were with the river and those who respected it—not with those who saw it as a commodity to exploit.

Jack's health was an unspoken concern around the marina. Marge—a woman with short, frizzy hair and clothes covered in a perpetual array of colorful flecks and smudges from paints, dyes, and other artistic endeavors—kept an eye on Jack, usually at a relative distance. Marge lived in a sailboat alone, not too far upstream from Jack's place. She came into the office occasionally to let Chad and Rick know how he was doing. Marge was helpful to a number of the older tenants at the marina, including Jack. After returning one afternoon from a trip to get Jack's hair cut—a trip that had turned into late breakfast followed by shopping—she came to the store and said, "Jack kept adding whiskey to my coffee this morning at McDonald's. Now my day is going to be shot. I ruined two canvases already." Later that afternoon she stopped by again. "Jack's out on his deck sleeping in the sun. I think someone should go check on him. Chad would you mind?" As kind as she was, even Marge had had her fill of Jack for the day. No one else wanted to check on him, so Chad agreed to. He wasn't sure which would be worse: waking him up or not being able to.

On the pretense of checking leaky abandoned trawlers in the lower marina down near Jack's place, Chad stood at a distance until he was sure he could see Jack's chest moving.

Jack opened one eye and then closed it again. "You can stop checking in on me, kid," he said. "You can start stopping right now."

Chad started to apologize.

Jack opened both eyes. "You're the kind of guy that needs Cliff's Notes, aren't you? Let me make it simple. Get the fuck outa here!"

When Chad returned to the marina store, Marge was there, waiting by the door. "Well?" she asked.

"He's seems alright. But I think he's running mostly on fumes."

Marge looked at Chad questioningly. "Oh dear. Did you wake him up?"

When she first moved aboard her father's powerboat after her divorce, Marge couldn't get used to balancing a canvas and paints and brushes on the water without all of them sliding and tipping and falling; it happened every time she stepped from one side of the cabin to the other, or whenever the wind blew, or when someone on the channel kicked up a wake. There was a path through some trees between the upper marina and the downstream boat ramps where she could set up an easel and get to work, but the labor of trudging up the ramp with supplies was just enough of an annoyance that she fell out of the habit of painting. Eventually, she packed up her supplies and canvases and hauled the bulk of them down to her newly rented storage unit in the lower marina.

After that, she ventured from one artistic craft to another. From drawing and sewing, to weaving, to brewing her own

vegetable and fruit liqueurs. She made curtains for other boat-
ers, and bottles of fruity sipping drinks. Then she started baking bread. She bought an Italian sourdough starter at a specialty
bakery in Portland. The starter had been developed in Venice,
and in the 1950s, came straight from that great floating city to
Portland via a traveling collector of yeast and sourdough start-
ers. The collector delivered the Venetian starter and then pro-
ceeded directly to a nearby hospital. Convinced exotic yeasts
were slowly turning his brain into a dense, thickening mass of
cheese, he committed himself for psychiatric evaluation. The
bakery never heard from him again.

Marge bought a large, gimbaled iron stove for her boat (causing the hull to rest several inches lower in the water) and began baking bread to sell in the marina store and give away at
birthdays and special occasions. She called them her Loaves of
Abundance. Those who received and relished the heavy, soft,
seedy bread began to call it, merely, the Abundance, as in: "A
little slice of Abundance," "Let's break Abundance together," or
"Bring any kind of sauce or fondue or salad dressing—any excuse for dipping the Abundance." She took the compliments in
stride, unaware of the culinary sensation growing at the marina
and spreading upstream and down.

Marge added to the starter and let it grow—it did grow, but
it also slowly dissipated in flavor and the ability to make dough
rise. She noted the decline as the weeks went by and went back
to the bakery only to find the business had changed hands and
no one remembered the starter she was looking for. When the
marina started commenting on the new taste, they chalked the
change up to the problem of familiarity. But Marge declared the
death of Abundance and moved on to other things.

"Good things never last," she said matter-of-factly to those
who asked her for bread. She sold the oven, had it removed from
the boat to make room for other things, and was surprised by
the sorrow that built up in the empty space it left behind. She
dropped the clay pot containing the starter into the river, turned
off the lights in her boat, and wept into her pillow for a good
while that night.

She used some of her Abundance profits to enroll in a class at an art college in the old industrial area north of downtown Portland. With renewed purpose, she learned how to balance a brush in her hands while on the water. The strapped-in canvas now moved with the boat, which moved with the water, the wind, and the weather outside. She learned to transfer her center of balance to the very tip of the brush, until she could paint a perfectly controlled, straight line as if she were using a ruler. There was still the trouble of getting her lines to be perfectly parallel with the edges of the frame, but in the meantime, the slightly askew compositions seemed appropriate for the world she lived in. By the time she had mastered painting on the water, she had trouble painting on land. She dropped out of her art class to avoid losing her momentum. She needed to seize this season and not think too much about it. She had trouble sleeping at night, constantly reworking the images in her head and thinking up new possibilities. So she painted at night and slept during the day, with the occasional trip to town to buy food and supplies.

The canvases piled up in the aft cabin of her boat, and she had to find creative ways to wedge new paintings into her packed storage unit. She gave away older work in order to fit in the new stuff, and that familiar question arose: what do you do with homeless artwork, especially when you live an already cramped life? Someday she wanted to write an essay called "The Artist as Non-Hoarder," if only to be able to teach herself.

One rainy night, as she drifted in and out of a dream, a looming sense of dread filled her. The river was in danger. The water was rising, and wouldn't stop. She imagined herself as a caretaker, offering paintings as sacrifices to mend the broken river. Without her work, the river would come apart and flow in all directions, dissipating everywhere and flowing nowhere. As she drifted toward wakefulness, her urgency turned into determination. She could summon more caretakers, work on publicity, contact the organization that planned the Time-Based Art Festival in Portland, invite other artists to join her in the effort—educated or not, young or old, the religious, the heavily medicated, the crafters, the arts-and-crafters, the

former-artists-become-former-architects-or-marketing-execu-
tives-or-graphic-designers-become-artists-again—the recov-
ering employed who chose to eat food and sleep under sloped
roofs and bear children rather than give themselves up to the
gravity of the sun and sail toward it until they burst into flame.
Everyone. She was more asleep than awake again.

She opened her eyes and the sun shone through a bright, ver-
tical gap between two mostly drawn curtains. She searched for
some inkling of what was required of her. Something had been
with her and was in danger of moving away. Like inspiration
does. Like the Venetian yeast had. Like her husband, like her
daughter, like the surges of painting in her life.

She had only an image in her mind, and she spent the next
eight hours committing that image to canvas: a picture of many
paintings strung together with rope in a long line and drifting
down a river toward the horizon. She was painting a distant, flat
memory of a deep longing, a shadow of an essential, glorious
purpose that at first seemed clear but was slowly becoming lost
to her—as it would be lost to anyone who thought twice about it,
lost to anyone unable to sleep without eventually waking. Next
time, she thought, she wasn't going to just move on from it. She
wasn't going to miss it by thinking twice, or preparing, or planning to share it, or expanding upon it, or observing, or describ-
ing, or even guessing. She would seize the evasive thing longed
for and never let it go.

On Chad's second week at the marina, a liveaboard named Barry
motored his sailboat, dubbed the *Stillwater*, from its slip several
spots upstream over to the fuel dock. Chad saw him and rushed
out of the store to help secure the boat, but by the time Chad got
to the edge of the dock, Barry was already done tying off the
bow and stern lines.

Chad said hi and tried to get a conversation going, but Barry
wasn't very talkative and walked away toward the store.

Chad asked, "Can I get some fuel going for you?"

"Nah, I'll take care of it in a minute," said Barry.

"I can get it started for you, at least."

Barry stopped and turned to look at Chad. "Fine. Ten gallons. Gasoline." And he walked into the store. Chad picked a nozzle off the fuel pump, unscrewed the fuel cap off the side of the boat, and started the pump. He waited by the boat and watched the numbers roll by on the pump's readout to ten dollars even. Barry came out the door just as Chad finished hanging up the green diesel nozzle.

Barry froze halfway to the boat. "What kind of fuel did you put in my tank?"

Chad's heart surged. "Diesel? You've got a sailboat. With a diesel engine, right?"

Barry closed his eyes.

Chad looked at the boat. "I thought all sailboats had diesel engines."

Barry opened his eyes and spoke calmly and quietly. "No. Not all sailboats have diesel engines. Mine, for instance."

Chad's heart sank lower in his chest. His eyes reddened. "We can pump it out of there, right?"

Barry opened his mouth then closed it again. He folded his arms. "Nah. No need to go to all that trouble. I can probably dip a hose in there and run it to the diesel outboard for a while. Don't worry about it. I've got a diesel heater inside too. I could feed it to that."

Rick came out of his office and stood behind Barry. Chad confessed what he had done, red-faced, looking down toward their thin, canvas deck shoes. "I'll fix it. I'll get a pipe or a hose or something and siphon it out. I'm really sorry, you guys. It probably could have happened to anybody."

"This isn't the first screwup like this," Rick said.

"That's a relief," said Chad.

"I wasn't talking to you," said Rick. He turned to Barry. "This isn't the first dumb-ass mistake Chad's made since he got here. How much fuel was in there when you came in?"

"Half the tank," said Barry, "But it's not a big deal."

Rick put his arm around Barry and drew him toward the store. "OK, no problem then. I'll give you a bottle of this fuel additive that will turn that mixture into supreme-grade fuel. Clean your engine out too. I've used it a hundred times."

The men disappeared into the office and shut the door behind them. Chad stood next to the fuel pump and looked at his hands, as if unsure what they were or what to do with them. His heart thumped in his ears.

He should just go. Moving out here was a terrible idea. Halfway to nowhere where he didn't know anybody. Where people eyed him with suspicion. Where he felt himself holding his breath on the walk down the ramp to this floating world because the transition onto water actually scared him. Where the rocking of the walkways and the bell-like tones of ropes banging into masts and the smell of diesel and all his fuck-ups and trying to fit in just reminded him of his granddaddy of a fuck-up and his wrecked marriage and his wrecked sailboat. That piece-of-shit boat that not even a salvage yard wanted anymore. Where he slept in a sleeping bag, like a hobo, not even making enough money to start paying down his student loans. He should just go. Leave the landlocked boat for Rick and his boatyard crew to break into pieces. Or he could set it on fire and walk up to the highway and hitch a ride to who the fuck cares.

A raspy female voice beside the fuel dock spoke loudly, more loudly than necessary. Chad jumped, startled.

"Wooohooo! That was great!"

Chad scanned the picnic tables and deck chairs over near the hot dog stand on the side deck for the speaker. He looked back and forth as if lost.

"Over here." Under a large yellow picnic umbrella, Doris stepped out from behind the main counter of the stand. "Come here, honey," she said, her eyes wrinkled in concern. Her bare arms reached out from her frayed jean vest. The leathery brown skin on her arms hung loosely around her bones, and it swung back and forth from where it sagged above the elbows. "If you can believe it, young man, that's more than I've heard coming out of Barry's mouth in all the years he's been moping around this place." She reached toward Chad with a hand that carried a lit cigarette between the pinky and ring fingers.

Chad watched out for the cigarette as she put her hand on his shoulder and shook him lightly. Chad opened his mouth, tried to speak, but no words came. Doris—they called her Dory on the docks—ran a hot dog stand now and then on the fuel dock. She was often there for lunch and part of the afternoon, but her hours were, as she put it, whenever the hell she felt like it, usually as long as the conversations on the dock were interesting enough.

Chad said, "You're Dory, right? Well, it's been nice knowing you. I think I'm fired now."

Dory threw back her head and cackled. "Are you kidding me? No, you're not. And even if you were, I wouldn't let it happen."

"How do you know?"

"I can just tell, honey. You just go right back in that store, walk up to Ricko-the-dicko, and tell him he's late in picking up my jars of sauerkraut like he said he would. Go on." She waved toward the store. "Don't you worry about it. Tell him I'm going to pour the nasty old sauerkraut my customers have been stuck with—all of it—right down into one of his file drawers if he doesn't hurry the hell up."

Chad looked Dory in the eyes and half-smiled. "Thanks."

Dory winked at him. "You're alright, Chad." And she walked back toward the picnic tables.

Chad went into the store and over to the shelf where Barry and Rick were discussing oil and fuel treatments and stood right by them, with his arms folded. He wasn't going to shy away from them, but he wasn't going to talk about sauerkraut either. They spoke for a while without acknowledging Chad, but he couldn't concentrate on what they were saying anyway. He kept searching back over the past few days, trying to think of what else he might have done wrong that would lead Rick to say "not the first time." What had he done? What had he fucked up? Put the wrong fuel in someone else's tank? Counted someone's change wrong? Something he had said?

Eventually Barry turned to leave. He reached out his hand to Chad, and Chad shook it. "Don't lose sleep over this," Barry said. "We all screw up sometimes." He sighed and closed the door behind him on his way out.

Rick returned to his desk, picked up the phone and dialed a number. He turned toward Chad while it rang and said, "I saved your butt, young man. Guess you won't do that again." Before Chad could respond, Rick spoke in a jovial tone to a boatyard customer on the other end about a boat repair job that was ready to be paid for.

Chad sat down at his desk and stared at the spreadsheet of boat tenants on the dimly lit computer screen. The rounded glass of the old monitor reflected more light from the windows and door behind him than it displayed from inside. He watched the reflection of gulls and the wind ruffling the canvas that hung above the doors and windows.

Before the marina hired Chad, Barry had helped monitor the fuel dock when Rick was busy. He often looked after the docks on weekends and holidays. In return, he got free moorage and a place to plug in and keep warm through the night. Right around the week Chad arrived, Barry was keeping an eye on things while Rick was away for Thanksgiving. Barry had his own set of keys to the building and would be sitting on the docks fishing anyhow. Why not keep the Open sign on and make a few bucks for the marina?

He'd just started in on the massive, Thanksgiving Day newspaper when the Lendaway family came by to fill up on fuel. They were the second boat he had seen all morning. Other than a couple fishermen, the marina was empty. Everyone, even the liveaboards, had climbed up on land and driven to where their families gathered for food and football. The sun was out. The river was quiet. He had the whole river to himself: fish moving under the dock, a blue heron's wings whispering through the air, a light breeze. Barry listened for the calm woven into it all.

When they pulled up in the early morning, there was barely enough room for the Lendaways to tie off their fifty-foot Grand Banks yacht near the fuel pumps and barely enough room on the dock for the half-dozen children to stretch their legs. The boat took on almost three hundred gallons of diesel.

Barry watched the numbers roll by on the pump. The kids laughed and chased one another around the dock, brushing by him roughly. Stuart Lendaway, the boat owner and father of the kids, introduced himself to Barry and invited him to join the family downstream at Coon Island for Thanksgiving dinner later in the afternoon. Barry looked up at the steam coming from the windows on deck. The aroma of the cooking turkey hovered over the stench of diesel fumes. He said he needed to watch the fuel dock. Stuart's wife, Amy, came down insisting—they were probably the only boat he would see that day. The children shouted their approval. It was decided even before Barry had agreed.

It took almost an hour to finish fueling up. When they were done and everyone was on board, Barry untied the bow and stern lines and passed them up to Stuart's father on deck. Barry shouted up toward the flybridge and heard the clunk of the engine engaging the two props. He placed both palms on the hull and leaned in, keeping the stern from brushing into the dock as the bow turned into the current. A sharp pain shot down his back and left leg, and he winced. Heavy boat.

Movement in the porthole between his hands caught his eye, and in his surprise he almost slipped into the river. It was a young girl's face. One eye met his, wide and blazing. The other listed, wandering to the side. She seemed to search right through him, her expression concerned—almost pitying.

It was only an instant, but the boat started drifting out with Barry still leaning into the hull. In a rush of panic, he pushed his body away from the water as hard as he could, twisting at the waist, reaching for the dock, both legs dangling in the water. He pulled himself to his feet, water pouring from his boots, darkening the dock. When he looked up again at the porthole, the face was gone. Light from an open hatch spilled into the room beyond the window. Through the glass he glimpsed a familiar shape hanging from the bulkhead. It was a crucifix. No plain Protestant cross either. The Christ was there, head hanging to one side, knees slightly bent.

Up on deck, Stuart and several children waved from the fly-bridge. "See you later," one of the children called. They hadn't seen him fall. The cold water sloshed in his boots. The window in the porthole went dark. Stuart Lendaway turned the bow sharply downstream and waved one last time.

Barry gritted his teeth against the cold, against the sudden pounding pain in his lower back and his knee, as he waved in return.

Shit. Catholics.

Barry's mother had been so proud when he signed up with the Catholic seminary. His father would have been proud too if he hadn't been killed in the Korean War. After seminary, Barry apprenticed in a Carmel, California, parish as the Vietnam War really began to settle in. He finished his studies and a year later signed up as a chaplain for the US Army. He never imagined he'd be close to the battlefield. Each time there was a request for him to go out in the field with the soldiers, he accepted. It was risky, but there were men dying and no one to offer them last rites or absolution. He figured that after the war, his experience would help him find a position in a big city parish, an important post close to nice restaurants and large libraries. He was twenty-eight at the time, older than most of the soldiers. They were like young boys to him, until they began dying and offering up their confessions. Then their confessions revealed long stretches of life and heavy burdens—the weight of unabsolved sins.

He knew all about sins. He'd been trained to know about them: venial sins, mortal sins, sins of omission, sins of commission. He had an ear for what penance fit each confession. He knew the Catholic language, those categories that separated him from any emotional connection to the sin: bestiality, incest, impure thoughts.

None of that mattered in Vietnam. There wasn't room for penance in war. The language he'd studied to articulate the state of a man's soul was of no use to him. The dying men he saw in the field used the words they could gather together as their lives bled out of them. He watched the life soak into the ground and spread out, soaking through his combat fatigues and into his knees where he knelt in the grass. His knees remained dark for days, the cloth thick and moist in the humid air.

The men told Barry the worst of their lives. In those last moments, their lives were defined by their worst acts. For some of them there was not enough time for absolution. Mostly they confessed sins committed back home, burdens they carried all the way here, only to lay them down in the jungle, in the grass, in the rice paddies: cousins they slept with, children they'd hurt, people they'd killed, bodies hidden, things they did to farm animals, things they'd stolen.

If the men confessed anything they'd done in Vietnam, it usually had to do with accidents. Once a week, a young, dying man would tell him about killing one of their own. Not many of these got reported. Barry didn't keep count. He tried not to listen for names. One night, an officer in the mess tent was talking about World War II. Supposedly, one out of five deaths in that war could be attributed to friendly fire. Friendly fire. And now Americans were coming over to a small country in Asia to kill more Americans. They told Barry about it as they lay dying. Barry listened and offered the assurance of forgiveness to those who lived long enough to receive it.

One boy had killed a fellow soldier in the crossfire and lied about it. Later, he tried to take his own life in the midst of the battle, but flinched when he pulled the trigger, killing the soldier standing next to him. He lied about that too. Some of the guilty ones ventured out into the open during a firefight, the shame heavy on their backs. Suicide runs. Those who lived to talk to Barry often told him why they had done it.

One scorching hot day, at the edge of a firefight, a soldier spoke to him from the ground. The soldier's left arm and part of his right were gone. His side lay open, blood seeping into the earth around him. The medic hadn't even bothered to cover up the wounds before moving on. The chopper had come and gone once already. The life came pulsing out where the boy's elbow should have been as Barry knelt by his side and listened. The boy was shaking violently. He spoke with the words he could find. Where words would not come, he spoke to Barry with his eyes. Barry didn't look away, and he heard it all.

"Bless me, Father. Listen. I killed one of our own. A guy from another platoon. They weren't supposed to be there. Thought he was a gook. Came up from behind. With a knife. He didn't hear me coming. After he died, I took his water, a chocolate bar, a picture of his woman. I took the picture. It's in my pocket here." The boy had stopped trembling, and his gaze struck Barry like a fist so he could barely breathe. "I have impure thoughts about the woman in the picture, Father. And I killed her husband. I keep killing him in my head and fucking his wife. It seems right to kill him and then keep killing him. I drink his water. I eat his chocolate. I fuck his wife. Why do I want to keep taking his life away? She is so beautiful. Please take the picture. Don't let me die with it."

Barry reached into the boy's clothing and removed several letters and the photograph. She was smiling, her hands loose at her side. He turned back to the boy. His eyes were still open, but he was gone.

Barry left the battlefield in the next chopper, keeping close to the boy's body. As they flew over a stretch of hills, he tossed the photo of the woman out the door. For the dying, there is no time for penance, and sometimes, not even for last rites. Barry said prayers for the boy there in the chopper and continued to think of him long after he was gone, long after the war was over. After that day, he knew he had come to the end of something. Part of his life was dead now, or buried. He couldn't keep to the structure of the sacraments in the chaos of war. If the sacraments were empty here, how could they work anywhere else? The confessions continued, running over, pooling at his feet, hardening over his skin in layers.

He never went back to church after the war. He just turned away and didn't look back. Not from God, really. In some ways, God's calm presence behind all things remained there for him. He tried to question the existence of God the way he'd heard others do so many times, but he couldn't. Even though it no longer filled the words of the religion he'd once believed in, it still filled other things. He didn't need the words of prayers and sacraments anymore to try and exert authority over it.

Even these days, he could see it in his surroundings, though he couldn't feel it in himself. Sitting, watching the river, Barry could see it in the current, the water carrying life below the surface. Barry felt impervious to that stillness, barely even a witness to it. But it was enough. It was enough to know it was there, enough to sit on the edge of a dock in its presence.

After the Lendaways had pulled away from the dock, Barry went back to his sailboat and found some dry socks and shoes. He sat in his green plastic chair gazing over the water. The morning had been quiet so far, peace hanging in the air. But the Lendaways had taken it away with a simple invitation.

He thought about biscuits and turkey and gravy and pie. He decided to go. He'd already winterized the inboard engine on his sailboat, and it would take at least half an hour to get downstream in the rowboat he used for his daily exercise. Barry filled his whiskey flask and shoved off.

He arrived at the island ten minutes early and marveled at the Lendaways' spacious cabin; inside a boat it was always much bigger than it seemed from the outside. Barry's eyes scanned the clutch of children and aunts and uncles and grandparents, looking for the girl. Stuart's father, Cliff, handed Barry a wineglass and asked if he drank. Barry nodded. He could feel the heavy lump of the whiskey flask in his jacket. Cliff asked where he'd worked over the years. Barry saw the girl coming up the steps from below and blurted out that he was a Catholic priest. He said he had recently retired, and he had come down here to the river to live the contemplative life that had eluded him at parishes along the West Coast. It wasn't altogether a lie. He still had some of his books from seminary buried on the boat somewhere.

Now that they had a priest in their midst, they were thrilled. Amy insisted Barry say the prayer before they ate. "Stu knew there was something about you back at the fuel dock, Father . . ." She paused.

"Father Palmer," said Barry.

"Father Palmer." She put her hand on his shoulder, guiding him to a place at the head of the table. He removed his jacket and hung it lightly over the back of his chair.

When the meal was ready and everyone had gathered, they all looked at Barry, smiling. The girl frowned, one eye on him. She crossed herself, and everyone else seemed to follow her lead. The rustle of clothing. The boat shifting—still settling from their collective movement toward the center of the vessel. Barry paused, said the words, his eyes open, watching the red wine move in his glass. He glanced up. The girl's eyes were closed, her hands folded. He pulled the words of the prayer up as if from a deep well.

She couldn't have been more than eight or nine. During the meal, she piled on potatoes and gravy, passing the other serving dishes along without taking anything. She paused between bites and looked at Barry. Always, one of her eyes seemed to focus on him until he could not tell which one was the good one.

When his plate was empty, Amy offered Barry second helpings. The potatoes came around to him, and when he looked into the nearly empty bowl, he saw a small fork next to the serving spoon.

"Did someone lose a fork?"

She got up and walked around the table until she stood beside him, her face questioning. Barry placed the handle in her palm. There were small chunks of potato on it.

"Gracie, why don't you thank Father Palmer?" said Amy.

Gracie didn't move.

Barry reached for his wineglass. As he turned, the flask hanging in his jacket behind him tapped once against the leg of the chair. Her gaze shifted down to the coat and then back to his face, her one good eye burning through him. Barry excused himself, asking where the bathroom was.

He made his way down a short set of steps toward the stern, entering the bathroom and shutting the door with a soft click. He rubbed at his face, wine on his breath. In his blood. Filling him like a memory. He relieved himself, twisted the outflow valve on the toilet, pumped it clean, and turned to face the mirror, both hands on the counter on either side of the sink. He smiled at his reflection. The whine of an outboard engine filled the small room with its soft hum and then faded downstream. Fishermen. The sound of the distant engine hummed in the belly of the boat. The air around him shuddered, the walls ticking, the counter buzzing under his hands.

She was just a girl, some kind of half-wit, and curious, that was all. He bent to wash his hands, and the boat rocked as the wake from the fishing vessel finally made its way to their side of the river. A movement on the floor caught his eye, something small rolling down at his feet. It was a tiny pearl, round and smooth. A small pinprick of a hole ran through its center. A keepsake. Something to remember the day by. These people were more likely to buy a new pearl before stooping to look for a lost one. Barry dropped it into his pocket where it clinked against the flask, a comforting, metallic sound. He winked at his reflection in the mirror and leaned in to whisper, "Bless me Father, for I have sinned."

Half an hour later, Barry was pulling away from the dock, waving up at Stewart and Amy and the children. They chimed like a chorus: "Come back next year!" Then they waved and hurried back into the cabin. All of them except Gracie. Barry gazed up at her. She waved to him, her expression grim, or sad; he couldn't quite tell. He tried to work his face into a smile. A string of pearls hung loosely around her neck and caught the light, glowing slightly. The pearls were evenly spaced except where one was missing—the necklace seemed to hang out of balance. Barry looked away and went to work on the oars.

Her voice came down to him, quiet but clear. "Come back next year, Father."

He looked up just as her mother called her name from inside. She turned and stumbled through the door. Barry waited until the yacht was a good ways off and pulled out the flask, sipping a little at a time but with few breaks between.

Two

Inside the marina store, there were bar stools for customers at the long counter that separated the office desks from the store shelves. On warmer days, marina residents would sit on benches under the wide awning just outside, until the sun was well above the horizon. Every day, all day, the store offered free coffee to whomever happened by and wanted some. The coffee was often part of what brought people in to talk, order supplies, or schedule boat repairs in the yard. Rick saw the business sense of it, but the free coffee also sustained something of the spirit of the place that he couldn't see—it was a different kind of drinking than all the beer consumed in the afternoon and evening at the fuel dock. Later on in the day, the talk seemed to orbit around the subject of alcohol, but the men and women who came in the late morning and drank the coffee didn't talk about drinking coffee. It was an occasion for something else. The kind of coffee didn't seem to matter; it was preground, generic stuff that came in a large bulk can. Pulling a mug off the shelf and pouring yourself a cup of coffee at the marina store was a statement, as much as an occasion for connection. In light of Portland's urban fascination with lattes and mochas that cost three or four dollars apiece, free coffee was a chance to maintain a social border between the marina and the spread of gentrification on land. It was a chance to emphasize the ritual of drinking, held in common among members of their floating tribe as they climbed their way into the day. Drinking coffee contributed to lingering, leisurely conversation. Men and women paused longer than they might have and told stories and made connections over the coffee in a different spirit during those hours before the bottles and cans of alcohol were opened—or at least before they were opened above the tabletops.

Since Rick was always either on the phone or away from the office, the tone of the marina was set by those who had lived there the longest. There were powerboaters and sailboaters and fishermen who respected each other's differences, but the physical space left between them was often big, even in a friendly conversation. It took Chad some time to understand the undertones. Certain people came in at certain times of the day in order to avoid running into certain other people for unspoken reasons. But mostly, people shifted to make room for whomever and whatever might drift by.

Then, one Monday morning, Rick told Chad to stop brewing coffee after 8:00 a.m., dump whatever was left in the pot, and put the coffeemaker away for the day. He said, "There are some people around here taking advantage of the gratuity." So Chad stopped brewing, and he put the coffeemaker away. Even Rick seemed to have no idea of the effect this would have on the place.

It didn't take long to see evidence of a kind of shifting social current. People stopped showing up at the store. At first, Chad welcomed the quiet and caught up on a lot of paperwork. He got work done early and took to writing at his desk. But the empty coffee urn spoke volumes that Rick had not intended. Only a couple tenants asked about it. The rest quietly started a kind of revolt. They brought to Rick a detailed account of every nail that was loose on the dock and every light bulb that needed replacing and made requests for more dock cleats along their slips. Mysterious cracks and holes started to appear in the sewage lines leading from the marina bathrooms and the floating homes. Rick remained unbending about the coffee, or else he didn't seem to see a connection between the coffee and the sewage suddenly spilling into the river. For about a week, everything at the marina changed. Rent was due that week, and a couple dozen faithful tenants didn't drop their rent checks off.

It was Jack who finally got through to Rick. Rumor spread that Jack had paid a visit to the office late one night at the end of the week, when he knew Rick would be "counting his money" alone. Some said Jack had brought his shotgun with him and started cleaning it on the store counter while he talked to Rick about whatever it was he talked to him about. Jack left the glass countertop pretty greasy and let a few spent shells roll from the counter onto the floor. Some people said Jack had asked Rick if he would be so kind as to brew him a cup of coffee. Others said he kept the barrel pointed at Rick's desk while he cleaned it. Whatever it was that passed between the two men, Rick finally understood what was already clear to everyone else: the unrest around the marina wasn't about coffee. It was about whose home this place was and the kind of home it would be. It was about Rick's sudden impulse to assert authority. Rick didn't live there; he was just passing through until he decided to sell the place, as the previous owner had done before him.

Rick didn't say anything to Chad the following Monday morning. He just started filling the coffeemaker through the afternoon until Chad caught on and took up the responsibility again. Tenants drank up the coffee with a renewed fervor, talking loudly and at length about the beverage, its rich flavor and the pleasant aroma in the store. Many caffeine habits started that next week.

Even after the coffee started flowing freely again, every once in a while, Jack brought his shotgun with him to the store in broad daylight. He would lean it up against the wall just inside the door and announce his arrival.

"Hello there, Ricardo," he said. "Good morning to you, young Chadwick! Have you heard? The geese are in season. I'll just check this old thing in at the door."

Spring arrived and the sun began to rise earlier. Chad started showing up to work at 7:00 a.m. instead of 8:00 a.m., since the morning light made it harder to stay asleep, and he enjoyed the quiet of the river before the marina had come to life for the day. When he arrived, there was usually a small gathering of men drinking coffee outside—inside if it was cold or raining. It wasn't until Chad started coming to work earlier that he understood the regularity of their meetings. They might be done by 8:00 a.m., or they might go on late into the morning. Most of the men who came before the store opened were retired or on disability. Jack was always there, and Barry. Moe, a Native American living aboard his sailboat nearby, came regularly. And there was Bill, the resident goofball who was married to the ever-patient Bernice and lived on a yacht one boat slip downstream of the fuel pumps. Sometimes the older shipwrights who worked in the boatyard stopped by. More rarely, there were unfamiliar faces who had sailed in from upstream or down.

Chad filled the coffeemaker at the end of each day so it was ready for someone to hit the "on" switch first thing in the morning. Jack and Barry both had keys to the store and could let themselves in before Rick or Chad got there. The morning congregation of men was a consistent thing. The women at the marina weren't unwelcome, but they never came.

Chad tried to give the men space. When they glanced in his direction, he understood that he was stumbling in on something not quite exclusive, where even Jack was hesitant to make him feel unwelcome—there was a vulnerability there the men didn't quite know how to guard.

Chad took to checking on things outside the building after he first arrived, to give the men time to adjust. Then he moved inside and took inventory of the refrigerators and freezers: beverages, a couple shelves of produce, live bait. Most mornings, Chad could catch parts of the conversation the men were having. He had a small notebook he kept in his shirt pocket for taking notes on details about the place or about boating. He kept his distance but remained attentive. He would turn to face his computer or go into the supply room around the corner and jot down a word or a phrase to remind himself later in the day, when he could fill in the gaps to form sentences and paragraphs.

The men might talk about the fights they'd seen between sailboaters and motorboaters. They might discuss the various alterations you need to make to a boat when you take it from freshwater to saltwater or vice versa. Jack told stories passed down from his parents about farming on Sauvie Island and how the floods came and went, leaving behind a mudscape filled with stacks of twisted bicycle frames, dying trees, and bloated animal carcasses.

Jack told once about a guy who dropped his keys in the water. They were on a hollow keychain that floated, and the guy motored downstream to get them, but a huge sturgeon gulped them down, floater and all. The guy got out his fishing pole and waited in the same spot all day until he caught the same fish and dug the set of keys out of its guts. No one seemed to believe the tale. Someone said, "You just read that somewhere."

"It's not my story," he said, glancing in Chad's direction. "It's just what I heard. Better to hear someone tell you a story out loud than to read it in a book all by yourself. A story should be a community thing, not some lonely practice of one ego reading into someone else's ego."

Chad logged on to the internet to check his email. The computer chirped out its long, garbled whistling sound as the connection came through.

Bill pointed toward Chad's desk. "You got to hand it to Chatty Chad over there. That kid can brew up some coffee-flavored coffee."

Chad whiffed a laugh out through his nose and said, "It's mostly hot water, with overtones of petroleum. Someday, I'm going to make you guys a nice cup of coffee, medium roast, in a French press."

Never one to be left out, Jack spoke up, "No *nice* coffee allowed! Don't you go messing with our recipe."

"Unless you put some strong medicine in it," added Barry. "Otherwise, it's fine the way it is."

The boatyard crew came and went. When Chad crossed the room to put on another pot, Jack started in on a story. He said he'd heard a few years ago about a young couple crashing their boat into the railroad bridge a few miles upstream on the Willamette. Chad's heart began to beat in his throat. He opened the cash drawer to count out bills. He flipped through them about ten times while he pretended not to listen. "They say he did it on purpose, to collect on her life insurance or get her inheritance or something. When she survived, he was so scared she might be wise to him that he jumped right overboard into the river, and she never saw him again."

Chad set the cash back into the register and turned toward the group of men. His eyes widened as he spoke, unsure of what he was about to say: "I heard about that one. In the news. I think... it sounded like it was a pretty straightforward accident though."

Jack glared at him and coughed once. Or maybe it was a laugh. "Straightforward, alright. Straight forward into a fucking bridge. I guess you think he just accidentally forgot to call in and have them raise the bridge span so he could pass under it, then? There are only two possibilities: he's either too stupid to be on the river, or he did it on purpose. You tell me which it is." Jack continued to look at Chad, unblinking. When Chad didn't answer, Jack asked, "He a friend of yours or something?"

Chad leaned into the counter and said, "No. But maybe there are options other than just deciding a young person in a boat on the river is either stupid or devious."

Jack's face wrinkled into a sly smile. "Atta boy," he said. "Maybe some of the bullshit is starting to drain out of you already. Stick around. We'll have you all cleaned up in a few years."

"Speaking of cleaning up," Chad said. He turned toward the far end of the counter and made his way into the back storage room. His hands were shaking. He could hear the men speaking in hushed tones on the other side of the wall, and then the sound of boisterous laughter.

Just before Keith's elementary school let out for spring break at the marina, Rick called Keith's dad to make sure they had a life jacket that fit the boy well and that he would be supervised during the break. His dad couldn't get the week off work, so Keith stayed alone and out of sight on the sailboat. His dad told him if anyone from the office gave him any trouble, just to tell them he was thirteen and he looked younger because he had been held back a couple grades. Keith rolled his eyes: what grade he was in had nothing to do with how old he looked. But he liked the idea of suddenly becoming thirteen. If people bought that, he could get away with ditching his life jacket for good.

At first Keith stayed inside the boat, then he started taking the canoe out for quick paddles down to the fuel dock for candy or fish bait. In the canoe, he strapped on the life jacket just in case, but once he got to the dock, he slid out of it and tossed it back in the boat.

Most mornings, when he went by the fuel dock, there were several old men sitting and talking at a table in front of the store. They usually paused when Keith pulled the canoe up to the dock. The first few times, Keith felt their eyes burning through him and practically ran past them. Then the oldest one, Jack, started asking him questions like "How's the fishing today, Captain?" and "What did you say your line of trade was, young man?"

None of the men ever asked about his age. Jack's gaze was fierce, even when he seemed to be smiling, as if he knew everything Keith had ever done.

Inside the store, if he was lucky, Chad was behind the counter, and he would always say something like "Hey Keith, you came on the right day. It's a two-for-one day on snacks." Then Keith only had to pay for one thing, and he could choose another for free. But if it was only Rick, the owner of the docks, or that other older guy, he only got what he paid for.

Outside on nice days, or inside if it was raining, the old men gathered on the fuel dock and told jokes and stories—stories from back before there were life jackets. Jack talked about how his parents had moved to the island a hundred years ago to farm and raise cattle. He talked about people and boats and whole marinas that had come and gone. He talked about Indians and steamboats in the old days. He would look out over the river while he spoke, almost as if he could see it more clearly when he watched the water flowing by.

Once, Jack told about a large ketch that sank on the channel a number of years ago. It was a beautiful boat, he said. It needed some work, but the owner wasn't interested in work. After the salvagers pulled the boat up, they found bullet holes in the hull near the engine room. The owner was trying to collect on insurance.

When they seemed to have forgotten him, Keith slipped away from the table without saying goodbye and made his way over to the canoe. The sun glared off the surface of the river. A man had shot holes in his own boat? Sometimes the old men just didn't make any sense. Most adults seemed to have forgotten what was important about life—they had grown too tall to see a lot of stuff lower to the ground that really mattered. The old men had a sense of humor sometimes, but they still spent a lot of their time talking about all the boring details of life on the river.

Late Saturday afternoons, whenever Keith took the canoe to the fuel dock, the men would be sitting there, quietly listening to a small radio that had only one speaker, to the show they called "Garris and Keeler." It made them laugh every minute or two, sometimes at things that were funny and sometimes at things Keith couldn't figure out. He liked to hear them laugh, though, so he sat for a while on the dock, with his feet in the water, until the band on the show settled in with their twangy country tunes. Then he dropped into the canoe and headed home. Every once in a while, the "Garris and Keeler" show would have a special episode, and for two hours there was nothing but jokes. Some of them made Keith smile. When the joke show aired, word spread throughout the marina, and people up and down the docks turned on their radios too. Keith could hear the jokes wherever he paddled up and down the dock. A lot of them were weird and not very funny, but sometimes there were really good ones. Keith tried to remember them to tell a couple of his friends who lived on boats nearby. But the only one he could remember perfectly was the one with the boy who needed to pee during church:

> A mother took her little boy to church. While
> in church the little boy said, "Mommy, I have
> to pee." The mother said to the little boy, "It's
> not appropriate to say the word 'pee' in church.
> So from now on whenever you have to 'pee,' just
> tell me that you have to 'whisper.'" The follow-
> ing Sunday, the little boy went to church with
> his father and during the service said to him,
> "Daddy, I have to whisper." The father looked at
> him and said, "Okay, whisper in my ear."

"It's not appropriate to say the word 'pee' in church" sounded
like something his mom would probably say if he and his dad
were still living with her in their house on land. Keith liked it
mostly because he knew his father would hate it. He tried to tell
his dad some of the jokes, but his dad never laughed and usually
told him he was telling it wrong. Keith didn't tell him the joke
about peeing in his ear though. He knew he would get it exactly
right, and his father would have nothing to say. He would probably just walk away and get a beer from the ice box.

Chad looked out the window to see a large powerboat leaving the
fuel dock. The winter sun was bright on the water. Reflected light
wavered on the massive hull as it pulled away. The deck of the boat
was so high above the waterline that the captain didn't see Jack's
skiff passing by to starboard. Jack swerved to avoid it, but the powerboat still bumped into his skiff, spinning it 180 degrees. Jack cut
the engine just before impact and fell hard onto his hands and knees.
One leg slipped over the edge of his boat into water up to his thigh.
Skookum spun around several times and barked. Jack pulled himself
up and threw a line to Bill, who had run to the edge of the dock. Bill
helped him to his feet. Jack shook his middle finger at the departing
powerboat, but its captain was looking off downstream, unaware.

When Jack stepped into the store, his face was white. Water
pooled on the floorboards at his feet. He leaned against the wall,

breathing heavily. There were several others in the room, boat-yard employees and tenants, but Jack turned to Chad. He let loose a string of highly articulate estimations of the fucking power-boater and recited several navigation rules about boats that were fucking docked and boats under fucking power, fucking signals, and who has right-of-fucking-way. He seemed too angry—and maybe even too shaken under all the rage—to weave his usual creative diversity of foul words into his sentences.

Jack removed a can of beer from one of the fridges and opened it with a pop. He shook his head, looking Chad in the eyes. He had come in shaking in fury, but now his face was wrinkled as if in pain. He labored to breathe. Pulling a handkerchief from his pocket, he wiped his forehead.

"Son of a bitch. I'm not afraid to call a man a son of a bitch. I don't care who he is."

The others in the room continued to talk, ignoring, or pre-tending to ignore, the two of them. Chad still hadn't said any-thing. Jack looked at him for a moment. Chad smiled. It was the wrong thing to do. Jack leaned over the counter and spoke low. Now he had something to say to Chad.

"What the fuck are you doing here, Chad?"

Chad's smile quickly drained away.

"Are you furthering your education? Getting material? You planning to write about me?"

Chad fumbled for words. "No. I mean ... I write about what-ever comes to mind. Mostly nothing and nonsense. I write for myself more than anything."

"Listen, kid. I've seen you pulling that little book out of your pocket there, taking notes when people leave the office. I'm not your fucking material. And I think you know I could knock you back into your diaper days if I have half a mind to. Your scrawny ass is so full of nothing you'd have to sit down twice in that of-fice chair just to make it squeak. Maybe I'll do you a big fucking favor and throw that damn booklet of yours into the river where it belongs."

They both breathed a deep breath at the same time. Jack seemed to sink down, like he had stepped off the bottom rung of a ladder. His arm was draped across the counter. Chad let his shoulders drop, thinking he must have said all that needed to be said, but Jack wasn't finished. When he spoke, the hard edge was gone from his voice, but he held Chad's gaze without blinking.

"You're not going to see anything worth seeing if you've always got a pen going in your head. If you can't sit still in a place for more than five seconds without taking notes, you're never going to end up writing about anything worth saying because you were never there to begin with."

He turned to leave and spoke loudly as if to everyone in the room. "Maybe you should write that down. Skook! Vámanos!"

Jack left the door open on his way out. A trail of watery footprints marked his path into and out of the store. Chad didn't write that down. He watched through the glass as Jack took a long drink of beer. Rick caught Chad's eye from where he sat at his desk, raised his eyebrows, and then went back to his conversation with the others. Chad sat down in front of the computer, pulled the small notebook from his shirt pocket, and put it in the back of the desk drawer behind a stack of files. Outside, Jack climbed onto his skiff, unwrapped the dock line with one hand and roared out into the current.

Moe woke to the sound of Jack's skiff roaring by his window. He waited until the sound faded then pushed the blankets to the end of the bed. He looked down at the empty bottles on the floor, and something like a sob rose in his throat—it came out sounding like a cough mixed with a yelp. Moe reached for his Bible on the shelf behind the kitchen table, next to a chunk of half-carved cedar that resembled half a bird in flight. The leather cover of the Bible, once black, had been duct taped so many times, it was mummified under layers of silvery gray strips. He'd kept it nearby since the sixth grade, a gift from the Indian boarding school some fifty years ago. He was pretty sure this was the same Bible, though he could barely recognize the scrawled notes in the margins as actual words. Verses and whole chapters were underlined in various colors and thicknesses of ink; often the lines ran over the words rather than under them, so certain passages were impossible to make out.

Moe ran his hands over the cover where the tape had frayed into a fine, soft netting and hung from the edges of the book. He fished a roll of duct tape from a drawer beside the calcified galley sink and wound fresh strips around the Bible's spine. Stopping to survey his handiwork, he discovered he'd lost track of the spine and had wrapped up the Bible entirely. He grabbed a rusted knife from a drawer and made three cuts. Then he opened the book to one of the passages he read when he woke up to hangovers like this one: "Though evil is sweet in his mouth, and he hides it under his tongue, though he spares it and does not forsake it, but still keeps it in his mouth, yet his food in his stomach turns sour; it becomes cobra venom within him. ... He will not see the streams, the rivers flowing with honey and cream."

Something about the honey and cream got him every time. He closed the book and wept.

Later that morning, after a tearful breakfast of hard-boiled eggs and toast, Moe stepped on deck and was surprised by the shadow of an angel perched on the stern pulpit. He gasped at the sight but then remembered: he had seen the large, plastic angel floating by the marina last night. He often found things in the river at night or during the day while he was fishing. A bird's nest once, like a small coracle carrying a frantic cloud of ants. An unopened six-pack of beer. A bobber fastened to a ring of mysterious, old keys. Several times, Moe had pulled out a flailing old alcoholic named Paul who drank more than anyone at the marina and sometimes slipped into the river when standing at the edge of the dock to pee late at night.

The memory of the previous night returned to him. He'd been praying outside in the dark when the statue's greenish, phosphorescent body brushed his feet where they dangled in the dark current. All he had to do was snag her by the head with his fishing net. She was several feet tall, hollow, made of thick plastic. Like a blank postcard arriving in the mail, she was an answer, evidence that something out there in the night was watching and listening. There were several gallons of water sloshing around inside her. Moe had hefted her onto the dock and pulled her aboard his boat.

It was late, but he'd worked quietly, mounting the angel onto the stern of his boat so she stood facing the river. Moe swore the angel glowed slightly when he turned off the lamp. Her wings rose above her head and draped down around her body, blending into the robes that pooled around her feet. Her expression was downcast, smiling slightly, savoring some understanding or pondering the deeper mysteries of the cosmos.

Her face was familiar and Moe remembered an almost identical statue of Mary outside the brick and mortar boarding school he had attended in his early teens. The nuns had him and some of the other uncooperative Native boys stand at her smooth marbled feet for ten minutes in the hot sun while they waited for the sweaty superintendent to finish his afternoon prayers so he could dole out punishment with a thick, metal yardstick. While some of the other boys risked spitting what little saliva they had onto the statue, Moe gazed at Mary's smooth, lidded eyes and savored the minutes of quiet comfort they brought him before the beatings began and left the boys with red and blue welts across their backs.

The plastic angel Moe had fished out of the river was probably made with the same mold used to make a Virgin Mary. He could see the white bead of plastic lining the base of the wings where they were attached. An angel but not an angel. Kind of like Moe himself. He'd lived the life of a Northwest Indian, but the list of his ancestral tribes began with Chinook, and Molalla and Nez Perce, and went on from there until his memory trailed off into the unknown. He liked to say that he belonged to the Columbia River itself.

Now, in the light of day, Moe could see the greenish film covering the angel. He got out an old T-shirt, filled a saucepan with soapy water, then started wiping scuff marks and algae from the statue's contours. When he was nearly done, he heard someone walking by. It was Marge. Moe paused, blushing a little.

Marge stopped when she saw him. "Hi Moe. Looks like you pulled something new out of the river. What did you find?"

"It's either an angel or Mary. Maybe both. Someone to watch over me while I sleep."

"It's a nice touch." Marge held her paint-smeared arms and hands out, away from her sides. A caption on her T-shirt read in black ink: "When in despair ... when in fear ... when in doubt ... make something." Marge continued, "I've gotta go to the laundry sink to clean myself up, but when I'm done, I think I'll tell Dory there's a beautiful woman hanging out on your boat. That'll get her revved up."

Moe smiled. "You're crafty—you brighten people's lives without even needing to think about it. Tell you what: I'll meet you down at the fuel dock and peek around the corner while you tell her."

Marge laughed. "Let's do it! Give me a five-minute head start."

Even from his perch halfway up the cottonwood tree, Keith had a pretty good view of the whole marina. He could get up even higher, high enough to see the Sauvie Island Bridge at the southern edge of the island and the spires of the St. Johns Bridge where his father worked renovation, scraping paint, loosening massive bolts with a fifty-pound wrench, leaning back into his harness over the river, balancing himself by the toes of his boots on the thin edge of a steel beam. Even during the day, spotlights illuminated his father's work from above and below. "No shadows," Keith had heard his father say once. "When you're up there, you don't look into the lights, not even the sun, unless you want to create blind spots and screw up or fall." He'd placed his hand on Keith's head. "There. Now you're already smarter than those young idiots twice your age working on the bridge."

In the cottonwood tree, Keith went back to his book. Through the leaves, the warm sunlight spilled bright wafers of light onto the pages. He read the paragraph for the second time:

> Well, it being away in the night and stormy,
> and all so mysterious-like, I felt just the way
> any other boy would've felt when I seen that
> wreck laying there so mournful and lonesome
> in the middle of the river. I wanted to get
> aboard of her and slink around a little, and see
> what there was there. So I says: "Le's land on
> her, Jim."

The school bus would be coming soon, down the road that snaked along the dike and followed the course of the river, which marked the western edge of the island. Every weekday, he waited by the road or up in the tree for half an hour before the head-lights of the bus appeared. He could slide down the rope well before the bus rounded the last wide turn and tie the rope off to a root at the base of the tree on the river side, where it couldn't be seen from the road.

From where he was perched, he could trace the journey he and his father took every morning in their small motorboat, from the dock across the channel to the flat spot on the shore below where his father dropped him off before heading to work upstream.

The mast and standing rigging of their sailboat glistened faintly in the sun. Ropes swung in the wind, tangled and knot-ted. No, wait, not ropes; on the water they were called lines. Lines. His faded-red canoe was tied off to the starboard side. Wait, port? No, starboard.

What used to be their main halyard was now the rope Keith used to climb the tree in the morning. No lines on the boat equals no sailing. They hadn't taken the boat out for a sail since moving aboard last fall. Not even once.

No breakfast again today. If his father would let him take the ca-noe over by himself, he could still be on the boat, eating, watching TV. Right over there on the boat with no running rigging. It would be some time before the lunchroom opened at school. He looked at the cottonwood leaves and wondered what they tasted like.

Keith heard the bus before he saw it, and when he looked down, the long, bright-orange shape roared by below him. Oh no. He slammed his fist sideways against the trunk of the tree as the sound of the bus faded away.

This wasn't going to sit well with his dad. It wasn't the first time he'd missed the bus. The school would call home. Maybe his dad wouldn't say anything, wouldn't do anything about it besides giving him a look that froze him for the rest of the evening. He started reading the paragraph again but only got to the end of the first sentence.

Sometimes his father worked double shifts on the bridge and was gone late into the night. Alone on the boat, Keith answered the phone. Sometimes it was his teacher, calling again, asking for his parents. If the teacher left messages, Keith erased them. On those late nights, his father came back and closed the hatch behind him. Keith had to get up and open it again slightly, otherwise the air inside the boat grew thick and stale. Sometimes the smell of beer hung in the air above his bunk, several cabins away from where his father slept.

Even when his father was home, Keith usually answered the phone. Sometimes his mother called from Salem, but not often, especially after Keith told her once that she was a complete bitch. She'd laughed then and said there was too much of his father in him. Their conversations were shorter after that, just a little talk about what he wanted for Christmas or his birthday, questions about school or what he was eating. It was more than he and his father usually said to each other in an entire day.

Even during dinner on the boat, his dad rarely looked anywhere besides down at his plate, or at the TV. Once, Keith had held his middle finger out at his father during dinnertime, just above the tabletop, for several minutes. His father never looked up once. When the news came on with a story about a worker on the St. Johns Bridge who had fallen and drowned, Keith brought his hand down below the table. He looked at his dad, who turned the channel and cleared his throat.

"That was Shane. Worked nights on the east end of the bridge. Stupid kid with long hair. He got too close to a safe light, and his hair caught fire. He threw his hard hat into the river and got the fire put out, and he would've been fine if he hadn't looked into the damn safe light for so long. If it was going to happen to anybody on that bridge, it was going to happen to him."

Keith asked him what a safe light was.

"The contractors call them safe lights," his father said. "When they're turned on in the evening, they make the whole bridge bright as daytime. But they're only safe as long as you don't look directly at them. You have to keep your eyes on your work."

Up in the tree, Keith read the paragraph again. Then he climbed to a higher branch to get the blood flowing into his legs.

The marina seemed to go on for miles. Directly across from his tree, Keith could see the end of the lower marina on the downstream side, timeworn boat houses and fishing trawlers, most of them abandoned, and then a small home, that old guy Jack's place. That whole end of the dock was a boat graveyard with an old caretaker. There were half-a-dozen rotting wood hulls and trawlers decomposing, most of them listing to one side.

And then there was the *Susan K*. Keith had heard about the *Susan K* around the marina. It was the largest of the trawlers. It had been partly renovated by an ambitious new owner who painted the topsides bright red and the trim white, cleaning up the boat from the outside in. Eventually, as the guy worked his way inward, he found most of the bulkheads rotted out and the engine completely seized up. He ran out of money, and the *Susan K* was abandoned for a second time, the clean, bright-red topsides betrayed only by the listing hull. From the island side of the river, where Keith watched, the boat flared in the sun next to the brownish rot of its neighbors. The name gleamed in black-and-white letters on the stern. The outward glory of the *Susan K* challenged the stories of its rotten center.

Keith turned back to the book and started to read the paragraph again. He couldn't get past it. Didn't want to. He didn't want to know what was going to happen. He wanted to keep the book where it was, keep the mystery where knowing couldn't touch it. Once you knew, you couldn't go back to the delicious state of not knowing.

A grain barge was coming down the channel. He could feel the hum of the engine vibrating the trunk of the cottonwood. The barge came by every Tuesday and Thursday. Sometimes it came by early enough that he was still in the tree waiting for the bus. Usually he was at school, but he could hear its horn blowing on foggy mornings. In the late hours of the night, the barge made the return trip upstream empty, its giant rolling wake rocking Keith's boat and startling him awake.

Keith stood up on the branch where he'd been sitting, holding his body straight and still against the trunk. He peered out from behind the tree. The golden mounds of grain in the barge were piled high above the water, but they passed far below him. The pilothouse hovered just about level with the top of Keith's tree. The captain sat in a straight-back chair above a panel of controls. He had a CB mouthpiece in one hand and a pair of binoculars in the other, scanning the trees on the island shore. He paused slightly when he faced Keith, but moved on, stopping now and again to focus on other trees along the shore. Searching for osprey nests, probably, or eagles. Keith didn't move until the barge had made the turn downstream on its way to Astoria. After it passed around the next bend in the river, only the pilot house was visible above the steep shore of the island, like a car floating along just above the road.

Keith read the paragraph once more, all the way through. Then he nodded his head decisively, slammed the book shut, and tossed it toward the river. It landed on the surface with a distant thump and hung there for a moment until it finally began to dip under the water. The book wasn't his anyway. He'd taken it from the teacher's desk at school after she read a line or two from it to the class.

Keith scanned the road below, grabbed the rope, and rappelled down the trunk. Across the road, and down the steep embankment, were rows of newly sprouting vegetables. Maybe he could find something to eat there. In the garage at the farm just down the road, the back doors were always unlocked, and there were freezers inside packed with Popsicles and ice cream. The sun blazed hot above him. Yeah. He'd go there.

He gazed back once at the river downstream from the tree; the book was gone.

Even several months after arriving at the marina, Chad still found it difficult to read Jack's tone or his mood. Exasperation sounded similar to gratitude or elation. Other times, he had the quiet intensity of impending volcanic activity.

One rainy day, when Chad saw Jack approaching the fuel dock in his skiff, he donned a rain jacket to help Jack tie off to the dock cleats. It was midday, but the light was dim outside. Everything far off was lost in the haze of falling rain. Everything close by was a dull gray. Jack pulled up, but the current and the wind pushed him too far downstream, so he circled back around and tried again. When he was within three feet of the dock bumpers, Chad set one foot on the deck of the skiff and reached for the bowline. Skookum snapped at his ankle and barked.

Jack shouted from behind the wheel. "Get off my boat, you asshole!"

Chad looked up through the pelting rain from under his hood. There was not a trace of humor in Jack's hard-set eyes. He lumbered out of the pilothouse and snatched the line from Chad's hands. Then he pulled his right arm back, making a fist, ready to throw a punch. Chad backed away with hands outstretched, warding him off in a mock gesture and smiling, but Jack was not playing around. He straightened up, suddenly taller than Chad.

"Don't you know anything about boats, you cracker ass? If you aren't invited onto a boat by its captain, then you stand clear and mind your own fucking business!"

Jack stood facing Chad for a moment. The rain rattled on the water and the dock all around them. With the flick of a wrist, he sent a small loop down the bowline until it hooked onto the dock cleat. Without bending downward in the slightest, his eyes fixed on Chad's, he flipped his hand two more times and pulled the line tight; his skiff was secure. It happened so fast Chad couldn't believe he had done it. Even with both hands, Chad usually labored over the lines when he helped secure boats arriving for fuel; he had to squat low to secure the lines around the dock cleats, re-adjusting them to pull boats in tighter—and that was on sunny days, not like this moment, in rolling waves and wind and the lines slick with rain.

Jack was done and moving past him as if he wasn't even there, toward the shelter of the office, glaring through his eyebrows. Chad had seen him punch other men playfully on the shoulder. They would chuckle and then walk away rubbing their bruised arms. Chad had seen Jack strike like a snake. This occasional roughhousing feigned lightheartedness, but it also held the understanding that Jack was no one to fool with. As Jack walked past Chad, Chad kept his eye on Jack's hands. They were clenched into fists, and dripping with rain.

Three

After the first wave of sunshine in the spring, the clouds set in again, and it rained every day for three weeks straight. In the midst of this season, Moe disappeared. Chad climbed aboard his sailboat, the boat Moe had named the *Great Beyond*, and peered through the windows, but Moe wasn't there. Chad tidied up the deck and polished some of the fiberglass in case Moe showed up. Bill went up to the parking lot and looked for Moe's van. It was still parked there, empty. On the third morning after his disappearance, Moe showed up for coffee. "I just went for a walk along the river," he said.

"For almost three days?" Barry asked.

Moe only shrugged, a confused smile on his face. "Oh, I wasn't gone that long. Just out for a walk. I've been around." The guys insisted they had searched everywhere, but Moe shrugged again.

Jack tried one more time: "Cut the act, Houdini! Just admit you were passed out somewhere and you're hard to find when you disappear up your own guano hole."

"I don't drink that much," said Moe.

Though Jack usually cut Moe a little slack, Chad could tell Moe grated his nerves.

One morning, Chad came in early to do inventory. He was changing the prices on the gas pumps outside and making calculations, taking his time. Jack shuffled around the corner first and disappeared into the store. He came back outside soon after with his coffee and sat down. His green, plastic chair was filled with a small puddle of water, and he jumped back up and shouted.

"Shit!"

Chad dropped his clipboard, and Jack glared in his direction, swiping the rest of the water from the chair with the palm of his hand.

"Kind of early aren't you, Chadwick? Here for the fucking show?"

Chad shook his head and pointed to the clipboard. "Work," he said. "Crunching numbers."

Barry came around the corner, went inside, and returned with a steaming cup of coffee. Jack pulled a handkerchief from his back pocket and coughed hard into it several times. Chad was about to warn Barry about the water, when Barry looked down at the chair, tipped it forward until the water had drained, and sat down. The air was heavy with the silence of the men. Chad considered going into the store and finishing up the fuel pumps later, but then Moe came around the corner. By the time Moe got there, the other two seemed to have genuinely forgotten about the water in the chairs. Moe barely flinched when he sat in the puddle; he just stood back up and tipped the remaining water from the chair onto the dock. As he sat again, he spoke exuberantly about a fish he'd found under the floorboards on his sailboat. He said he kept hearing a swishing sound under the floor throughout the night, and when he pulled up the boards to look, there it was, a tiny fingerling salmon leaping in and out of the bilge water. He checked for holes on deck but found none. He said he hadn't brought any fish onboard for a while, so how it got in there was a mystery.

Chad scratched away on the clipboard with his pencil. The other two men looked up from their coffee, waiting for Moe to offer a punchline or speculate further. But he didn't.

From where he stood, Chad could only see the back of Moe's head. Was Moe just messing with them? The layers of fiberglass inside the hull of a sailboat—even one as rundown as Moe's— had to be sealed well enough to create a fairly closed system. The inevitable condensation, or rain dripping through tiny cracks on deck, would slowly drain to the lowest point in the hull. Chad shook his head. Unless there was a catastrophic leak in Moe's outer hull, big enough for a fish to get through, water would just do what water does on boats—accumulate slowly, over weeks or months, until there was enough of it to trip the float switch on the bilge pump and get sucked overboard.

Jack tilted his head and stared at Moe.

Bill came around the corner, said good morning, and hesitated when he saw the faces of the men around the table. He stood with his hands on the back of the last empty chair.

"Who died?" he asked.

Jack spoke to Moe as if he hadn't heard Bill arrive.

"Did you find the fish before or after you threw it in the bilge?"

As Moe drew in a breath to answer, Barry cut in. "It couldn't have been there very long—it would never last in sludgy bilge water."

Jack set his mug down on the table. "You're both full of horse shit! Either you've got a hole in the bottom of your boat or a hole in your head. Out with it! If there really is a fish in there, how did it get in?"

"I don't know."

"Quit farting around! There's no way a fish could get in there. You were probably just jerking off into your bilge, and you spawned a freak-fish that's about as dumb as you are."

"Sheesh, Jack," said Bill from where he stood. "No need to get all romantic about it."

Chad looked again at the back of Moe's head and walked quietly over to the diesel pump a dozen steps down the dock, where he unclipped the top page from the stack of fuel forms and placed it behind the others.

Moe shrugged his shoulders.

Jack slammed his hands flat on the table. Coffee sloshed out of mugs. "Moe. Before we all go make sure you have a bilge pump on your boat—one that actually works—let me tell you something about talking with words and sentences to other human beings. Don't make other people try to puzzle out what you are saying. If you're going to tell a story, at least tell something that has an end and makes some sense."

"I'm just trying to tell you what I saw. Events, not stories. Just what it is." Moe shook his head. "Do you know that there are colors and light waves that we can't even see? There is light that passes through objects at a subatomic level."

"Yeah, it's called television. It's called radio." Jack's hands waved in front of Moe's face. "There's music and debates and sermons broadcasting all over the place. Right here." Jack snapped the air in front of Moe's face with his thumb and forefinger. The sharp crack echoed off the shore on the other side of the river.

"And there's more than that too," said Moe.

"Yeah, you better believe there is. But a good story has some kind of conclusion. It comes full circle. It has a beginning that sets us up for what the rest of it's gonna be. You come down here every day and say things like, 'Hey fellas! There's a fucking fish swimming in my bilge water!' and then you expect us to oooh and ahhh and clap our hands like you're some kind of Holy Houdini?" Jack slammed the glass tabletop again with his palm. "*How the fish got there*, that's where your story is."

Moe leaned forward, smiling. "How the fish got there is one thing, talking about how it got there is another. It's guesswork. Just something to pass the time until the coffee is gone. I'm interested in the truth—it's gonna be way more interesting than all the guesses in the world." Chad smiled to himself. Moe was on a roll. Not backing down even though he could surely see Jack coming to a boil.

"Your truth would have Crazy Horse flying out of my ass." Jack's finger shook inches from Moe's face. "No truth, Moe-Moe. Only stories." Jack leaned back into his chair satisfied, claiming final say in the matter.

Moe spoke again, calmly. "But the fish got in there somehow before I told you about it and before you wanted me to tell about it in a certain way. It's too much talk. We should let our lives do the talking for us."

The men grew quiet. The dock swayed under their feet. Chad's heart thumped. Barry held a cup of coffee to his lips, squinting into its heat. Moe's head tilted up toward the sky, and even though Chad couldn't see his face, he could tell Moe was smiling. Jack wasn't.

Bill, still standing, finally slid the chair out from under the table and sat down. Everyone jumped a little when he leapt to his feet again with a loud yip. Chad broke the pencil tip on his clipboard. More coffee sloshed onto the tabletop.

"Who put the puddle of cold water in this seat?" Bill asked. The others chuckled, a little harder than the situation warranted. Bill glanced around, searching their eyes. Then he gave a wry smile and sat back down. "Oh, what the hell. Sure feels good on the hemorrhoids, at least."

Jack was smiling now too. "I'm surprised it soaked so quickly through those diapers you're wearing."

Barry spoke. "You almost missed it, Bill. Moe here was just about to tell us how a salmon got into his bilge."

"No, I wasn't. I was just saying that one was there, that's all. Why don't you guys come and take a look if you don't believe me."

They all shuffled into the store to fill up on coffee and then walked up the dock toward Moe's slip. They carried their steaming coffee mugs in silence, hoping not to wake anyone up along the way. After they climbed aboard, they gathered in a circle in the main cabin. Sure enough, there was a little fingerling in the bilge—but it floated on its side on the oily green surface.

That whole next week, the men made guesses about how the fish got there. The inquiry came to a close with Bill's theory. The key, he said, was in all the fishing that went on aboard Moe's boat. "Maybe, at some point Moe dropped some bait—a salmon egg—in the main cabin, where it rolled through the cracks in the floor and into the bilge. Then, with all the gutting and washing of fish out on deck and all the rain we've been having, the appropriate seed washed its way into cracks on the topsides, and ran down into the bilge where it spawned our little friend." It was the best idea anyone could come up with.

Moe never offered any suggestions; he only added more of the unnatural into the mix. He said that the night before he found the fish, he dreamed he was trying to climb the fish ladder up at Bonneville. He'd get almost to the top and then some guy in big boots would kick him in the head, causing him to slide all the way back down the ladder and into the river again.

Jack said, "Kicked in the head is right," but stopped short, shaking his head. "It's the damnedest thing, really," he said, and let it go at that.

Chad got to know Moe, little by little, whenever Moe stopped in for M&M's and menthols, or, as he referred to them, his three Ms. Chad asked what tribe he belonged to and if there was a story behind his name. Moe said his real first name was Morgan, but his last name had been lost to time and tribal displacement. He'd been called Moe for longer than he could remember. When he entered boarding school, he told the school his last name was Molalla, after one of his tribes. "Morgan Molalla" eventually became "Moe" for short.

Before his people were displaced by the progress of dams along the Columbia River, his family lived within walking distance of Celilo Falls. Before that, they'd lived in a village near a Catholic mission further south, until someone set fire to the mission buildings, and his family fled to avoid being blamed. Most of what Moe remembered was growing up among the Yakama Indians who lived on the fringes of Celilo village on the Columbia. The Yakama tribe allowed his family access to a couple fishing spots near the falls. At first, Moe wasn't allowed onto the platforms or near the edge of the rocks. Tribal relations were becoming more and more contentious with the shifting of fishing rights along the river—his family's permission to fish there was a particular honor that Moe couldn't explain.

Moe spent months watching the dam go up, watching trucks drive by carrying gravel or cement or supplies. The builders put stakes in the ground and painted red, orange, and yellow lines along the river; straight lines and right angles that crossed over rocks and trails, abandoned shacks, and the ancient drying racks that smelled of a hundred generations of salmon. The Army Corp of Engineers drove steel posts and small metal disks called benchmarks into rocks along the shore in invisible grids that turned sacred places into a kind of geometric landscape.

The elders of the tribes met. Their conversation ranged from anger to cool acceptance and back to anger again. There was talk of sabotage. There was talk of negotiation. There was talk of moving sacred remains from the ancient burial sites. There was talk and more talk. Moe, his brother, and their friends listened to the meetings and heard the words amounting to nothing as weeks and months and trucks went by. So they decided to do something about it. The boys wandered their old trails, dizzy in the presence of painted lines marking out unfamiliar shapes and signs: maybe they were future roads or outlying buildings or power lines. They tried to pry up the benchmarks, but couldn't. They took to pissing on them instead.

Moe's brother came up with other strategies. They went to the dam site with stolen paint to add their own lines and shapes until they had created a web of confusion. At night, they spread fish oil over rocks and scaffolding, hoping that workers would slip and fall. They roamed the hills with pellet rifles, shooting at supply trucks that roared down newly carved roads through ancient gathering places and sacred sites. On the top of a hill overlooking one road, they rolled large rocks down on the trucks, denting their sides. If the trucks came to a stop, the boys ran, giddy with their small victories. They kept it up as long as they could—little things to hold back the inevitable.

Moe listened to radio bulletins about their futile attempts to sabotage the building of the dam. The news made it out to be a matter of national security, an act of violence against the Army Corp of Engineers. Beyond that, they mostly stayed clear of the "Indian problem" out at Celilo, reserving airtime instead for the successful progress of modernization on the river.

Months went by. The steel framework and concrete grew up out of the rocks downstream. Even with the size of the project, the dam seemed quiet next to the roar of the river. Almost like it wasn't happening at all. More men were hired to paint more lines and hammer in more stakes, and then more men came to guard those lines and stakes. The boys turned their attention to fishing.

In March of 1957, two weeks before the completion of the dam, Moe's brother drowned while fishing the falls. When he fell in, their father jumped in after him. Someone caught Moe's father's body in a net downstream, but the life was gone from him. He was the last person to be buried on sacred grounds along the old shoreline before it was submerged. They never found his brother. Some said his body must have been caught under the rocks and was still there.

The dam builders used dynamite to blast away at the falls and make a passable channel for the barges and ocean-going vessels that would soon bring goods from overseas. Then they closed the dam gates. It took six hours for the waters to rise up and cover Celilo.

A crowd gathered some eight miles upstream from the dam. On the day the waters rose, there was a lot of murmuring. Some of the Natives were singing and banging on drums. Then the crowd went silent. They wanted to hear the last sounds the thundering falls made before they grew still. The roaring that had filled the valley for thousands of years fell away and was gone. The hiss of traffic on the highway and the distant hum of the dam rose up to take its place. It was a mournful sound, even a little consoling, and it droned out a new tune that echoed through the Gorge. Moe's mother died the same week the dam closed its doors on the river, drowned in her grief. Moe liked to think about his brother, still down there somewhere, his bones resting on rocks under a soft layer of silt.

The state and federal government used celebratory language to mark this moment of progress, and Moe remembered the excitement in the air, especially on television. Vice President Nixon came to the ribbon cutting of The Dalles Dam, and the river suddenly became important to the success of democracy all over the world.

Giant barges with foreign symbols painted on their sides rumbled along the Columbia. Moe began to catch more sturgeon and squawfish. They were multiplying below the dam, feeding off the eggs of salmon unable to make it upstream. Fish runs dwindled, and he and his people were blamed for overfishing in their areas.

Further upstream, where the river was now a series of unbroken lakes linked by navigable locks, new official rules were established for Native fishing. A new language of unofficial, unspoken rules soon followed. Officially, Natives kept the rights to their fishing areas. Unofficially, there were fewer fish to catch, ancient sacred sites were gone, and Natives were expected to get out of the way. Rules of the road changed on the newly bloated river. A vessel using paddles or under sail (you could set sails on the river now), supposedly had right of way over vessels under power, but the commercial vessels couldn't stop quickly, so you got the hell out of their way to avoid being overrun. If you fished, you were always looking over your shoulder. Barge horns echoed off the surrounding hills, adding to the new sounds of railway and highway traffic that had replaced the pounding voice of the river.

People fished from newly built platforms along the shore, or in boats, sometimes at night under the bright lights of the dams, but their catches were paltry compared to the ton or so of fish they used to catch in a day. Officially, Natives couldn't fish with nets from certain rocks near the dam on either side. Fines were handed out, but they went unpaid. Some Natives fished and refused to carry identification, or they used the names of dead relatives when they were caught. The government created incentives to draw them into urban life.

After Celilo was flooded, and his family along with it, Moe moved from one foster home to the next, until the state government placed him in a Catholic boarding school with other Northwest Natives. Some of the Native teenage students ran away. Moe stayed put. He learned a foreign, Caucasian history of westward expansion. He learned Latin. He learned to play the trumpet in the tiny school band until the day he tripped and bent the school's only brass horn. When he finished high school, he joined friends in Portland, following the tide of Indians who moved into the city looking for work.

Moe told Chad about living on the streets in downtown Portland. He told Chad about finding Jesus and getting a job at a music shop cleaning instruments. At the end of each day, he took one of the store's trumpets with him and played late at night along the Willamette River. One night another homeless man, tired of Moe's noise, grabbed the horn from him and threw it into the river. Moe worked extra hours to pay for the lost horn. He started drinking heavily and eventually lost his job. He lived on the streets and slept in parks. He was beaten badly more than once over the years. He was stabbed twice. He said his longest bout of pneumonia lasted two full years. Moe told Chad about finding a winning lottery ticket, and about his injured hip being healed in a church downtown. "I couldn't go to that church anymore when they stopped praying so much and started mostly preaching and talking a lot, instead of listening to what the Holy Spirit wanted to say." There were tears in his eyes. "There I go," he said. "I usually cry in the mornings."

One Friday evening, Keith's father climbed the mast to try running a new main halyard through the pulley at the masthead and down its hollow center. Without any explanation, he grabbed a tool belt, a plastic bag filled with unopened beers, and a bosun's chair; then he strapped them all to himself, threw some lines over the spreaders, tied the chair to a come-along, and started ratcheting himself up. When he was standing on the spreaders, he worked his way up the shrouds and lashed himself to the masthead.

He was up there for a long time. Keith yelled up to him, but his dad didn't seem to hear. An empty beer can clattered into the cockpit. Keith walked from the port side to the starboard for a better view of his father's face. The boat rocked under his feet, and the top of the mast swayed from one cloud to another.

"God dammit, kid, you're flinging me around up here!"

Keith froze.

"Stand still and don't move your feet from that spot. If I drop anything, it'll be your fault."

His father was up there so long, the night began to settle in. Keith didn't move from his spot. His neck hurt from looking up. Another beer can bounced off the deck and fell with a splat in the water. In the fading light, Keith could just make out the silvery shape bobbing along.

From where Keith stood on the deck, the sky was a deep blue, filled with patches of stars. A flashlight clicked on among them. One of his father's hands, ghostlike in the beam of light, held a shimmering can. Keith heard a grunting sound, and the empty can landed in the current with a light tap.

Then Keith heard a nervous rustling and clanking. "Son of a bitch," his father said, and Keith looked up to see the flashlight spiraling down toward him. It spun through the air forever before he felt the sharp blow to his shoulder and heard it bounce from the deck into the water, where the beam of light quickly faded. Keith dropped to his side, his shoulder humming with pain, his back pressed against the shrouds rising from the deck to the top of the mast. His father cursed again, somewhere in the darkness. A new can hissed and cracked open. Keith waited for his father to say something to him about the flashlight, waited for his father to ask him if he was OK, waited to feel something else fall and hit his arm or his foot or his head. Maybe a wrench or a hammer. Or maybe his father would fall. Keith reached for a life jacket resting on a tangle of line nearby and pulled it over his head. A metal tool clinked against a bolt high above him, the sound vibrating down the length of the mast.

Just three years earlier, when Keith had fallen and broken his leg, his father had scooped Keith into his arms, his face wrinkled in horror, tears in his eyes. But that was a different time. He was just a kid then.

The man at the top of the mast shifted his weight and pounded hard several times on the masthead with something heavy. "Son of a bitch," he kept saying, over and over. The shrouds shivered where they pressed against Keith's back, humming against his ribs and spine through his clothing.

His father must have heard the flashlight when it hit him. He must have known. But he didn't say anything.

The next day, the forward cabin was quiet. The tools sat in a pile in the cockpit among half-a-dozen empty beer cans. The new main halyard hung from the boom in a tangled web of knots.

Four

"How had Marge known?" Moe wondered. He must have said something at the fuel dock about his nightmares, and Marge had overheard. After the sun went down that evening, she'd come to his boat and tapped lightly on the window. Handing the dream catcher to him, she said, "I made this for you."

Moe looked through the dim evening light into her eyes, and she looked into his, and the minutes went by and neither of them looked away. He'd never felt so calm, or understood, or fully known by another human being.

Marge was the first to look away, down at her hands, as if she expected to find something there. Moe took one step back and opened his arms. She stepped aboard, and they wrapped their arms around one another and stayed that way for a long time, feeling the warmth between them in the cool night air.

They were up all night, talking. They drank a little whiskey, but not too much, and only because he offered it when he didn't have anything else onboard to drink. They lounged in the forward berth, arms wrapped around each other, and spoke of the loneliness of the day before, trying to make sense of their joy in the present moment. They tried to put words to what was happening between them and spoke the names of those they would see on the dock in the morning, guessing at each person's reaction to seeing the two of them walking hand in hand. Jack. Barry. Dory.

Marge looked at Moe's face. "Oh, she won't be surprised a bit."

"Really? I guess she knows just about everything before it happens around here. We should all be drawn to this like Dory seems to be. Drawn like magnets."

"Drawn to what? You're talking up a fog again."

"To love. We're all so hungry for it. We should recognize it more."

Love. It was the first time the word had been spoken between the two of them.

"And the fog thickens." She kissed his cheek. "But I get you."

"You get me?"

"I just mean: you and I. Two souls who don't need to make sense of everything at every moment. Let's stay here, on this boat, and never leave. Unless we take the boat somewhere. Let's go downstream and watch a movie together at the old theater in Astoria."

"We could take your boat so you have your oven handy. Astoria is a good place, and it would be even better if we could introduce it to some of the Abundance."

"You mean, the bread? It's no more, I'm afraid."

Moe looked at her expectantly.

"The yeast, the starter I used, just kind of faded away on me. Maybe it's the flour I added or the humid air on the water…"

Moe said, "The kingdom of heaven is like yeast that a woman took and mixed into flour until it worked all through the dough." He stared off into the distance.

Marge asked, "What religion is that from? Where did you go?"

Moe looked at her. "Maybe the yeast was going through a season of some kind."

"It was probably homesick. It came from Italy, from a city on the water there."

"Venice is a nice place," Moe said.

Marge's eyes widened. "Have you been there?"

"I dreamed once that I lived there."

When the sky brightened on the horizon, they bundled together in blankets on the back deck and watched the sun rise.

Moe realized, as the sun blazed over the hills, that he had passed through the night without one of his increasingly frequent nightmares. Morning was arriving, and here he was with a calm fullness in his heart unlike the shock of waking from his recent dark dreams. When he shifted his weight, Marge pulled him close. He thought, surely those nights were over now.

Marge hadn't spoken to anyone about her daughter in many years, but she told Moe.

"My husband and I planned to take her on a cruise across the English Channel when she was only four years old. We'd been waiting since..." She paused. "Well, since my surprise pregnancy during my last year in art school. We'd been saving for it, or rather, he had. He worked at a bank. A cruise on a floating metropolis isn't my idea of fun, but I'd always wanted to go to Europe, so we compromised. But we never even made it onto the plane."

She stopped.

Moe said, "You don't have to talk about this if you don't want to."

"We lost her at the airport while we were waiting to board. She was sitting next to us. She fell asleep. My husband watched her while I went to buy a couple books. I was gone for too long. Too long. Buying a book on parenting, of all things. And some magazines. I came back to the gate, and my husband was asleep, and she was gone. They never found her. We never found her."

Moe remained quiet for a long time. "What was her name?" he asked eventually. "Marge?"

He looked down at her face and saw she was sleeping.

They spent the following day on the *Great Beyond*. When they'd finished eating what little food Moe had on board, they moved over to her sailboat. Her father had named it *Margaret* back when he first bought it. Moe took to calling it "The Margaret." She thought it sounded funny, so she started calling his boat "The Moe." They went back to *The Moe* as the evening sky dimmed. He hung the dreamcatcher from a hook in the galley, and they fell asleep in the forward cabin. First her, then him.

They spent the next entire week on board *The Margaret* and the following week on *The Moe* again. Then his nightmares came back.

One night, he dreamed he was drowning and trying to call 9-1-1 underwater, but he couldn't get them to hear his voice. The dream came and went, but the pounding in his chest didn't stop. Terror and dread surrounded him, and then his dreaming self was looking up at the sky from the deck of his sailboat. From the boom to the top of the mast, chords were woven in a grid-like pattern. They dripped with thick fluid, and a hulking black shape crawled down them. The pulsating creature approached him on many legs, and its hairy body filled his vision. He felt his limbs go numb, his heart beating painfully. The creature carried him up the mast.

He woke and looked around frantically. A saccharine smell in the cabin. Someone next to him. A look of horror on her face. She shrunk back from him. The floor underneath his bare feet swayed as he stood up.

That look of horror.

He asked Marge to leave, and his heart continued to pound in his chest and ears, even after he had closed the curtains and shut the door behind her. He gasped for air. He drank whiskey. He paced and rummaged through drawers. He needed something to do with his trembling hands. He fumbled through a closet, pulled out a ball of string, and wound it tightly around his wrist until his hand grew numb and purple. He unwound it and wound it again, this time around the rim of the dreamcatcher until it was a round disc of string.

Moe heard a soft tapping sound on the window twice that day. The first time, he listened to Marge's trembling voice. He couldn't make out her words—just the bird-like softness of her voice. The second time, he covered his ears and shrank to the floor until he was sure she was gone. The boat rocked lightly. The world swayed around him. He gasped for air. He felt like he was falling and falling.

This kind of love was a trap. It would be the end of him if he let it. He drank whiskey until his weeping stopped.

The next night, Moe woke with a sense of urgency from another terrifying dream. He itched with an impulse to do something. Up on the boat deck, in the dark, he patched a couple of holes in his mainsail with duct tape. Glancing at Marge's boat, he saw her lights were still out. He folded the sail on top of the boom and secured it. He wound a whole roll of duct tape around the backstay, then got out another roll and secured some other lines that often came loose in the wind. He wound back and forth between the boom, the side stays, the mast, and the rest of the standing rigging.

The wind picked up—a river of invisible currents. It hissed through the taut web of tape. He wound more tape around the mast and down at angles to the boom. When he couldn't reach any higher up the mast, he hoisted himself up in a bosun's chair and continued making a web of crosshatches, until he had woven a massive sail-shaped triangle of tape.

He dangled from the chair halfway up—for how long, he didn't know—listening to the wind humming through the translucent sail, feeling the boat lean and rock lightly until the wind calmed and then stopped altogether. All was quiet. The surface of the river was still and dark. "What am I," he thought. "Predator, or prey?" The memory of Marge's frightened face in the forward cabin made him wince. He lowered himself to the deck and looked up at the web-sail he'd made, half expecting to see the menacing shape from his dreams outlined by the starry sky above.

What unseen things would he catch in this net? Some wind in the spiritual realm that still blew despite the calm? To be open to the unseen light of Love was also to be vulnerable to a terrifying darkness. He pulled his cigarette lighter from his pocket and started small flames in the tape just above the boom. They spread upward, glistening. Molten tape dripped and loosened, hissed, snapped, and burned upward, where the flames finally faded to smoke between the fiberglass mast and the steel backstay. The boom fell to the deck. A number of ashy threads wavered from the rigging in the light, early-morning breeze.

Moe walked up the marina ramp to solid ground, then turned

and followed the muddy shoreline downstream into the rising sunlight.

In the morning, the deck of Moe's boat was littered with ash and pockmarks where melted tape had dripped. Gray threads dangled in the wind among the halyards.

No one saw Moe for a week.

Bill and Bernice sat at a table under an umbrella around lunchtime, all by themselves. Chad glanced out at them every few minutes. Bernice was looking down at one of Bill's hands, held in both of hers, as if in conversation with it. They were both drinking something neon green from a massive cocktail glass. Dory came over every few minutes with a new, oddly shaped bottle, and soon the table was littered with bottles of various heights and colors. Bernice continued her conversation with Bill's hand.

Chad called over to Rick's desk across the room. "Hey, Rick. Do you know what the hell is up with Bill and Bernie out there?"

"Enough to know I don't give a shit. Those two are like a couple of teenagers. Better off not knowing."

Chad stepped outside the sliding glass doors. "OK," he said. "I've got to ask. Are you guys having some kind of Wiccan session or Mary Kay ... Holy shit, Bill! Your finger!

Bill's ring finger was purple and twice the size of any of his other fingers. His wedding ring had sunk into the skin above his knuckle and was barely visible.

Bill tried to chuckle, but it came out as a choking sound instead. "I wish."

"Did you smash your finger with something?"

Bernice was trying in vain to get the ring to slide or spin. "All he did was try to put his wedding ring on."

"How long have you guys been at this?"

"I don't know," said Bernice, "twenty minutes?"

Bill looked at Chad, his face shining with sweat and twisting into an unconvincing smile. "It's our anniversary today. This is just how we celebrate. We've tried every type of cooking oil and motor grease known to man. Man, you've got to stop Dory. She wants to try sauerkraut and hot sauce next."

"I do not," said Dory, returning from the cabinets behind the hot dog stand with a lantern, lamp oil, and a razor blade.

"Get away from me!" Bill yelled when he saw her approaching. Chad backed up a step to avoid Dory's bony elbows, shoulders, and whatever lethal things she was carrying. "Alright, guys," Chad said, "I'm going to call paramedics or someone. You needed to cut that ring off, like, ten minutes ago."

Bernice looked up at him. "That's what I'm trying to tell him. He keeps saying we'll try for one more minute, and then we'll go down to the jeweler and get it resized."

Bill shrugged. "I don't want to lose this ring. It would blow the mood for the whole romantic day I have planned."

Bernice took both Bill's hands and looked into his eyes. "They can fix it—resize it—after they cut it off, Billy."

"She's right, Bill," said Dory.

Chad nodded and said, "You can have them make it so big, it will just slide on and off like nothing. That's what I did with my wedding ring, only then it was too big, and it slid right off and fell in the river."

They looked at him.

Bernice smiled and said sweetly, "So, you're married, huh? Still married?"

Dory gaped. "What? OK, everybody. That's it. The hot dog stand is closed for the day! Everybody go home. Chad's married."

Chad backed up a step.

"Get your ass back over here." Dory grabbed him by the elbow. "How the hell long were you going to wait to tell me about this?"

Chad held up both hands in front of him. "Wait. Wait. Stay focused," he said. "We're having an actual emergency here. I'm going to go call 9-1-1."

"Don't bother, Chadwick," said Bill. "I'm headed up to the parking lot." He and Bernice stood in unison.

"I'm driving," said Bernice.

"Great, we'll never get there."

"Oh, now all of a sudden you're in a big rush."

Dory looked at Chad. "Don't go thinking this conversation is over, young man."

Chad turned and opened the sliding door. "It is. I'll talk to the whole universe about it when I decide to." He closed the door behind him.

Dory and Bernice met each other's eye, and Dory said, "Did he just get pissed? Is that him getting pissed? He's pissed, isn't he?"

Chad lost his wedding ring to the river when he and Abby still lived on the water. It had been his grandfather's ring, a gift he'd received from his grandmother.

Chad and Abby had been cleaning the boat on the day it happened. He was shaking out a small, round rug over the water. The dust and food crumbs from the rug collected on the surface of the river and held there. It was a cool winter day. His fingers were stiff and cold, unswollen. On the final shake of the rug, the ring slipped off his finger and bounced three times on the dock—ding, ding, ding.

Its shadow passed beyond the wood planks of the dock, and its inverted reflection flashed on the surface of the water. It was only an instant, but the image of the reflected ring hung suspended in his mind. For a brief, confused moment—before he could label with words the thing that was happening—he saw two rings, rather than the one he knew. A stab of wonder and grief pierced his chest as one ring rose and the other fell—they joined with a small, underwhelming "plop."

The flecks of dust settling on the surface of the water slowly moved away with the current. He was left gazing into his own wavering reflection. Up on deck, Abby turned her head when she heard the sound and saw him leaning over the stern, staring at the water, not moving.

"Oh," she said.

She said it flatly, nodding her head, almost like an admission. She knew what had happened and seemed to know what it meant.

She faced moments of loss and pain like that—nodding like she had seen it coming and could receive it for what it was.

Chad closed his eyes.

Gone.

They hired a diver to go down into the river after it. The diver was a man old enough to be Chad's father. His hair was mostly gray, his weathered face the color of wet sand. When Chad pointed to where the ring had gone in, the diver removed his own ring from his left hand, fed a thin fishing line through it, and dropped it into the river.

"That ring was from my ex-wife back when we were married," he said with a grin. "It'll sink down to the river bottom, landing roughly where your ring is. It's good therapy throwing it into the river over and over again. Someday, maybe I'll actually lose it for good."

They waited while the fishing line ran slowly through the diver's fingers until it finally grew still. Then he wrapped it tightly around a dock cleat and lowered himself into the water, following that thin line down to the bottom. For half an hour, Chad and Abby watched the river current bubble and churn from the expelled air of the diver's oxygen tank.

When he resurfaced, he shook his head. His wetsuit was torn slightly at the shoulder, a hole the size of a silver dollar revealing a blood-red gash surrounded by red, pimpled skin. He removed the dark gloves, untied the fishing line from his ring and worked it back onto his finger. Chad asked if he'd seen anything. The diver smiled and said there was no seeing anything down there, even with his headlamp. The light of the sun faded into darkness at about ten or fifteen feet below the surface. During the spring runoff, he couldn't even see the fishing line that led him down into the depths, though he kept the line mere inches from his mask. You just get to know where the line is, he said. Going down there wasn't about seeing anything, it was about feeling and sensing what you could, which was quite a lot if you spent enough time below the surface.

He said he was pretty sure he knew where Chad's ring was, but he couldn't get to it. A large mass of twisted metal had dammed up a lot of stuff below them—trees, tires, a shopping cart—a mound of debris over ten feet tall and several times as wide. There was no way to pull it all apart. Rust and years of pressure from the river current had locked it together.

Chad pointed to the hole in the diver's suit where blood ran in a thin line down his arm. The diver nodded and told them he'd better get going so he could clean out the wound. He said he'd been infected a number of times from the toxins in the water. Once, he'd almost lost a leg to parasitic infection.

Chad pulled out his wallet to pay him, but he shook his head as he tossed the oxygen tank over his shoulder and turned to walk away. "Tough luck," he said, "but look at it this way: you'll always know where your ring is."

The diver was right. Chad would always know where his ring was—the one he'd worn. The one that had begun to reshape the skin and flesh of his finger. The other ring, the reflection, seemed just as real for all its brief existence. It hung suspended in Chad's mind like a sharp sting. Lost. It seemed absurd, but a small portion of his loss was also in the other ring—the one he'd found for a brief moment before it vanished into the dark water at the same time it ascended into the gray sky. He tried to tell himself the other ring was not worth noting. He dismissed it, and yet, to his relief, it remained in his mind.

Clouds hung black in the sky over the channel, and wind whistled in the rigging above Moe. His mouth was dry, his skin sweating, and his heart racing. The lights from the dock glistened on something in the water upstream. He reached for his net and pulled a bottle out of the water as it floated near. There was a note inside. He made out a phone number—Portland area code. Since he didn't own a telephone, he walked to the pay phone on the fuel dock. The phone purred in his ear. He waited for an answer.

It had been a while since Moe had shown up at the marina store with one of the many strange things he'd found floating by in the current. This time, it was a bottle with a note in it. Jack unfolded the note and looked at the phone number written there.

"You call it yet?" he asked.

Moe started a coughing fit that went on and on. Chad winced to hear it—he hadn't seen Moe in days. Moe held his chest. Between short breaths he said: "The number was disconnected." He said it was time for him to head upstream, back to the source of things.

Chad said, "You shouldn't be going anywhere. Except to the doctor."

"I have. He said I'm falling apart at the seams."

"Is it something serious?"

"Oh, no. Just the old flesh doing what it does best. And too many of these damn things." Moe waved a half-smoked cigarette in the air and shook his head.

Chad handed Moe his "three Ms," the pack of M&M's and the pack of menthol cigarettes. He hesitated before handing over the cigarettes. Moe popped some M&M's into his mouth, then coughed again.

Jack asked about the note in the bottle, if it had something to do with his sudden urge to travel. Moe said, "No, it's just the right time for me to go."

Jack turned a suspicious eye on him and said, "I'll believe it when I look toward your boat slip and see it empty. And if it ever really is, we're holding that slip open, because you're just gonna be back in a few days."

Jack followed Moe on his way out the door. Moe shifted to avoid someone who had just rounded the corner, and he lost his balance, dropping the bottle. It was Marge. The bottle rolled under a table where Barry was sitting, and Moe hurried away. Jack watched him go, then joined Barry at the table.

Inside the store, Marge approached the counter and spoke softly to Chad. It took Chad a second to realize she was even addressing him. He leaned closer so he could hear.

"Chad, can you do me a favor? Can you tell Moe I said it's alright?"

Chad sighed, then nodded.

"Thank you. He doesn't have to worry about it, about me. I'm alright. Tell him I'm not going anywhere and that I'll always be his friend."

"I will," said Chad. "Are you really OK?"

"More OK than not," she said.

Moe left the next day. Bill and Barry helped him shove off while he raised the sails. It turned out his boat didn't have a working engine. Barry tried to give him a small outboard but Moe refused. He'd follow the wind and set anchor when he needed to, tie off to other boats when he got to the locks. Other sailors would have spent months in preparation for this trip. Moe prepared by selling his van and moving the plastic angel from the stern to the bowsprit so she could gaze out ahead of the boat.

In the afternoon, Chad walked over, handed him a bulk box filled with M&M's packages, and said, "They're on me."

Moe reached out, and they shook hands. Chad asked why he felt he had to leave, but Moe only shook his head. He placed a trembling hand on Chad's shoulder. His eyes welled with tears. "I'm sorry, I don't usually cry in the afternoon."

"Call us when you find a place to stay."

Moe nodded and said, "You'll hear from me."

After school and again after dinner every weekday, Keith met Nick and Steve at the top of the ramp in the upper marina, where the three of them hid their life jackets behind a rhododendron, then wandered into the forest between the channel and the highway, just upstream from the upper parking lot.

Nick and Steve had known each other all their lives. Nick had a picture of the two of them sitting on a lawn in their diapers.

They'd been through Cub Scouts together. Steve had earned about ten times the badges as Nick, who'd focused mainly on Morse code for two years straight. Nick taught Steve enough of the Morse language for the two of them to tap out messages to each other at school or around others they wanted to keep things from.

Nick was a thin boy with a mop of blond hair who always wore a soccer jersey with the number eleven across the chest and back. He said eleven was his lucky number, just two ones side by side, and when the number eleven was multiplied by one of those ones, you got eleven again. He said it was a solid number he could trust.

Nick could talk for hours if uninterrupted. Sometimes he described confrontations between people who didn't even exist. Today, he told them about two older students (who probably didn't exist) from the high school across the street, who were at each other's throats over their mutual love for a beautiful, blond-haired teacher (who probably didn't exist) with large breasts (which seemed to exist everywhere in Nick's life), until one of the students shot the other—the violence of this story shook Nick back to himself and he reconsidered. "No, wait, that's not quite right, but you should have been there. It was amazing."

Steve spoke out of his long, habitual silence, "Maybe you should have been there yourself, taking better notes."

"Screw you, Steve. You can't even remember what you had for lunch today, much less who the hot teachers are."

Steve was quiet but attentive. He was always on the lookout for the perfect skipping stone. Even when he seemed to be lost in his rock collecting, though, he could interrupt and point out the contradictions in Nick's verbal wanderings. Steve wore the clothes passed down from his older brother, always a little too big or too small. He had recently learned to juggle; he could juggle three things at a time: coins or wads of paper, sometimes, but usually three small stones. When Keith tried to convince him to juggle four things, Steve only frowned and shook his head and said, "No, three's plenty."

Steve could skip stones all the way across the channel, from the dock to the island shore, when he wanted to. Neither Keith nor Nick could even come close. Steve would follow slightly behind the other two, head bent down at the base of his neck so he looked like he was sleeping on his feet. Sometimes, when Keith found what seemed to him a perfectly round, flat skipping stone, he'd hand it to Steve, who'd hold it up to the light between two fingers and bounce it in his palm before passing it back saying, "Nope. It'll never make it." The others never doubted him when it came to rocks, and he never offered them reason to. He could balance larger rocks on top of each other until he had a stack towering above his head. He had several of these stacks in progress along the river, and when they wandered near one, he might stop and make it a little taller.

Keith's life at the Sauvie Island School on the opposite shore, just across the Multnomah Channel from the marina, was a complete mystery to his friends. He could make up pretty much whatever he wanted about his life during the day—girlfriends, crop circles, cattle mutilations, dinosaur remains—and the others could only listen or ask questions. Sometimes Steve would smirk and shake his head in disbelief, or Nick would offer elaborations and guesses, but mostly they listened or tried to express contempt for the "hay-seeders" over on the island.

The other kids living at the marina went to school in Scappoose. Keith would have gone there too, if it weren't for his mom. She had done her research. The homely schoolhouse on the island might do him some good, she said, and she knew it would piss his dad off to have to drive out of his way to cross the bridge to the island every day. She didn't know about the car breaking down. She didn't know about Keith crossing the channel in the motorboat with his dad and waiting for the school bus on the island by himself either.

The first Saturday after Moe left, Chad paid a guy in Scappoose way too much for a motorcycle. He rode upstream along the Columbia into the Gorge on the Oregon side. He crossed the river at the Bridge of the Gods and headed back along the Washington shore. He brought binoculars, stopping frequently under overpasses or thick stands of evergreen so he could look out over the river. His eyes searched the wind-churned channels and bays. But he couldn't find Moe's sailboat anywhere.

Eventually, a few answers came over the shortwave radio stored above the coffeemaker at the marina store. As summer had come to an end, rain had settled in for weeks without a break, and the river was swelling against its banks. The dams upstream let out water with machine-like precision, spillways roared, and the Multnomah Channel ran high. "Unusual weather," local news reports said, "with record levels of precipitation."

A story had been running for several days out in The Dalles, but it was a little off-kilter for the likes of Portland broadcasting networks. It didn't make the news in Portland until cracks started appearing in The Dalles Dam.

When Chad heard about the cracks in the dam, he searched until he found a station broadcasting from The Dalles. For the past three or four days, the news out there had been following the story of a crazy Native American who was trying to fish in the off-limit area around the dam's spillway. Whenever the guards went down to look for him or arrest him, he evaded them. In a radio interview, the guards claimed that he seemed to disappear in the mist.

One morning, a week or so after they first spotted him, guards at the dam heard what sounded like a trumpet down near the spillway. One of the employees at the dam said it sounded like an old hymn. When they went down to investigate, they found a silver trumpet dripping with water at the shore's edge, but there was no sign of the man. They never heard or saw him again. Later that same day, news of cracks in the dam reached the broadcasters in Portland.

In the days that followed, the cracks in the dam lengthened. Then the rain stopped, and the water level slowly came back down. Contractors started bidding to patch up the dam. Trucks arrived, bringing workers and supplies. They filled in cracks and reinforced the dam's foundation.

Chad left the radio dial tuned to The Dalles station for the next couple of weeks, and eventually they heard about the body found downstream from the dam. A few members of the Yakama tribe had identified the remains, and Moe was buried in a small graveyard next to his mother. Local tribes were hailing him as the Indian Joshua who almost brought down Jericho. In the following days, the radio told how The Dalles Dam security had their hands full finding and arresting Native Americans congregating at the foot of the dam with trumpets, trombones, and whatever other instruments they could get their hands on.

The news eventually died down. Chad turned the radio dial back to something more local.

Standing in the mist and the rain, the concrete walls towering above him, the salmon churning in the river before him—water all around—Moe pressed the stops on his trumpet and blew. At first the notes seemed lost in the rushing water, but when he paused, notes echoed off the dam walls, filling what room was left in the air. Water falling and water rising. The river pushed upward, joining the sky, joining the notes of the song. The earth rumbled and shifted. Moe coughed, water filling his lungs. He blew into the trumpet again, the song carrying through his coughing. Water swallowed everything. Solid ground dissolved under his feet. Bright red salmon brushed past his arms and legs and chest. Then the salmon drifted away and were gone. All was gone. No rain. No air. No song. Only the river.

The Coast Guard had been called shortly before the Indian fell into the river, so they arrived only a couple minutes later and fished his body out. The man was unconscious and breathing only occasional shallow breaths.

He was taken to The Dalles Hospital and rushed into the ER, where several nurses and the paramedics crowded into the small room and shouted out vital signs.

"Do we have a name?" asked one nurse.

"No. No name," said a paramedic. "It's some lunatic who was down at the foot of the dam and fell in."

"I need a second pair of eyes on this guy's pupils," said another. "They look dilated. Hard to tell. Emma, can you take a look?"

The nurse named Emma pulled back one eyelid and aimed her flashlight into the patient's eye. The other eye snapped open, and the patient focused on Emma's face. He breathed one deep, raspy breath and said, "Angel … You were there all along."

"What?" said Emma. "What did you say?"

He breathed one more short breath and said, "Thank you …" Then his eyes went dark. The monitor reading his pulse flat-lined, and the room erupted in more activity.

After some time, Emma said, "We should have stopped a few minutes ago. Where is the doctor?"

"I couldn't find him. I'll try the cafeteria."

"Run, please." She placed a stethoscope on his chest, paused, and shook her head. She lifted one of his eyelids again and said, "That's a first."

"What's that?"

"He called me Angel."

"Emma, you alright? Why don't you go take a break?"

"No," she said. Then she whispered, "Why the fuck couldn't I have been on lunch or something?"

"Go on. I've got this."

Emma pulled off her gloves, slapped them down onto the floor, and shouted, "Somebody get the fucking doctor in here to give us the fucking time of death!"

She left the room and walked down the hall. Opening the door to the storage closet, she closed it behind her, put her hands over her face in the dark, and cried.

Five

For the third day in a row, rain kept most people at the marina indoors. Chad was just about to put on a fourth pot of coffee when Jack called out to him from across the room.

"Hey, Chad! While you're over there near those supply shelves, how about you measure out a good dozen yards of double-braided line for me? Solid white. Three-quarter inch."

A few minutes later, Chad returned to the main counter and set the coil of soft, bright-white line in front of Jack. "You really want more rope?" he asked. "I've seen how much you already have looped and hanging from the outside walls over at your place. Not a bare square foot of wall to be seen."

Jack sighed, shook his head and said, loud enough for the other people in the room to hear, "Since I know the doctor dropped you on your skull after you were born, I'm gonna cut you some slack. But don't ever let me hear you say 'rope' again while you're down here, floating on water."

"OK. Line then. Not rope. You can never pass up a chance to school a person, can you? You know what I meant."

"Do I?" asked Jack. "Do you know what you meant? And nobody needs to answer to your sorry ass about why they want more line in their life."

Chad rang up the bill for the cordage on the register and said, "Let me guess, Captain Hornblower. Put it on your tab."

Jack didn't answer. He settled onto a stool next to several others who were there for coffee. Finally he said, "I tell you what,
I'll tell a story that will be worth a hell of a lot more than some
of your damn 'rope.' Chad here thinks he's already been schooled
more than anyone else around here, but I'll bet he hasn't heard
shit about that guy who used to strap a motorcycle onto the deck
of his sailboat way back when. I know some of the rest of you
have. Happened right here on this river. My old man lived in this
story. Played the fucking hero, the way he told it.

"Back before you could expect to have electricity or phone
lines on this stretch of the river, it was nothing to see guys
walking around with hundreds of feet of line hanging from their
belts. My old man never left the house without it. I never thought
to ask him why. There was just that deep-rooted instinct that a
length of rope is rarely a burden and usually a help. What help a
length of rope might become is hard to know before you see how
handy it might have been when you don't have it. My father grew
up around both horses and sailboats, and he knew by instinct: on
or near the water, you could never have too much line.

"Sometimes a line is all that stands between you and the chaos
that the wind and the river can bring. It doesn't matter how big
or how fancy your boat is. If you don't have lines, you're fucked.
You've got no way of tying yourself off to anything, and life on
the water just isn't possible unless you're hanging on to something else, whether it's a dock or an anchor or your own damn
balls. Without the line, you're just drifting.

"OK. So, there's this kid. Liked engines and speed, but he also
liked sailing, the ancient power of wind in the canvas. He decided it was a good idea to strap a motorcycle up on the deck
of his sailboat. Word on the river was he thought he might sail
down to San Francisco and have himself a pair of wheels to zip
around the hills with once he passed through the Golden Gate.
Couldn't decide whether he wanted to be a sailor or a power-
boater or a damn motorcycle demon. So he tried to do it all at
the same time—the speed of revved-up engines and the given
pace of the wind. I mean, this guy was a real fucking accident
waiting to happen. As it happened, though, when the accident

was no longer waiting but actually happening, it was happening to his small daughter, some four or five years old, and to his wife.

"You gotta understand that this was the 1930s. Way before all this shitstorm of speedboats and those damn—what do you call 'em?—impersonal watercraft. There were still folks around for whom an internal combustion engine on any boat smaller than a battleship was a brand-fucking-new marvel of industry. Outboard engines ran like shit in a barrel, but you counted yourself fortunate to be able to spend all your time trying to make it run. Either that or you were like my old man and didn't bother with new junk just because it was new, especially if what you already had was working fine. He stuck to steam and coal or hitched up a team of horses to long ropes and pulled flatboats up and down the river from the shore. You could run a length of rope across the channel and pull everything from one side to the other with a couple of pulleys and some horsepower. But that was just my old man holding out against the tide of progress. Most folks were hypnotized by the ability to make fire in the belly of an engine. People were still trying to figure out how to run the damn things, making boat engines out of spare car parts or whatever washed up on shore, wearing the parts out until they could find something else. Those days, you poured hundred proof into the tank when you ran out of fuel since there was more of that around on the river than any other flammables.

"The tensions between powerboaters and sailboaters were still new back then too, and stronger. There were no such things as lawsuits like we got now, and you could still express some of your thoughts with your fists or just by keeping a gun lying around. There were lines you didn't cross then—partly because people knew where the lines were, and they respected them.

"So anyway, this guy was young enough he couldn't remember before everybody had an engine on their boat. Imagine what he looked like to some of the old timers that were still on the river. He's got this sailboat. A fancy, new fiberglass thing, and he sticks a huge, fucking prop on the end of his shaft. I mean, this prop was a monster. It was almost as big as some of your dumb puffed-up heads. Never mind that the speed of a displacement hull tops off at around seven knots or so depending on the length of the boat; this guy thought the more noise he made, the more he was getting somewhere.

"I used to see him going by, careless bastard, fenders still bouncing in the water long after he'd left the dock. Of course, the prop was mounted all wrong—too high an angle—so it blew water into the air behind him as he went along. Today you'd call it inefficient motoring. Back then, you just called him an asshole. You'd hear that engine revving and see the water frothing up in his wake like a damn fountain while he pushed his puny six or seven knots' worth of hot air and fumes. Not that he noticed the big mess of water blowing out his backside—too busy with the wind in his hair and places to get to up ahead.

"He'd do it with the sails up too, flapping away, boom swinging back and forth just above his head, canvas all ready to fill with wind for when he decided to slow the hell down. He'd see a patch of water somewhere with more wind wrinkling up the surface than in the patch of water where he happened to be, and he'd go racing over to it, his sails all ready to go. It got to where he didn't even bother to turn off the engine when he was cruising, even with the sails full of wind. Just throw her in neutral and milk that fucking breeze until a better one blows over the water someplace else.

"What finally did the guy in was that old Harley Davidson. All the motorcycle ever did was weigh down the port side and hang up the jib sheets and leak oil all over the fucking deck. And did the guy ever clean up the mess? Well, I don't know, but my father had a horse out for a run on the beach at Sauvie Island one day and saw the idiot taking his daughter and his wife out on the boat for a revved-up sailing trip to who the hell knows where. They're churning up the Columbia, guy's wife is in the cabin, and he's looking for wind somewhere on the horizon, when the guy's poor daughter slips on the oily deck and falls in the river.

"She goes down under the hull and back, to where that big prop is spinning away. For the first time in his life, the guy stops to turn around, and he sees red foam spraying up out of the water. By the time he gets the engine disengaged, her body is drifting in the wake. The engine stops, and the sails start scooping wind, pushing his boat away from the mess he's made.

"What's a guy to do after he's killed his own daughter? I don't know, but this particular guy stops long enough to see that his life isn't worth crap. He locks the tiller to keep the boat on a level tack. Then he climbs onto the motorbike, unstraps it from the shrouds, and uses the straps to lash himself to the handlebars. He fires it up and rides into the drink. The mother pops her head out of the cabin when she hears the motorcycle engine, and when she sees the mess and it hits her what's happened, she falls back inside—dead or unconscious, we'll never know.

"So, right about when the guy climbs on the motorcycle, my old man sees what's happened and what's about to happen, and he digs his heels in and takes his mare for a run downstream fifty yards or so ahead of the boat. Then he jumps down from the horse, tosses his boots toward the shore, grabs a length of rope, and ties it around his waist. He hears the motorcycle engine and the splash, and he turns to see the bike hovering for an instant on the surface of the water before it goes down. He sees the woman falling into the cabin, and he dives into the water.

"So the boat's still sailing downstream, and my father is swimming for all he's worth to intercept it. His clothes are heavy with water by now, and he sees the boat's probably gonna pass him by. The bow of the ship is sliding along in front of him, and the deck is way above the surface—it's not like he can jump up and grab on, so he ties himself a big bowline and tosses the line toward a deck cleat—of course he misses the entire boat by a nautical mile.

"He's watching the stern fade away downstream, wondering about the woman onboard—whether she's hit her head or broken her neck or if she's sitting down there pulling her hair out—when something brushes into him from behind. He turns and there's the girl, floating face up, feet forward, pushing into him. Her clothes are torn, her skin is bone white, and one of her arms is gone above the elbow. He retches a little and feels bad for barfing in front of her.

"He's getting pretty tired by now, swimming in all his clothes, but he reaches out for the girl's leg, thinking to tie the line to it and tow the body so he doesn't have to touch her.

"The leg moves. The girl groans. She's alive. My father holds her and tries to keep her head above the water. He sees blood's still pulsing out into the river and wraps his line around what's left of her arm, pulling down tight on a couple half hitches—that seems to stop the bleeding a little. The girl coughs. Her breathing is shallow. My father shifts her around onto his back, her body facing away from his, her arm up out of the water and her head lolling back over his shoulder. His back, pressed against hers, grows warm. He wraps the line around the both of them, cinches it down with a slip knot, and starts swimming toward shore, his strength having come back to him now that he's swimming for two lives rather than just his own.

"When they hit Sauvie Island shore and both of them were balanced up on his horse, speeding off toward civilization, my father turned to look back—the unmanned boat was only a spot of sail on the river just about out of sight downstream.

"The story leaves the river at that point, as far as the little girl's part in it. She lived. I knew her for a little while right after. She visited our place on the island a couple times when she got out of the hospital, one sleeve draped across her chest and pinned to her opposite shoulder. Her eyes were always wide open. Whites all around the edges. I never saw her blink. Not even once. Some of her relatives came up from California to claim her; otherwise, my dad might have tried to adopt her.

"Back on the river the story goes on. The Coast Guard couldn't find the sailboat. It seemed to have disappeared. The wind had kept filling its sails, blowing it all the way down to St. Helens Island where it slammed into the ground on the upstream side, tipped over, and sank. They found the mast sticking out of the river at an angle, slapping sideways in and out of the water as the waves came along. The mother might've died in the crash maybe, trapped inside the cabin. There's a rumor that her wrists and throat were cut, though, so who knows.

"Twenty or twenty-five years later, some diver said he found the motorcycle when he was down there looking for something else. People thought maybe it'd landed on the bottom and just kept rolling along, The bike was all corroded out and there was a skeleton strapped to it, still sitting in the chewed-up seat—all the crap long since washed out of his damn skull.

"Never heard that one? Well, I guess you guys weren't even in diapers back then. Aren't many people left down here who'd remember to tell that story, or to tell it right.

"Let's get one thing straight about this tale. Somewhere in there, the whole thing starts to turn into so much bullshit, right? That story's at a delicate point in its history. Been told a number of times before it got to us. It's probably been blown way off course. But when? My old man is the only one who was there, but his version has carried over water and time, dragging in other things from other tellings.

"Maybe my old man embellished what he saw and what he did. That girl is in the water bleeding out, and my old man just comes along and ties a few knots and saves the day? Maybe the bullshit comes from others, people who weren't even there. I mean, that sailboat damn sure didn't keep her course into the wind all the way down to St. Helens, right? Into the wind and around a couple turns without luffing or tacking at all? Come on. Maybe nobody ever really saw the motorcycle flying into the river or that damn skeleton sitting on it all those years later. Maybe there wasn't really any motorcycle to begin with. I was just a little crapper back then, and I'd swear the motorcycle was there—I can see it in my mind's eye—but talking about it over the years might have put it there. The only shred of decent, living history left in the tale might be that my old man saw a body floating in the river once, or that I used to have a distant, one-armed cousin.

"That tale has become a wide tale. You know tall tales? It's kind of like that, except tall tales are for the landlubbers. You wouldn't call them tall tales on the water. Things don't go up here unless it's to borrow from the old gods in the wind, weather, or stars. Floating homes, docks, boats—they spread over the surface. They tie off to other things that are tied off to pilings or an anchor wedged in the river bottom or they drift away or they go down into the drink.

"That story might be reaching the end of its life. Maybe this is where it dies, on this dock with you all. It's got the smell of bullshit all over it, already. You've got to have a nose for bullshit if you're going to tell history instead of just the version you think people might want to hear. Grains of history are embedded inside people and in their stories. The best you can hope for is to keep those grains alive for a little while. They're decaying all around us as we speak.

"It's a delicate balance, telling stories on the water. Stories are on their way to being the truth, the whole truth, or almost nothing like the truth. You've got to get them to stay afloat without turning it all into so much bullshit. You're guardians, all of you, not just a bunch of idiots tipping back booze and shooting the shit, yammering about whatever floats along.

"So, does it matter if you have a rope handy? Or a line? Or that you call it one thing or another? Abso-fucking-lutely! Here, here, and amen!"

Jack lifted his coffee up to his mouth, saw that it was empty, and set it down on the glass countertop with a light tap. The floorboards creaked as Chad walked to the coffee pot and lifted it from the burner. The wind pressed into the windows, bending the light that reflected off the glass and back into the room. Chad sighed. A little more loudly than he'd intended. Still facing the coffeemaker, he spoke loud enough to be heard across the room. "So, Jack. Should I go ahead and put fourteen ninety-five on your tab for that ... *rope?*" Several men snickered.

Someone yelled, "Duck!"

Chad turned, smiling, just as Jack's mug crashed into the large aluminum can of ground coffee on the shelf above his head. Coffee grounds sprayed in all directions, hissing like a torrent of tiny hailstones. Chad dropped to the floor. Coffee rattled off windows, lights, and ceiling fans. The grounds took several seconds to finish settling through the dozen stands of wire shelving.

Nervous laughter around the room. From where he was sitting on the floor, Chad looked at the steaming coffee pot, still in his hand. He breathed a sigh of relief: it was intact. He felt around with his free hand. Somehow, he hadn't spilled any.

He heard Jack's voice fading, "Shit..."

By the time Chad had picked himself up off the floor and started brushing coffee grounds from his clothes and hair, Jack was no longer in the room, though you could hear his heavy, limping footfalls on the wood walkway outside slowly fading into the distance.

Emma knew she wasn't supposed to be this close to the spillway, but she kept paddling toward it anyway because she didn't give a shit what she wasn't supposed to do. She could finally see them: the cracks she'd heard about on the news, newly filled and surrounded by structural supports. Water roared from gates just below the mended wall. She'd told herself she would turn back the moment she could see them, but that was a moment or two ago. Could it really be called a death wish if she hadn't intended to come this close?

She was here with the beginning of a plan still forming: a hundred-mile excursion she intended to make down the river in her late brother's kayak as a way to remember him, or honor him, or something like that. She wasn't planning to spend every single moment thinking of him, picturing him in her mind and shedding a tear at each mile marker. She couldn't think of him so constantly without facing all she loved and loathed about him. She needed relief from the mental shrine of him.

On the journey she had planned, loathing her brother would be a necessary part of her grieving. Grieving. After a year of it, she couldn't stand the word. She'd started smiling and even laughing at pictures of her brother her parents had discovered in boxes above the garage in recent months. Frivolity could be a relief. Relief from her parents and their indulgent, stoic grief. "I grieve by smiling," she'd told her mother once. And that had been the beginning of the drifting.

She was intentionally drifting away from her parents after the big *D*, Death in the family. How often could you be around someone else's tears at moments when you had already spent your store for the week? And when you yourself were moved to tears, how comforting was it to cry on your father's shoulder when it felt obligatory, and he started to lean in the direction of some project in the garage?

It got worse when they discovered the empty box of wine in the trunk of her car and freaked out about it. She worried she might return late one night and quietly open the back door to find a kitchen full of concerned loved ones staging an intervention, so she didn't drink for a week. When she thought the coast was probably clear, she resumed drinking every night after work.

Wasn't someone supposed to have stopped her on the spillway by now? Coast Guard speedboats with lights flashing? Spotlights? Black helicopters?

She felt mist blowing across her face on the wind made by the torrent of water.

Fuck this. She turned the bow of the kayak toward the stony shore and paddled up onto the rocks. The tremor of the scraping hull vibrated through her. Not a good place to land her brother's beloved kayak. But it wasn't his anymore. He was free now from his obsessive, tender care of it. It wasn't up to him how much she banged it up when she borrowed it. She wasn't borrowing it. It was hers now, fair and square. Emma climbed out of the kayak and held her arms out to get her balance on the stones. She walked right up to the dam wall. Well, actually, it was concrete attached to some more concrete that supported the dam wall, but this was as close as she could get. The mist beaded on her eyelashes.

That crazy Native American probably stood right about here when he blew his trumpet. Her eyes started tearing up. "Oh, hell," she said. Over the past year, she'd gotten to where she could choose the time and place for tears. Or choose to not even bother. Then this guy … People had died right in front of her enough times now that she'd stopped counting. But this guy? He arrived in her thoughts and precipitated these stupid sobs. Some deeper well of grief, untapped all these years, had only now re-vealed a sorrow she couldn't reason with or anticipate or avoid.

She picked up a stone and threw it toward the river, where it disappeared into white water. She shouted, "Motherfuck you, you Native motherfucker!" Then she stooped to catch her breath. It was hard to breathe in this cool, thick air. Her movements felt numb and dreamlike.

This would be the start of her journey then, here at the foot of The Dalles Dam with a single unexpected sob and the most irreverent set of words she had ever strung together at the ex-pense of indigenous cultures on the shores of their most sacred river. It would take her more than just this week she had off work to plan and execute the whole journey. She would have to make it in stages. Maybe a weekend here and there this spring or sum-mer, when she could get time off. She picked up another stone, and on the smooth concrete she scratched out the curved shape of the Columbia River. It was something her brother had often done. He'd map out a rough sketch of the river and its tributar-ies to show her where he was making his next kayak trip, or to make suggestions when she planned trips with her own friends. He told her what she should look out for. Where hard-to-find channels of navigable water were that only he knew about.

On the wall of the dam, she scratched several routes she'd paddled with her brother. There. There. And there. She'd stop by these places. She'd pause in the heart of the Gorge where he'd drowned. She'd end in Astoria after almost two hundred miles of river.

She wouldn't tell her parents. They hadn't been down to the river yet except to identify the body. This trip would not sit well with them. They would insist she bring someone with her. But how could she share this with anyone? She could share this with Ko. Of course, Ko would come; he was amazing on the water, sitting still and quiet in the front seat, even in deep water.

Emma climbed back into the boat and kicked off. She closed her eyes and let the current carry her down. Her pants and shirt were soaked through. Cold, even with the sun beaming down from a cloudless sky.

An alarm high above the shore blared in loud, even bursts, and she covered her ears, wincing at the painful sound. It kept on, once per second. Dark forms peered from the summit of the wall.

"Now you decide to give a shit?" Emma dug the paddle in and got the hell out of there.

Keith tied both ends of the canoe up to the fuel dock and grabbed his fishing pole from where it was propped over the gunnel. He carefully laid it in the bottom of the canoe and climbed onto the dock. He passed by the old guys at the table on his way into the store. They didn't seem to notice him. Inside, Chad set aside the broom handle he'd been sweeping with and said, "Hey, Keith. How's the canoe holding up? Still floating?"

Keith looked at the broom where it leaned against the counter. The straw bristles were bent in all directions.

"I've been sweeping a lot. I made a big mess a couple days ago," said Chad. "So, tell me what's new. Did you catch anything this morning?"

"No. I need more bait. And hooks. I keep losing hooks."

Chad grabbed a box of hooks from under the counter, then walked over to a fridge and pulled a small Tupperware container filled with soil and worms out from the bottom shelf. He handed it to Keith and asked, "What kind of knots are you using to keep the hooks on?"

"I don't know. A basic knot."

"Here, I'll show you a couple sailing knots you can use. Pretend this string is your fishing line."

Keith watched Chad twist and loop the string a couple of different ways, then he tried it. When he had one of the knots down, he thanked Chad and got out his wallet.

Chad shook his head. "How about you pay me later if it actually works and you catch something?"

Keith picked up the supplies and thanked him.

"You know, if nothing is out there biting on these, we also have salmon eggs and some little herring you could try. Check with Barry outside. He's the one wearing a coat even though it's warm out. He's pretty good at knowing what's out there, where they are, and what they are biting on. Though, maybe wait until Jack's not around. Don't let those guys get to you if they give you a hard time, OK?"

Keith nodded.

Back outside, he watched the men. Maybe when they were done talking, he would ask Barry about the fish. In the meantime, he sat down on the front seat of the canoe and tried to untangle the line that had twisted itself around the tip of the pole.

Over at the table, Jack said to Bill, "I see you and Bernie finally stopped dithering and named your boat. What the hell is it supposed to mean? Tooee?"

Barry chimed in. "You sure you spelled it right? T-U-I-T?" Barry's voice came out slow and slurring. His hand holding the coffee mug shook slightly.

Jack said, "T-U-I-T? What the hell is that? French for 'dumbass'?"

Barry cleared his throat, met Jack's gaze, and nodded toward Keith.

"Don't give me that. You can tell this kid is no idiot just by looking at him."

Keith tried to keep from smiling too big, but he couldn't stop himself.

"So give it up, Bill," said Jack.

Bill said, "Maybe it is French, but I don't know. I don't speak French. Did you notice the circle painted around the word 'Tuit'?"

"Clever," said Barry. "You should have just painted, 'To Be Decided.'"

"Bernie wouldn't agree to 'Floating Fart Bucket,' or 'Master Baiter.' That's B-A-I-T—"

"Yeah, I think we got it, Bill," said Barry.

Bill finished, "In any case, now I can say we finally got 'a round to-it.'"

"Stop it. That hurts my ears," said Jack.

Keith watched as Barry reached into his coat pocket, pulled out a silver container, and poured something into his coffee mug. He tried several times to slide the container back into the pocket before it finally settled in. Then Barry said, "It's not a terrible choice. What do you think, young man?"

Keith's face burned when the men all looked at him.

"I don't know," Keith mumbled. "Kinda funny."

"See?" said Bill. "He knows a good idea when he hears one."

Keith's fishing line was now in several knots around the pole. Forget it. He could bother Barry some other time.

Marge entered the marina store with a thin, rectangular package she said Chad might like to hang near his desk. "I thought you could use something to brighten up your week. Call it a Thanksgiving present. I heard some gorilla was throwing his shit at you the other day."

"Wow. Thanks, Marge. It was just a coffee mug. Missed me by a mile. And I was asking for it."

Chad opened the package. It was a painting. He recognized a rough map of the upper marina, with various floating structures strung together by a maze of docks and walkways. Where some of the boats should have been were various familiar-looking faces, animals, and symbols. A smiling hot dog with a cigarette hanging from its mouth was obviously Dory.

Chad ran his finger up and down the length of the painting. There were prison bars on windows of one of the floating homes further downstream. When he asked, Marge said, "Bad marriage there." There were flags from foreign countries, flying fish, sandals, broken bottles, and crushed cans. There was a sailing ship steered by a two-headed person with one male head, one female head, and two hands on the wheel. It was in Bill and Bernice's slip. Further up the dock, where Moe's boat used to be, was a bright yellow sun; its beams shining into the slips all around. Across the walkway was what Chad took to be Marge's boat—a cloud of mixed colors drifted out from it in the water, carried downstream through the rest of the painting. At the bottom were wild-looking creatures and an arrow reading, "Here be dragons."

Chad whispered, "So King Kong climbing this small building near the end of the dock. Let me take a wild guess. . ."

Marge said, "The paint is still wet on that little touch-up. I just added a tiny diaper to the mighty Kong there."

Chad tilted his head back and laughed, "Oh, that's mean."

"Maybe. But it fits."

"Now you're the one asking for a mug to the head."

He looked over the painting again and asked, "What's this up here on land? This eye floating in a boat? Some kind of compass rose?"

"That's you living aboard the Looney Bird," She said.

"So, I'm an eyeball? It doesn't look like I'm pointing anywhere even close to true north."

"If you say so," Marge said.

The two of them talked for some time, pleasantly surprised by their similarities. Marge found the community on the docks to be a rich source of ideas and inspirations that fueled her creativity. She filled Chad in on some of the backgrounds of people he barely knew. There were lots of less visible tenants: shut-ins in the middle marina and at least three boats scattered around growing "certain illegal plants," as she put it. One house used to be a meth lab that housed half-a-dozen disheveled residents until the police caught wind of it.

By the time Marge left the store, after trading a couple book titles with Chad, most of the afternoon had passed. Chad turned to where Rick sat on the phone. Then he saw Barry sitting in a far corner of the room, close to the rack of magazines, reading a book rather than his customary newspaper. When had he come in?

"Hey Barry, you should check out this painting Marge dropped off."

"Yeah, I saw it."

Then the door opened and Jack walked in.

Chad turned around, set the painting on his desk, and sat down at his computer.

Jack walked over to Rick's desk. Chad glanced in their direction.

"Hey Rick. I figured it was about time for me to catch up on my tab."

"I'm on the phone," Rick said. "Talk to Chad."

There was a pause. Jack walked toward Barry and said, "Barry. You've been watching the books on weekends. . ."

"Not really. Talk to Chad."

Chad went back to his computer screen. About ten seconds later, Jack cleared his throat from the other side of the counter. Chad stood up and turned to face him.

Jack slapped his checkbook down on the counter. He had already signed his name in tight, shaky scrawl on the bottom of the first check in the book and asked Chad to fill in the rest if he didn't mind. "My penmanship is getting worse than a blind doctor's," he said. Chad pulled out the ledger from under the till and started adding up the charges. Jack stood silently for a moment, gazing out the glass door to the fuel dock and the river beyond. Then he started toward the door and said, "I'll let you finish filling that out. Whatever I owe. Just roll it back to nothing. So we'll be even."

"I'll take care of it. Thanks, Jack."

"Thanks for what? You and your manners. ... We'll see you in the morning."

The room fell quiet while Chad punched numbers into the till. Rick left for the day before Chad was done adding.

After Rick was gone, Barry looked up from his book and said, "If you like Marge's painting, you should take it up to your boat. Rick will probably just stow it up in the attic with the others Marge has dropped off over the years."

Chad said, "He doesn't even put them on the wall for a while first?"

Barry shook his head and returned to his book.

"You doing anything special this holiday weekend?" Chad asked.

He thought Barry wasn't going to answer, but after a few seconds he said, "Holiday? Oh, right. Turkey Day. Probably not."

"Can you watch the dock for me on Thanksgiving Day? I'm hoping to go for a motorcycle ride. Get away. Unless you've got plans."

"You go. I'll tell Rick and close the place down if we go a couple hours without any customers."

Chad looked at the painting again, counting the slips until he saw where Barry's boat would be. There was a man standing at the end of his boat slip behind what looked like a podium. The man's face had two eyes but no nose or mouth. His eyes, small as they were in the painting, held a vivid expression of astonishment.

Barry glanced at the surface of the water through the thick layer of fog. He tried to watch the current, listen to it, and feel its many turnings under the hull as he pulled at the oars. The lane of swift-moving current had a way of shifting from one shore to the next on its way downstream, splitting in half to flow around Coon Island. The oarlocks rattled and squeaked, rattled and squeaked. In his coat pocket, he could hear the pearl clinking against his whiskey flask.

Barry winced a little each time he pulled at the oars, his back and neck complaining as his muscles took the strain. The island would be coming into view around the next bend, and then he would know. The Lendaways' massive powerboat would be there off in the distance, tied to the transient dock on the eastern side of the island, or else it wouldn't be. If the boat wasn't there, he would drink the whiskey. If the boat was there, well, the Lendaways would have wine on board just like last year.

Last Thanksgiving, the sun had warmed Barry on the half-hour row to the island. There had been a breeze. This year, the air was still and cold. It was one in the afternoon, and the fog hadn't lifted yet. Barry pulled at the oars. His shoulders ached.

He aimed the bow of the rowboat toward the center of the channel. Canadian geese honked in the distance, above the fog.

Then he remembered last year's prayer. Shit. They would probably ask him to say a prayer again. Maybe he should turn around and head back to the marina. He tried to think of the first few words for a Thanksgiving Day prayer. The rest would follow faithfully after the first few words. Nah, forget it. The words would come in the moment with the smell of food and the kind of silence that can only happen in a room full of people. Just like last year.

What if they weren't even there? They said they came every year, but they hadn't stopped by the marina for fuel today. Last year, they told him to come again next Thanksgiving. Lunch had been at 1:30 p.m., and the food was almost ready to go, everything but the biscuits. Barry looked at his watch. It was 1:15. Maybe he would be too late, and they wouldn't ask him to pray for the meal again. Perhaps they hadn't believed his story. Maybe that was why they didn't stop by the marina for fuel this year. Maybe they went the long way around, along the main, in order to avoid coming by. Perhaps this was their way of telling him to stay clear. Maybe they knew about the pearl.

Barry stopped rowing and listened again to the water passing under the boat. He couldn't concentrate. The current was playing with him. He would never make it in time. They probably weren't even there. His shoulders ached. His mouth felt dry and swollen. Why the hell hadn't he brought any drinking water?

He didn't drink much water these days. Last year, he was in the habit of reaching for the whiskey around noon. Now, he started his days pouring a little into his coffee. The other men must have known but said nothing. They'd turn to look out across the river, their voices not quite drowning out the glug, glug, glug of the whiskey as it splashed into the half-filled mug.

Last year, Barry had gone down to Coon Island sober. This year, he figured he would do the same. The river turned around a bend. The fog hid the shoreline from view.

Would they even remember him? It's not like they were his family. How embarrassing, borrowing a family for one day a year—renting them for the price of half-truths. And then there was the pearl. It was stupid, really, but he had to return the pearl. He'd pull it out of his pocket and place it on the floor in the bathroom as if it had never been gone.

Barry turned to look downstream over his shoulder. Through the fog, he could just make out the dark form of Coon Island and the Lendaways' boat tied to the dock.

Every year, just like they said. He tried again to remember the first words of the Thanksgiving blessing but couldn't. They would ask him to pray. His heart was beating fast now. He would never remember the words. They would see right through him. Shit. He let go of the oar on the starboard side and brought the silver flask from his coat pocket, fumbling with the lid. He took a long pull on the whiskey, tipping his head back until he almost lost his balance, letting the current pull him toward the island.

A few moments later, the Lendaways' boat loomed quietly above him. The cabin windows glowed dimly. Even after he pulled up to the dock, Barry couldn't hear any noise coming from the boat. No children. No sound of clinking dishes. He wrapped the painter around a dock cleat and waited. Gracie. What if Gracie knew about the pearl? Maybe that's why she asked him to come back.

No, that was ridiculous. He would put the pearl in the bathroom and have some pie and leave and never come back. This wasn't his family. No use pretending to himself that he wasn't using them to hold loneliness at bay. This would be it, then. No more Thanksgivings. Barry risked one last pull at the whiskey and stepped confidently from his rowboat onto the dock.

He reached the foot of the retractable steps and rapped two knuckles on the hull. A moment later, the small face of a dog peered through the railing above. A toy poodle, its fluffy ears tied with ribbons. For Christ's sake, they'd gone and picked up a ridiculous little dog for their big boat. A few seconds later, he saw Stuart's face.

Silence for a moment.

"Is that you, Father?"

"I was just out for some exercise in the rowboat. Looks like you were telling the truth. Every year down here."

"Come on up. We were just about to serve up dessert, but there's still plenty of other food."

"I don't want to intrude. I thought I would stop in and just say hello."

"No, please, come up for something to eat. I was hoping you would make it." Stuart extended his hand, and Barry took it, a firm grip pulling him up.

Barry made his way up the stairs and onboard. He felt in his coat for the pearl, hoping to transfer it to his trouser pocket before he removed the coat inside. He felt around the flask but couldn't find the pearl before he stepped up to the main cabin door where Amy stood. The dog yapped behind him. Amy greeted him with a weary smile.

She came in close and wrapped her arms around him. He staggered a little then accepted the embrace, folding her in his arms. He held his breath, partly from fear she might smell the whiskey, partly to hold down the sadness that suddenly welled in him. They parted, and Amy looked into his eyes, thanking him for coming. She smiled again sadly. She must smell the whiskey.

Stuart's parents were still at the table. So were the aunts and uncles and most of the children. All their eyes were on him. Two of the children came over and gazed up at him, smiling but saying nothing. He placed his hands on their heads. Their mother called to them, and they skittered off to their spots at the table. Most of the plates were finished, utensils resting on them haphazardly.

Stuart guided him to the one empty chair. Everyone wanted to know how Barry was, how the fishing had been this past season, how the marina was treating him.

Amy offered to dish him up some food, asking him what he wanted. Barry told her to surprise him.

Something was off. The kids weren't as loud maybe. Maybe it was the fog and the dull, gray light coming through the windows. Maybe it was the whiskey. They hadn't offered him any wine yet. Maybe they knew about the pearl. Where was Gracie?

Barry looked around the table for her. He removed his coat to hang it on the back of his chair, feeling in the pocket again for the pearl. It was gone. His heart began to beat wildly. Where was it? Where was she? Something brushed up against his leg, and he jumped. When he looked under the table, there was the little dog face again.

Stuart poured him a glass of wine. Amy brought in the plate of food. He started in on the potatoes. One of the boys asked if he was going to pray for the food before he ate it. Amy shushed him.

Barry looked down at his fork. "No, he's right. I should pray."

Amy sat down next to Stuart. "Will you pray for us all? For all our food I mean?"

Stuart was gazing at the table.

"Sure, I can do that. Is everyone here? Anybody missing?"

Everyone looked at the table. The boat rocked slightly in the water. The dock lines stretched and groaned.

One of the girls, the youngest, said, "Gracie's with the angels. She's flying with them and with Jesus."

The dog brushed against Barry's leg again, and he bumped his arm into his wine glass, tipping it over. It spread across the table and poured into his lap. The dog barked from under the table, a small yap. Several people ran to the kitchen and to the closet down the hall for towels. When Barry stood up, he could feel the wine soaking through his trousers and rolling down his legs.

Amy apologized. Stuart apologized. Barry looked down to see the dog come out from under the table, its legs shivering, red drops hanging in its fur. He noticed the dog was wearing a life jacket, padded on both sides with a handle protruding from its back. It looked like a large rat in a space suit. Barry reached down and grabbed at the handle, pulling the animal up easily. The beady eyes stared back at him. Fear in those eyes. A slight tremor in the handle. Barry laughed softly. Then he saw that everyone was looking at him. Stuart's father, Cliff, was glaring. Barry set the dog down, one-handed, and rubbed his eye. His head was pounding. His cheeks reddened.

"It's funny. At the fuel dock, the bigger the boats that come in, the smaller the dogs." He kept rubbing his eye.

"Actually, I had a beagle once, a long time ago. We used to live up in the hills. That dog kept me alive. He'd catch cottontails, and we would eat off 'em. It was winter, and he would go out and come back with a cottontail, and we would both eat off 'em. I tell you that dog was unconditional." He paused. "Shit. I don't know what I'm saying."

Barry put both hands over his face and stood for a moment listening to everyone's silence until the boy spoke up again.

"Father Palmer ate rabbits?"

Barry took his coat and headed for the door. "I'm so sorry for your loss," he said as he pulled his arms through the sleeves, "and sorry for butting in on your grieving."

Stuart met his gaze. "Don't go, please. It's all right. Don't go." There were tears in Stuart's eyes, his face pleading. Amy's voice echoed her husband's. Some of the children chimed in, "Don't go." "Where is he going?" "Did he eat rabbits?"

Stuart held Barry's forearm. "We need you to be here. Please come back to the table."

Barry pulled his arm from Stuart's grasp, opened the door, and stepped through, speaking back over his shoulder. "Thank you for your hospitality. I'm so sorry." He closed the door behind him and ran down the steps. Losing his balance on the last step, he fell to one knee and winced, but he was up again quickly, moving to his rowboat, untying the painter and stepping in, scrambling for the oars. The skin on his knee was broken under his trousers, and the blood beaded through the cloth, mingling with the wine stains. He pulled at the oars and aimed the bow upstream, watching the island and the boat fade into the mist. When he was a ways off, he pulled the flask from his pocket and worked down several gulps. The throbbing in his knee subsided.

Just before the Grand Banks faded away, he saw a dark form moving on deck, lowering a boat into the water from the stern-crane arm. Someone was coming after him.

The yacht was lost in the fog, but he could hear the sputter of an outboard engine carrying over the smooth surface of the water as someone pulled on the starter rope to get it going. Barry aimed his rowboat toward shore. The outboard engine turned over in the distance as the bottom of the rowboat hissed into the sand near a grassy bank. He leaned back and waited, drinking whiskey.

Keith looked down at the steaming plate of food in front of him. A pool of instant mashed potatoes, still settling. Perfectly round slices of turkey meant for deli sandwiches. A pile of barely boiled frozen peas. The boat rocked in the wind, and several peas rolled into the potatoes.

His dad looked at him from across the table. "Well, here we are. We've never really done Thanksgiving or anything like that. But maybe we could say a couple things we are thankful for before we eat?"

Keith frowned. The boat groaned into the inflatable bumpers that cushioned the hull against the dock outside.

"OK," his dad continued, "how about just one thing we're thankful for?"

Keith said, "I'm thankful we don't live with Mom anymore."

His dad picked up a fork and stabbed at a thin slice of turkey. "Fine. Let's not do that."

They ate in silence for a while. Keith's dad turned on the small black-and-white TV. The wavering image of a marching band came slowly into focus.

"Really, Dad? A parade?"

His father turned to a channel where sneering, cartoon faces glared out from the screen—*The Nightmare Before Christmas*. He and his dad had seen it in the theater together. It was a lot more impressive in color.

Keith asked, "Why are they even playing this on Thanksgiving? It's about Halloween and Christmas."

His dad changed the channel again.

The picture came and went between fuzzy black-and-white lines. It was a bowling tournament. Soft murmuring voices were punctuated by the clattering of pins and the hiss of applause.

Keith stirred the potatoes on his plate. "Dad. Why do you always just give up when something doesn't work the first damn time?"

Keith's dad pointed his fork at him. "Because I know when to shut my damn mouth, that's why," he said and turned the volume up on the television.

Bowling pins clattered.

After a minute, his father sighed. "You never notice when I try. You can't blame me every time something doesn't work out."

"Yeah, it's not your fault we live on a sailboat and never go sailing . . ."

"Hey."

". . . because you only tried to get the boat ready once . . ."

Bowling pins. Applause.

". . . and then you just threw things at me and gave up."

His father stood up, walked over to the chart table, grabbed the telephone, and set it in front of Keith.

The TV cut to a hissing, black-and-white haze.

"Maybe you should call your mom to pick you up. She's got a color TV. Maybe that would make you happy."

"Maybe *you* should call her."

His father turned the TV off with a click and went back to his meal. "You know where the phone is, and you know her number." He kept his eyes fixed on the plate while he tried to scoop up his watery potatoes with a fork. After a dozen scoops, he walked to the icebox and pulled out a beer.

Keith stared at the phone and then at his plate where the phone cord was slowly sinking into his potatoes.

Barry's breath came slowly. Fog floated by, and time along with it. His mind grew still in the presence of the river, the fog, and the warm flask in his hand. The hum of the small engine came and went, moving up and down the river. Finally, Barry saw the skiff passing close to his shore. He felt a kind of hope moving inside him. Strange. A sensation he hadn't felt since he was a boy:

he wanted to be found. When he saw that Stuart was going to pass by, unable to see him, he waved with both arms and blurted out, "Stu!"

The engine died down, and the bow of the skiff turned toward Barry. Stuart's grim expression materialized out of the mist. The engine sputtered to a stop, and their boats met with a bump. Stuart spoke first.

"You're not a priest, are you? At least not now."

"No, not anymore."

"But you used to be?"

"A lifetime ago. Before Vietnam."

"Then I have something to ask you."

Barry leaned forward and offered the flask to Stuart who unscrewed the cap and took a quick sip. "Bless me, Father, for I have sinned." Stuart took another drink and passed the flask back.

Barry ran his fingers through his hair. "That doesn't sound like a question to me. Why don't you take your 'bless me, father' on downstream to the next drunk priest you find along the shore?"

"No, I'd like to talk to this one here. I don't have a regular priest anymore. And Gracie would have wanted it to be you." Both their smiles faded. "She liked you. She was always asking if you'd come for Thanksgiving again. I don't go to mass anymore. Not since she's been gone."

"What happened?"

Stuart's voice wavered. "She had a tumor in her brain. We could have caught it a couple of years ago if we had known. We thought it was more of the same old disability—she was deprived of oxygen at birth. After they found the tumor, the doctor gave her a couple of weeks to live, and she lasted four months."

Barry shifted his weight, straightening his leg out. The little water in the bottom of his boat flowed to starboard and there was the pearl in the brownish puddle. He picked it up, holding it out to Stuart between his thumb and forefinger.

"I need to give this back to you. I found it last year. I think it was Gracie's. I was wrong to take it."

Stuart furrowed his brow and shook his head. "No, I think it's yours. Gracie wanted you to have this." He reached into his coat pocket and pulled out a necklace, six small pearls fixed at intervals around the thin chain. Barry looked at the gap near the tiny clasp. "She said to make sure Father Palmer got this. She was adamant."

Barry reached for the necklace and put it in his pocket. He offered the flask to Stuart. "You want the last bit?"

Stuart shook his head.

Barry straightened his back, stretching a little. The pain in his knee was only a dull throbbing now. "So, what was it you wanted to say?"

The mist floated between them; a thin veil folding and swirling in the air. "I'll start over," Stuart said. "Bless me, Father, for I have sinned."

Barry looked him in the eyes. "Technically, I can't do this anymore, you know."

"Bless me, Father, for I have sinned," Stuart repeated, lowering his head as the tears rolled down his cheeks.

The words poured out and Barry listened. Stuart had slept with another woman, and soon after, the family found out about Gracie's cancer. He was carrying the guilt of the affair and blaming himself for his daughter's death. He felt his sin had killed her in the crossfire—God's punishment to get his attention.

Did Amy know? No, not yet. Stuart promised to tell her. No penance. Just go tell Amy. Barry offered him absolution.

Once he and Stuart were speaking the words, it was as if water flowed back through some dry, forgotten part of himself. Under the layer of dullness from the whiskey, under the layers of sound along the river, under the words of absolution, something stirred inside him: a grain of hope, or the longing for hope—he couldn't tell the difference.

After Barry told Stuart to "go in peace," they shook hands and headed quietly in opposite directions. By the time they parted ways and Barry was rowing back toward the marina, the fog had begun to lift a little. Patches of blue sky came and went.

Now that the fog wasn't so thick, Barry could see the marina up ahead. He paused and lifted the flask to his lips, the last drops of whiskey burning dimly on the way down. Pulling the necklace out of his pocket, he lowered it into the mouth of the flask. Then he took the single pearl and held it between his thumb and fore-finger. He said a blessing out loud for Gracie and let the pearl drop into the flask with a clink. When he had twisted the lid down tight, he put the flask into his pocket and reached again for the oars.

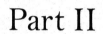

Part II

Six

The story the marina had to tell about Moe seemed to have no end. During the winter, there was still more to tell—more for memory to find. Chad began to see that no one would have strung the pieces together, though, if it weren't for Barry.

Through the winter, Barry sobered up in more ways than one. At first, it seemed to Chad like it was Jack who kept bringing Moe up, telling the outrageous stories there were to tell about him. In the mornings, over coffee, Moe's name came up often. No doubt, he would have been in the conversation anyway, but Barry seemed interested in keeping the man alive in a purposeful way—his stories, his habits, his perspective, even his quirky faith. So, while Jack told and retold Moe's stories, Barry was creating a space for those stories to exist. The stories placed question marks in people's minds and challenged them in the way Moe's presence used to.

On New Year's Eve, a handful of people met on the dock for drinks. The occasion was partly to ring in the new year and partly a sendoff for Tom, a retiring lawyer from the middle marina who was leaving for warmer waters in the South Pacific. Earlier in the day, Barry had stopped by the fuel dock to invite Chad, even though Chad didn't know Tom well. It wasn't clear to him whether Tom was intentionally bringing his career to an end or if his law practice had foundered for long enough that he was finally done pretending to work.

Chad arrived late. Someone had brought a large basin and started a small fire to create a little warmth. Someone had brought several jugs of wine. Barry handed him a glass and filled it, spilling a little onto the wood below their feet. Chad sat next to Barry on a large cooler. Tom and Jack were arguing about the types of people who live on the water. Jack thought everyone was either hiding or running away from something. Tom suggested there were only two kinds of people on the river: people who would eventually head downstream toward blue water and people who were stuck in an eddy somewhere. Jack tried to speak, but choked on a mouthful of wine instead.

Barry spoke up, "What about that other kind of person down here, the one who leaves and heads upstream instead of down?" No one spoke.

Jack cleared his throat. "What is there to see upstream once you get past Beacon Rock? A dead river, that's what. A bunch of windsurfers and grain barges stirring up the lakes that go from one dam to another up beyond Cascade Locks."

Several people started speaking at once. Conversation seemed about to split in several directions. Barry met Chad's eye and Chad spoke, more loudly than he'd intended. "I think Barry's talking about Moe, isn't he? The other kind of person we have down here who goes their own way."

The air grew still again. Jack coughed, spilling a little red wine on his white T-shirt. "Moe, huh? I guess Moe belongs to a type of person that includes only Moe himself and no one else I've ever met. So much for types of people."

"I wonder who of us had known Moe the longest," said Barry.

After a few seconds of silence, Jack said, "I bet I've got you all beat. I must have crossed paths with Moe out there on the river at some point when Moe was still a boy. Before the dam went in, everyone used to drive out there to buy fish and watch the Indians balancing out over the churning water on those wood platforms. My dad and I went on fishing trips up the Gorge, and we always stopped at the falls on the way home to watch. Once, when I was just a scrawny little monkey, my dad took me to fish the falls late at night. We must have caught a dozen fish in half an hour. How we were going to haul all those fish up to the truck, I wasn't sure. One of the Indians must have seen us out on the rocks, fishing on Native land, because we saw a dozen dark forms heading our way. My dad yelled to me over the roar of the falls to drop the fish and run. I clutched onto one fish, dropped the rest, and scrambled over the rocks back to the truck under a starlit sky, not daring to look back. It must have been a thirty-pound salmon I was carrying, still twitching in my arms."

As the conversation about Moe continued, Chad noticed Marge at the edge of the group. She quietly hugged Tom goodbye, then Dory, and then she walked down the dock toward her boat.

"You know that plastic angel Moe had mounted on his boat?" Jack said. "Well, let me tell you something about that angel. I threw that damn thing in the river at the boat ramp upstream. God's messenger: that's what I am. My sister put that damn angel on my mother's grave. An awful thing it was to see it there. Mom never cared for religion, and it would have twisted her in knots to see it. When my sister died, I sent it on its way down the river. The next day I was doing my rounds, and wouldn't you know, there was that angel on the back of Moe's boat giving him some kind of sign for who knows what. It took a couple weeks for him to realize the holy hunk of junk was made of glow-in-the-dark material. Until then, he said it glowed with an inner light."

Jack chuckled and looked around. No one was laughing. His shirt was splattered with red from the collar down to his stomach, where the wine had spilled. He coughed again.

Barry said Moe had told him something else about the bottle he found in the river before he left. "The note in the bottle was from a young boy who wanted to know who found it, but the phone number belonged to a music shop owned by the boy's father. It was the same music shop Moe had worked in years ago." Barry paused. "When he left us, he sailed up the Willamette into Portland to return the bottle. I went by the shop after Moe was gone. The owner remembered him. Moe dropped off the bottle and bought himself a trumpet before heading up the Columbia."

Chad talked about the church where Moe said he was healed, about him leaving because people talked too much and didn't listen. He explained the letters from the doctor he'd recently found at the bottom of a drawer in the office. He'd opened them since there was nowhere to forward them. He told about the doctor asking Moe to get in touch right away, about the malignant tumors that were growing in Moe's lungs. "Moe never received those letters," said Chad, "but I think he knew about the cancer."

The group was silent for a long time.

Jack reached for the jug. "Well, I can't seem to suck any more wine out of my shirt here, so I'm going to pour another glass." He looked over to Chad and then over to Barry. "You know, sometimes I wonder if Moe put that fucking baby fish in his bilge just to piss me off."

At the end of a late-winter day, Chad finished stocking the shelves and headed up the ramp, reading over a shopping list. He started to climb the ladder up into his boat when something in the parking lot caught his attention. A woman was standing near the highway just out of sight from the road, slightly behind the large wooden sign advertising Rock Creek Marina. Beside her on the ground were two suitcases and a cardboard box. She stood up straight when she saw him, with the stiff, determined posture of a woman from a black-and-white photograph. He thought he should help her in an official capacity as a marina representative—somebody in the community, not just someone who received the monthly moorage payments. Drawing closer, he saw it was Bernie.

Chad had often envied the warm, knowing looks Bernie and Bill shared with each other, holding each other's gaze for long stretches, barely speaking. They reminded him of his relaxed first weeks with Abby. Bill and Bernice had been together since the 1970s, when they'd met in the Bay Area. He was from Berkeley, and she was from San Francisco. They seemed like an odd match, she with her poise and directness and he with his playful verbal dodging. But they shared a level of patient grace with one another and made it look easy.

But here she was, waiting by the highway with suitcases and Bill nowhere in sight. Chad asked her if she was alright, if she needed help with anything. She said no; she was waiting for Bill, who was bringing the car around. She said they were going on a short trip. One of the suitcases was partly open, the latch bent upward like a tiny shoehorn.

"I really shouldn't keep you from your work," she said.

A cab pulled off the highway and slowed to a stop, the gravel under its wheels crunching loudly. Bernie started to pick up the partly open suitcase. Chad stepped up and told her he would help. She nodded. The driver came to the front of the car and picked up the cardboard box. Chad followed him back, hefting the suitcases into the trunk. They were surprisingly light. Bernice was already sitting in the backseat of the cab when he came around the car. Her door was still partway open.

She looked up at Chad and then averted her eyes.

"Bernie. Are you OK? Do you need me to call anyone? To write up a report about anything?"

She looked at Chad. Her eyes were watery. "No, nothing like that," she said. "You've always been kind. Don't let them ruin you." Then she quietly closed the door. The cab pulled out onto the highway toward Portland.

Chad walked back down the ramp to the dock and then realized he had left his keys to the marina store back on the *Arctic Loon*. He headed back to get them. There was a heavy weight in his stomach and a vague feeling of betrayal, though he couldn't picture who might be the victim and who the betrayer. He might be helping or hindering Bernie, or Bill. He didn't really know either of them well, but he could feel the unexpected absence of the two of them together, their calm grace lighting up the dock whenever they were there.

Chad didn't see Bill that day or the next two mornings, but on the third morning after she left, Bill showed up. He was barely recognizable, wearing sweatpants and a T-shirt, his thinning hair waving like smoke in the air above his scalp. The other men greeted him. Jack asked him what was with his new hairdo. Bill poured a cup of coffee and sipped before answering. "I thought I might start trying to blend in a little more with everyone else around here." Barry changed the subject. Bill didn't say much of anything for the rest of the morning.

"No, really," Bernice said. "I just needed a vacation. Just a vacation." She gazed through the cafe window where sunlight filtered through leaves high above the crowded street. Her sister copied phone numbers onto a white slip of paper—work phone, cell phone, the salon, the tennis club, other clubs—all the places where she could be reached. Outside the window, people rushed by or lingered on the sidewalk waiting for the streetcar. Several tables lined the wall under the awning on the other side of the window. Women and men were laughing in their black, cast-iron chairs and stirring their coffee or tea with spoons that flashed silver whenever the sun broke through the trees. A woman with a large potted plant—a cactus of some kind—strode by, dust motes trailing in the air behind her, making sunbeams in her wake. Across the street was the library, the massive stone structure reaching up through the roof of branches and leaves. A man carrying a stack of books shuffled slowly down the steps, pausing for a moment to balance the weight of them while reaching into his pocket.

The dizziness passed over Bernice again. She closed her eyes to hold it at bay. Her sister didn't seem to notice. Bernice took another sip. The tea trembled in the white, porcelain mug. She had lived on the river for too many years. This frantic spinning in her head might hang on for a while. She had packed her bags that morning and left. Bill was on his own now—for a few days, maybe longer.

He would run out of insulin soon, and then he would probably call her for help, since he didn't know where she went to pick up refills after the old pharmacy in Scappoose closed down. He probably wouldn't even remember to take it while she was gone.

But she wasn't going to call him about it. He could call her. He had the number. If she called on the first day, it would mean she was checking in on him. It would confirm to him that this was indeed a vacation rather than something more serious. How serious was it? She wasn't sure herself.

Elizabeth passed the slip of paper across the table. "There you go, Bernice. If you can't reach me at the office or any of these other places, then I'm not reachable at all. The cell phone's just for emergencies."

People called her Bernie at the marina, but it wasn't bothering her so much anymore. And not being bothered was starting to bother her. It's not like the name Bernie was any shorter than the name Bernice, or any easier to say. That was the whole point of familiar names, wasn't it? Convenience. It was the same with Doris. Everyone called her Dory. What was wrong with these people?

A name was a treacherous thing. Everything stemmed from there. She'd read about it in a magazine recently. Good economic standing could be traced back to certain successful-sounding names. Names were likely to affect intelligence. Your name was often the first impression in new relationships. It determined the kind of people who would be attracted to you and even the quality of your relationships as they went along. Nicknames weren't the problem. It depended on what the nickname was, or what it suggested. Men named Richard who used the familiar name Rich grew up more financially successful. There were statistics to prove it.

How different it would be on the river if she had become friends with a "Doris." You would never have tea in a downtown cafe with "Dory."

When Bill had convinced her to move onto the boat five years ago, she'd tried politely to hold people to the name Bernice, but Bernie had stuck. It was a stubborn, masculine name that put people on the defensive, as if she were an insolent, presumptuous woman who needed to be put in her place. At least for the next few days or weeks living downtown with her sister Elizabeth (and Jeffrey, the newest husband), she could listen to people say her real name for a change.

Elizabeth picked up her cup by the small handle and asked if Bernice was alright, maybe tea had been a bad idea so soon after arriving, maybe they should take their time, let her settle in a little before they tore up the town?

"No," Bernice said. "It's good to be anywhere as long as it's on dry land."

She brought the tea slowly to her lips. A blue-and-green streetcar hissed to a stop outside and the doors opened. A young couple at one of the tables outside stood up, fishing through their pockets. Bernice dropped the cup into the saucer with a clink.

Her sister asked if everything was alright with Bill.

Bernice said Bill was fine, just about to start a new job. They had both thought a short vacation for her was a great idea.

The woman on the other side of the glass tossed several coins onto the tabletop, grabbed her young man's arm, and ran with him through the door of the streetcar just before it closed. The train hissed as it rolled out of sight.

She was on vacation. That was the name attached to what she was doing here. That was what Bill called it earlier that morning when Bernice had packed her bags and called her sister looking for a place to stay. He said a few vacation days would be good for her, especially before their upcoming trip.

Vacation days. Days to decide what to do, whether to join Bill on his trip down the coast to Southern California or let him go alone. Next week he was starting a new job with the boat brokerage, a position delivering boats by water up and down the coast. And he couldn't make these trips on his own. It would mean that they'd spend more time on the water instead of less.

Bernice let out a sigh and gazed out the window. "It's just so good to be on land, having tea in the city again, away from that floating trailer park."

"Take your time with it all," Elizabeth said. "We can talk whenever. When I'm not around, I'm always near a phone." She reached for Bernice's hand across the table, her eyes wrinkled with concern. "I'm glad you knew you could come to us."

Bernice looked into her sister's eyes. "I'm on vacation, really, a getaway trip for a few days. Don't try to make this into something it's not."

They grew silent for a while. The glass of the window radiated the heat of the afternoon sun. Perhaps Bernice had overdone it a little by wearing a heavy sweater. Elizabeth was wearing a thin silk blouse and a skirt too short for someone as old as she was. A breeze moved through the trees on the street. Small, round strips of light and shadow danced over the tables outside, over the cars and people passing by, over the bricks of the library walls.

A man in baggy, gray clothes staggered up to the table outside, scooped the couple's change into his palm, and stepped away. A coin rang as it hit the sidewalk and rolled into the street. Elizabeth didn't seem to notice. Of the things Bernice had seen since arriving downtown, that homeless man, with his loose stride and meandering way, seemed the most familiar. He could have been a liveaboard from the marina. He could have been Bill even, minus the boat to live on and their savings account.

Elizabeth stiffened and looked at her watch. She'd forgotten something at the office. She would have to go back, but she wouldn't stay there long. She slid a single key across the smooth glass tabletop and told her sister to go ahead and make herself at home. She asked if Bernice wanted help getting back to the apartment.

Bernice shook her head and reached for the key. She said she would stay and finish her tea. Elizabeth leaned across the table and put an arm around her shoulder. Their cheeks touched for a moment. Bernice caught the heavy scent of her sister's perfume, the same old stuff—that officious, secretarial smell. Then Elizabeth stood up straight, "Bernice, I'll tell you what. I'll give you some space. I don't want to crowd in when you need some room to breathe. You let me know when you want to talk again. Jeffrey and I can head out of town for a few days so you can have some time to yourself. We've both got plenty of vacation time of our own. I'll see you, alright?"

When Elizabeth had passed out of sight down the sidewalk, Bernice stood up and walked toward the bathroom. Most of the tables on the way were empty. Several people huddled close, speaking softly. A photograph of the Portland skyline and the Willamette River hung on the wall behind the register.

The floor rocked under her feet. The dizziness again. She tried to correct her balance and overcompensated, placing her hand on the shoulder of a woman sitting at a table. The woman turned around, brow wrinkled. "I'm terribly sorry," said Bernice.

She breathed deeply, walking to the bathroom, holding onto the backs of empty chairs along the way. After locking the stall door, she sat on the toilet, eyes closed, head spinning. She rocked back and forth on the seat trying to make it stop. She tried to tell herself that land sickness wasn't the same thing as homesickness—that it was nothing compared to seasickness—that Bernice was a lovely, elegant name, and that she longed to hear people say it.

Barry searched the first floor of the downtown library for the card catalog, but all he could see were computers, shelves of books, and more computers. He walked among the shelves instead, reading titles to get an idea of where the sections were on the first floor, then the second. By the time he got to the third floor and found the section he was after, he was hungry, but he stayed for a while anyway, scanning the shelves. There were a few titles he remembered from seminary and some books on Augustine and Merton he'd been meaning to read for years. He pulled a bunch of those off the shelves.

At the checkout counter, the scanner wasn't able to read his decades-old card, and when the librarian eventually found his account in the computer system, the number showed up as canceled. Some of the other librarians gathered around to look at the old card. They gazed back and forth between it and Barry, as if perhaps he had only just woken from fifty years of sleep. They asked for his Multnomah County address, and since he lived in Columbia County, a ways downstream, he made up a PO Box number on the spot using an old zip code. He didn't have identification to match it, nor an email address, but they gave him a new card anyway. He appeared harmless enough; an old man checking out books on theology.

He'd been spending more time in the rowboat, exercising and fishing. Sometimes he brought books along and sat at anchor for hours reading. He read Plato, Milton, and some Christian mystics. The mystics reminded him of Moe, fixing their eyes "not on what is seen." The effusive thoughts of the old manuscripts meandered like Moe did. Moe had been gone for almost six months now. Barry wished he hadn't been so quick to dismiss him when he'd still been around.

Moe had looked Barry right in the eye one morning, after Barry had added half-a-dozen glugs of whisky to his coffee, and told him that the world needed him around. Moe said, "There's still some good work for you to do in the world."

Barry replied, "I hope you don't expect payment for your vague fortune telling."

Moe smiled. "It's just something that needed to be said. But if you want to pay me for the advice with some of your coffee spirits, I wouldn't turn you down."

Later that day, Moe had disappeared, and no one at the marina could find him for several days. Barry'd figured he was probably floating facedown in the river somewhere downstream, so Moe's final words and the shared coffee-with-spirits had rested heavily in his mind.

Moe showed up eventually, wandering along the shore with half-a-dozen monstrous steelhead in a long net draped over his shoulder, even though the season for steelhead runs had long since passed.

Bernice called Dory from the pay phone in the lobby of her sister's apartment. The security guard who'd helped her with her bags when she'd arrived was a man even older than she was. He sat behind a tall oak counter beside the elevators nodding to those who came through the glass doors from the street outside.

He threw stern glances in her direction as she searched her address book for Dory's phone number. That was why they called them "guards," she guessed—that was what they were paid to do.

The other end of the line rang four times, and Bernice worried the hot dog stand might be too busy for Dory to pick up. Men and women paced over the plush carpet near the elevators; the men jingling coins or keys in their pockets, the women standing up straight and confident, heads tilted up to watch the numbers changing on the digital display above the elevator doors.

The hot dog stand had recently reopened after a long stretch of bad weather. Dory'd had to toss a bunch of bad meat, replenish her supply of Polish foot longs and local sauerkraut, and paint a new sign. It said Let's Be Frank and hung on the front of the red-and-white-striped condiment cart.

Bernice could always count on Dory. She pictured her on the back deck of her boat or at the hot dog stand, smoking. Dory always insisted, with a wink, that she wasn't a chain-smoker because she never lit one cigarette off the red coal of another; she always used a lighter to get the next one going. As she puttered around the fuel dock, she lit cigarettes. Sometimes she had several going at once, balanced on the rims of ashtrays at tables where she had several conversations going. Bernice once saw her stab out a cigarette absentmindedly on the top of a fuel pump by the one official nonsmoking table.

Dory knew the marina news, the news of found romance, dwindling romance, or lost romance, and what people were saying about it. People came to her boat to talk. Bernice visited Dory several times a month. She couldn't stand all the cigarette smoke, and Dory didn't take a shower every day, either, but Dory treated everyone the same. Names and background didn't matter. The rich kids cruising through on their speedboats and the alcoholic bachelors at the marina all got the same hot dogs from her at the same price. Her sense of equality came across as effortless. Bernice put up with the cloud of tobacco smoke to listen and learn.

The phone purred several more times in Bernice's ear before Dory finally picked up.

"Dory? It's Bernice ... No ... Look, I can't talk long. ... No, I'm fine ... Yes, well, he'd better be ... Yes ... Well, we're separated ... No, I don't want anyone else to know about it ... I just wanted to talk to you about it. But I can't right now ... No, I'm at my sister's ... No ... I'll call you back soon ... No, I'm fine ... No, I don't want you to give him a piece of your mind."

Barry shifted his weight back and forth on the library steps, waiting with a couple dozen others for the doors to open for the day. A strange, quiet urgency came over him to be the first to get inside. He stood close to the door. Others inched closer. It was a stupid crowd impulse, with a gravity he couldn't shake just by recognizing it. He smiled to himself. It wasn't as if someone was going to go beat him to all the good books. The air was quiet, even with all the people. An Indian stood at the top of the steps by the door, his arms folded, like a man guarding the entrance. He was a head or two taller than everyone else, staring fixedly down the steps at the sidewalk below.

Barry looked at his watch. Two more minutes to go. Then he heard a sound like a large animal panting at the bottom of the steps. All heads turned to look. A man wearing rags paced over the sidewalk, his breath seething loudly through his teeth. He grunted, meeting gazes one by one. He looked in Barry's eyes, and his wild look set Barry's chest burning like a match struck behind his ribs. Barry held his breath. The man looked away and started shouting.

"What the fuck are you fuckers looking at? You know I could fuck you all up?" His pants were shredded at the cuffs. They were huge on him; a thick belt with a silver buckle barely held them up. A woman on the bottom step slowly moved away. He looked at her and she stopped. No one else moved.

"You know who I am? I could do it. Fuck the shit out of any one of you. That's right. I know. You think I don't know?"

Barry didn't move, hoping he wouldn't have to look into those eyes again. A man on the other side of the steps yelled that he should quiet down or go away.

The disheveled man paced. "How about you, fucker? Yeah, you, big guy. You know what I'm talking about, don't you?"

The flames spread in Barry's chest. But the man was pointing at the Indian. He pointed with one hand, and with the other undid the buckle at his waist. The belt jangled and the man whipped it from the loops around his waist in one quick sweep.

"You know, don't you, you big fuck?"

The Indian remained still, his eyes darting back and forth. The man folded the belt in half, snapped the two ends together, and let the belt dangle at his side, just brushing the sidewalk by his bare feet. When his pants slipped, he grabbed the waist with his free hand. Then he started up the steps toward the Indian. It occurred to Barry that he should pray quietly in his mind, but there was no room in there to think the words. He wanted to pound on the doors a couple of steps away and scream. Why hadn't they opened yet?

The Indian's eyes were red. He looked at the ground. The man with the belt yelled on his way up the stairs.

"That's fucking right! You know, don't you, big guy."

Then a low voice spoke.

"Put the belt away," it said.

The man with the belt whirled in Barry's direction, his gaze moved just over Barry's shoulder. He started wrapping the belt around his fist.

"What the fuck do you mean, put the belt away?"

Barry turned his head to see who had spoken. A short man stood beside him. Skinny, wearing a brightly colored plaid shirt. He spoke again, softly. "Put the belt away. Put it back on."

"What do you mean? You don't think I know shit? I'll put the fucking belt on!"

"Just put the belt away," said the man beside Barry.

The belt guy screamed out obscenities, at nobody in particular, but he slowly fed his belt back through the loops in his pants. Briefly, he stopped and sneered at the man in the plaid shirt and said, "You don't know who I am. Don't fuck with me."

"Put away the belt," said the man in the plaid shirt.

The belt man looped it through the buckle and started grunting again. He turned and leapt down the steps and panted away down the sidewalk. Several people on the steps clapped. Everyone breathed.

Barry turned to the guy in the plaid shirt who shook his head and spoke up toward the Indian. "Well, they let that guy out of detox a little too early, didn't they?"

The library doors opened and people poured inside. In the lobby, Barry saw the Indian striding toward the bathroom. He looked around for the man in the plaid shirt but couldn't see him in the crowd.

Before she and her husband left for the weekend so Bernice could "have some space," Elizabeth served a quiet dinner of noodles and vegetables with tofu. "Comfort food," she said with a half smile. Elizabeth's husband, Jeffrey, asked if Bernice needed any money. Bernice excused herself for a walk, stopping at the pay phone downstairs.

The security guard sat behind the counter, his head bent forward. He snored once loudly then sat up straight, but his eyes soon began drooping again.

When Dory answered, Bernice whispered into the receiver, "Hey, it's me."

A cigarette lighter flicked once on the other end. "Talk to me, sweetie. I'm dyin' here."

"We had a fight," said Bernice.

Sort of. They had never fought like this before, throwing things, raising their voices, but Bill turned it into a kind of game. Bill could laugh his way out of anything, and he usually got her laughing too.

They were never supposed to stay on the water. That had been their agreement from the beginning. They were supposed to just try it out for a little while in order to save money. "A little while" had come and gone. Then Bill had been laid off and out of work, until he'd found this boat delivery job.

The night of the fight, after Bill poured treatment chemicals into the toilet to clean out the holding tank and accidentally splashed some all over her one and only evening gown, Bernice just lost it. She smelled the chemicals and discovered several big holes in the bottom of the dress where it'd been eaten through. They hadn't used the toilet on the boat in years, having turned it into a closet for clothes that needed hanging—the nicer clothes they never wore anymore. Why would he need to pump chemicals into the holding tank when it was empty?

Bill said he was cleaning out the boat a little, getting it ready for the trip to Newport, where they would switch boats for the delivery to California. He'd thought maybe they could go on a short cruise to Portland next weekend, visit some nice restaurants downtown before the long trip down the coast. She reminded him that she would have nothing to wear to a nice restaurant anymore and then marched over to the dresser, pulled the boat ignition keys out of the drawer, threw them out the hatch into the river, and thanked him for letting her in on his plans. She went into the aft cabin for her purse and said she was going for a drive into town to spend some of her own saved-up money. Bill strutted over to the key box by the main hatch, pulled the car keys out, and threw them outside into the river too. He smiled after he did it—out of relief, or awkwardness. Neither of them had ever done this kind of thing to the other before. They were in uncharted territory.

Bernice started throwing more things into the river: a couple screwdrivers, his deck shoes, a bag of corn chips, the TV remote. Bill was still grinning, and she started smiling a bit too, which made it worse, dissipating the anger she wanted to feel. She turned to face him, narrowed her gaze, and called him William, which only made them both laugh. Bernice had to leave and go for a long walk down the dock in order to stop smiling, in order to call attention to the seriousness of what had just happened.

Later, Bill took the dinghy downstream and came back with a few things that were light enough to float. He even brought back the bag of chips. The boat keys were on a bright yellow floating key ring, so he got those too. The car keys weren't. They were somewhere on the bottom of the river. She spent the better part of the evening searching through the boat for the spare set, but they never turned up.

The next day, Bernice packed her bags and stood silently by the door with her arms folded while Bill stood by the TV, flipping through channels. That's when he used the word vacation, as if to clarify for them both what she was about to do.

She imagined Bill sleeping on the boat without her. Night was when Bill needed her most. She was the one who gave him his insulin shot, after he was asleep. Bill hated needles but he usually slept right through it. It was getting harder to catch him in deep sleep recently, since he was getting up to pee more in the night. She lay waiting, watching his chest rise and fall, his body twitching with dreams. Sometimes he pretended to be sleeping, and when she reached for the needle, he'd whimper or hum a mournful song.

The common bathroom in the upper marina was fifty yards down the dock. He couldn't really make it that far and was tired of walking up and down the dock all night, so he relieved himself in the forward cabin sink now, rinsing it out afterward with hand soap. In the morning, she wiped the dry spots of urine from the floorboards and the counter top. It had bothered her at first, but not anymore. She didn't say anything about the spots or the smell. It was hard enough for him. He usually had a hard time going back to sleep afterward. If Bernice rubbed his back, he could drift off more quickly. Sometimes they would make love in the dark, but more often they talked, sometimes until the sun came up.

The security guard snored loudly in the lobby where Bernice stood at the pay phone. Her knees ached. She told Dory about the fight, about Bill throwing the keys into the river, about how he had laughed at her. "I had to carry my luggage from the boat by myself, all the way up the hill to the highway where the cab was supposed to pick me up. I'm pretty sure only Chad saw me go up there. I don't know what I would have done if anyone else had seen me. Do people know? Has Bill talked with anyone?"

Dory's lighter scratched over the line. "I haven't told a soul, sweetie, though I think people heard me on the phone with you

earlier and know something's up, so yeah, pretty much everybody knows. And pretty much everybody knows that Bill doesn't
know that they do, so nobody's saying anything." The lighter
flicked again. "To Bill, I mean."

Bernice told her about the insulin, wondering out loud if Bill
would remember to take it, wondering if she should call home.

"Listen girl. If you're going to do this, and let him know
you're serious, then you need to really do it, you know? If you
don't mean what you say, then who will? You want me to have
my husband stop in and check on him? Or I could talk to him."

"No, you're right Dory. He needs to know that this isn't some
vacation."

Seven

It was the first day of spring when the Coast Guard called the marina with the boat ID of a sailboat abandoned in The Dalles: a Catalina with a big plastic angel strapped to the bow. Not many of those on the Columbia. They'd found a reference to Rock Creek Marina on the boat only recently and were planning to auction it off unless someone from his estate claimed it. Chad worked out how to claim it for the marina as compensation for freeing up the moorage where it had been docked in The Dalles. To his surprise, Rick agreed. He found out later Rick had made up a few bogus unpaid charges Moe owed the marina to persuade the Coast Guard to hand it over. Chad wasn't happy about being part of the scheme, but by that time the deed was done. Moe's sailboat was property of the marina, and Chad would be the one to bring it home.

He caught a ride out to The Dalles early the next morning from Dory's husband, Mark, who was headed to Idaho with a load of lumber. The mechanics in the boatyard sent an outboard motor with him for the trip back. They arrived midmorning. Mark dropped him and the outboard off at the private marina just downstream from The Dalles Bridge. Chad met with the Coast Guard and the marina owner to sign the paperwork, and they handed him a set of keys for the ignition of the nonworking motor on Moe's boat.

"Good luck with that floating heap," said the marina owner. "It's at the far end of the dock. Just follow the smell."

The boat was a horrific mess. On deck, bits of tangled thread hung everywhere in the standing rigging. Something like glue or pitch spots riddled the deck. Moldy lines were draped everywhere. The bilge pump had shorted out, and the rain and sweat between the layers of fiberglass had drained for several months so there was about a foot of water on the cabin floor below deck—a pair of shoes and several cushions were floating in the brownish water. Chad reached through the viscous water and pried up several floorboards so he could pull out the bilge pump and rewire it. By the time the water was pumped overboard, he'd discovered rancid food in the tiny fridge, half-a-dozen soggy books, a Bible wrapped in duct tape, and a soggy mound of foul-smelling clothes on the floor of the forward cabin. After an hour or so, his gag reflex drove him to buy cleaning supplies and face masks. He hauled out garbage bag after garbage bag to a dumpster up on land. No doubt he was throwing out treasures of great significance to Moe. He apologized to the memory of him as he threw out cracked Simon & Garfunkel records; a dozen rosaries; soggy, unreadable journals; music sheets; and bags of moldering M&Ms. He found booze stashed here and there: two bottles of cheap vodka, a couple unopened bottles of beer, some gin, and several bottles that had long since lost their labels.

Chad dried out several black-and-white photographs he found in a cupboard. One was the image of a man fishing the falls at Celilo. The smile on his face was familiar—not Moe but probably his father. Another photo was of two boys, one unmistakably Moe, his eyes wide, wearing a wide-brimmed straw hat and a thin vest of feathers with bones dangling from the collar in rows. The other boy wore a grim expression and was dressed in similar garb. He held Moe's arm in a tight grip. That must be his brother. The final picture was of a woman with long, straight hair, dressed in pleated pants and a loose blouse, her brow heavy and furrowed. She was holding a small bottle. A splash of sunlight shone on the dirt floor around her. The light struck the edge of the bottle in her hand, casting a sliver of light at the camera.

By the time Chad finished scrubbing the cabin, night had fallen. He dropped the salvageable loops of rope into a bucket filled with bleach water. The only things left of Moe's were a number of dishes, three cans of sardines, half-a-dozen rolls of duct tape, a few tools, an aerosol air horn, and the bottles of alcohol. Maybe some folks at the marina would like to share them in Moe's memory.

The boat still smelled of rotten food, so he left the hatch and all the windows open through the night and slept on deck beneath a tarp. The sky was cloudy but without the threat of rain. Enough heat was trapped beneath the clouds that it was still warm out. When the sun rose, Chad awoke. Birds were alighting on the rigging, singing loudly.

He mounted the outboard onto the stern, brought several gallons of gasoline on board, along with water and food, turned the bow downstream, and motored away from the dock.

Barry went to the library one Friday in March. Barely anyone was there. Not even children. It was strange. Returning to his truck with an armload of books, he found the downtown streets almost completely empty. Television cameras were scattered here and there, and the police seemed to have taken over. He hadn't known there were that many police in the whole state.

Then he heard the drums. He stopped when he reached Broadway and looked north. The protestors began pouring around a corner, signs denouncing the new war in Iraq: 9/11 IS NO EXCUSE, NO BUSH WAR PART 2, REPUBLICANS AGAINST ANOTHER IRAQ WAR. Giant puppets bobbed in the air above the crowd. Barry walked toward the marchers to get a better look. Hundreds of faces peered from windows. The drums thundered. Several rows of dancers spun long, silky flags and tossed them in the air. Here and there, protesters turned to

Barry and smiled. There were children among them, as well as elderly folks.

Barry needed to get back to his truck with the heavy books, but the marchers were headed the opposite way. The crowd thickened. In the crush, he started walking in the same direction along the sidewalk, keeping pace with them. To avoid a newspaper box that appeared in his path, Barry stepped off the curb into the street. He was walking beside a group of children, their faces painted with cat whiskers, peace symbols, stars and stripes. A young girl pulled on his sleeve and handed him a rock with a peace symbol painted on it. She carried a small basket of them. A woman, hair in a hundred braids, placed her hand on the girl's head and looked at Barry. She said something and smiled. Barry couldn't hear her above the drums. She pointed at the books he carried and gave him a thumbs-up. Something cold landed on his cheek. The ominous, gray clouds from earlier had drifted away. Rain? No. He grimaced when he recognized it as spit from one of the open windows. The pace of the marching slowed and sped up again. People stepped in time with the drums. Barry kept stepping on the heels of the people in front of him and apologizing.

They were moving leisurely enough, but Barry slowed down even more and let the children go ahead. He looked around. Long lines of Arab men and women were holding hands. He saw more children and more parents, an old woman with a cane, a black man in a wheelchair, the elderly also in chairs, and handicapped children holding knots on a long, colorful rope, all looking somehow like they belonged here. Several people were weaving through the crowd, handing out small slips of paper. One of them carried a sign that read, Poets Against the Iraq War. A woman two decades older than Barry handed him one of the slips, nodded once, then moved on. He read the words to some kind of poem: "I'm saved in this big world by unforeseen friends, or times when only a glance from a passenger beside me, or just the tired branch of a willow inclining toward earth, may teach me how to join earth and sky." Barry felt something roll and flutter in his chest, another heart starting to beat a strange, uneven rhythm next to the one already there. His stomach fluttered, like there was another heart beating in there too.

The stone in his hand grew warm. He looked again at the peace symbol on it, a broken, inverted cross. Several decades ago he'd seen this symbol everywhere.

It had struck him like an insult the minute he'd stepped off the plane onto US soil—his first time in over a year. The air in the terminal was thick with a strange silence. He kept trying to relieve the pressure in his ears even after the flight was over and his hearing had cleared. He felt them clearing and reclearing, the sounds of jet engines, people, and distant music crackling then ringing clear. Soldiers in uniform met their wives and parents and friends. They were quiet reunions. Even the families of the soldiers seemed to have suspicions about what these young men may have done on the other side of the world. Barry encountered protesters inside the terminal shouting, "Murderers! Animals!" He saw a sign that read Love Thy Enemies. Airport security escorted the protesters outside, where they continued their clamor.

Barry remembered a woman and her young daughter asleep in a chair in each other's arms. A Welcome Home sign leaned against a table beside them. The mother was lovely, even with her bright lipstick smudged and her hair slightly unkempt. How long had they been waiting? He removed his Bible from his pack and set it on the table beside their sign before walking away.

The marchers slowed down again. Barry's eyes watered as he pictured the woman and her daughter sitting next to the table where his Bible had rested. His throat tightened. This peace march was so dissimilar to the cynical protests he'd seen all those years ago. A spirit of joy was in the air, as if people of all ages were laying hold of something not even wars could stifle: the affirmation of life, of diverse lives joined by joy. His sobs were lost in the noise around him, so he let himself cry freely. He pulled out a handkerchief with a free hand and wiped at tears, snot running from his nose, mixing with another wad of spit from the windows high above. It felt to Barry like a strange kind of baptism, wiping it away an act of cleansing and healing. His crying shifted to laughing, and he met the gaze of several people who looked about his age. They smiled back at him with a mixture of joy and pity.

Then, just ahead of Barry, a large group of young adults marching behind the drummers began tying black bandannas over their faces. They branched off the main group. Police in riot gear stood on the side streets, waiting. Barry heard shouting, and a roar rose from the crowd up ahead. The music stopped. Some of the marchers turned with worried faces and started back the way they'd come. Others walked quickly down side streets.

Barry stepped down a side street and walked several blocks over to where he had parked his truck. He dropped the books in the back seat, sat down in the driver's seat, and shut the door. Tears filled his eyes again, and he held his face in his hands for a long time. The sound of a roaring crowd and sirens drifted between the buildings from several blocks away. He wondered whether he should have stayed with the march, suffered the same fate as the other marchers. A man in a dark uniform knocked on his side window with a nightstick. A muffled voice on the other side of the glass. Barry started the engine and pulled away from the curb. Luckily the officer stepped out of the way. Barry checked the mirror to make sure he wasn't writing down his license plate number, but the officer was already walking in the opposite direction. The empty park blocks rolled by, and he drove into the west hills, following them north toward the Multnomah Channel.

When he arrived home, he placed the stone with the peace sign in a drawer, next to the flask full of pearls.

Bernice kept close to the phone on the last day of Bill's insulin supply, in case he called. She turned Elizabeth's black leather couch to face the TV and watched *Perry Mason* then *Murder She Wrote* then *Oprah*, hoping to hear the phone ring each time the credits rolled.

Late in the afternoon, outside the tall windows, clouds hung heavy in the sky, almost black along their bottom edges. According to the weatherman, the wind would carry them east before they could drop their rain.

When the drums started pounding in the streets outside, Bernice removed her glasses and pulled some binoculars from a peg by the window. Her sister had called that morning from the coast to warn her about the protest, but she'd already heard about it on TV.

Should you call it a protest, she wondered? A march? A peace walk? A rebellion? Democracy? Everything depends on what you call it.

Several city blocks were visible through the tops of the trees and between the buildings; the river hung like a dark ribbon, wrinkling faintly in a light breeze as it wove through the city blocks. From the apartment, the color of the river multiplied the effects of the sky, carrying a deeper blue, or duller gray, than what it reflected. In the morning, the surface shattered into a hundred dancing suns. People paid good money for a view like this, a view of something they wouldn't want to get close to if they knew how foul and green the water was.

The dizziness came over her with renewed strength. Even sitting, if she got too close to the windows, the floor tilted down toward the river, and she had to close her eyes to make it stop. She felt more at ease looking through the binoculars. If she wanted to see the streets below, she had to walk right up to the windows and look down through the binoculars. During the day, there were people everywhere. The homeless. Businessmen and women. You could tell a lot about them by what they carried, or how they carried themselves: their posture, the quickness of their pace, their confident weaving along the crowded sidewalks. You could even guess their names and probably not be too far off. Some men still yielded to the women, letting them go first off the curb when crossing the street, but mostly, people kept clear of one another.

The drums were getting louder. The streets were strangely empty.

Just below her building, riot police began to arrive. She had to lean into the window to see them. On TV, the news said that police were prepared to use tear gas and pellet guns.

Outside, the sun started to push through the clouds. It looked like the weatherman would be right for once.

Bernice stood up on her toes to better see the street below. She leaned into the glass and waited.

Dozens of riot police climbed out of black vans, pouring out one by one, an impossible number of circus clowns jumping out of impossibly small cars. She'd never thought of police this way, clowns pretending to be soldiers. Call them cops. The fuzz. She sensed her own perceptions shifting slightly under the different names. Law enforcement. Police force. Portland's finest. How strange and laughable they looked through the high window. They were like toys, or pawns, fanning out in groups of five or six, lining the intersections along the parade route.

Light spilled into the streets. The tone of the gray river shifted and deepened into blue. Cloud shadows climbed from the streets, over trees and buildings, and fell flat on the pavement again. The pounding of drums came louder through the closed windows and echoed off surrounding buildings.

Bernice held her breath. The first of the marchers appeared. She lowered the binoculars for a moment. A river of rippling color poured slowly around the corner and over the gray concrete, swallowing the staggered yellow traffic lines. Her head swayed. Lifting the binoculars back to her eyes, she swept them up the street and away from the marchers to where police on motorcycles passed back and forth across the parade route. Red and blue lights spun dimly under the glare of the sun. Several banners waved from open windows. People leaned out into the air. Heads above and heads below all turned toward the drums.

Bernice paused. There was something familiar about the man approaching the march from the opposite direction. His arms were heavy with books, his shoulders bunched up under their weight. She couldn't place him, a face from another world, another life. Her head lightened and her body swayed—the dizziness coming on, even with the binoculars. She pressed her palm against the window frame to hold herself still.

He was from the marina. What was his name? Oh, come on. She saw him all the time. Sloppy clothes and hair. What was his name? The guy looked exactly like him: the untrimmed beard, the thick canvas pants and flannel shirt, cloth wrinkled into a web of shadows in the bright sunlight. What was his name? The resemblance was amazing. But no. He rarely left the docks except to putter around in a rowboat or to go buy booze.

It was him, even though it couldn't possibly be. He would have spent the morning with Bill over coffee. Only hours ago. They would have been laughing together. Bill might've even confided in him. Christ, what the hell was his name?

No. It couldn't be him. It might be his unkempt hair and unironed clothes, but he had all those books in his arms. The only thing he ever read was the paper and the tide tables. Everyone knew that. And everyone knew his name. It was on the tip of her tongue.

The guy became even less like himself when he stepped down off the curb and into the river of colorful clothes and banners, his head nodding to the rhythm of the drums, his face smiling. That settled it. There was no way. But she watched him. There were children beside him. What were children doing at a protest? And there were older folks in wheelchairs. The man balanced the books in one arm and handed something to a child next to him. No, the child handed something to him. A woman next to the child seemed to know him.

The soft carpet tilted under Bernice's bare feet, and her head rocked violently. The window seemed to fall forward in front of her. She leaned into the glass, a windless wind pushing her down toward the crowded pavement. Shutting her eyes, she listened to the drums until the floor felt firm again.

Collapsing onto the couch near the window, she rubbed both hands over her eyelids. Had he followed her here? Was it really him? Or was the real guy back at the fuel dock, where he always was, fishing?

The drums stopped. The second hand on the clock above the kitchen counter rolled around the clock face in a smooth arc. The crowd below roared. Sirens blared. Bernice looked up at the spinning ceiling, then made her way over to the phone. The room tipped.

The drums sounded sporadically, then stopped altogether. They might have been gunshots. Bernice dialed. Even with her eyes shut tight, the darkness rocked back and forth. When Dory picked up, Bernice tried to speak slowly, tried to calm her trembling voice.

"Dory?"

"Yeah, sweetie? You OK?"

"Dory. How can I go back? I can't go back to him. I can't go back on what I said. What are we going to do? Bill and I can't laugh our way out of everything all the time. If you are really paying attention, you can't just smile at everything."

Bernice held the mouthpiece away from her face, breathing deeply. The noise of the crowd outside faded.

Muffled sounds in the receiver. And whispering.

"Dory? Are you there?"

Bernice heard the scratching sound of a lighter firing up, and then Dory said, "Yeah. Sorry. I had a customer."

There was another pause. More whispering. Then Dory said, "I wish I could talk to you in person. Can you come back, and we'll sit down and talk this out?"

"What? But I'm sticking to my guns, I thought. Bill has to know I'm serious, right?"

"Are you trying to convince Bill you're serious, or yourself? You're pretending you've really left him, Bernie, and making it sound more complicated than it is. You guys are crazy about each other. I haven't seen Bill crack a smile since you left."

"I'm not making it complicated. It *is* complicated."

"You might think about calling him, honey."

"Wait, you've been talking to him, haven't you? After I said not to?"

"Bernie, wait a minute."

"Bill is there with you right now, isn't he? What did he tell you?"

"Bernie."

"My name is *Bernice*, you got that?" She paused, shaking. "You and everyone else down there disgust me, but especially you, Dory. You and your damn hot dogs!"

Bernice hung up the phone and grabbed her purse, letting the door slam behind her. Waiting for the elevator, she remembered

Barry's name. But what did that matter? She didn't really know him. Just his name.

As Chad traveled down the Columbia, he watched the brown and yellow grass slopes along the shore give way to dry, rocky cliff faces and towers of carved stone. Upstream of the Hood River– White Salmon Bridge, he hailed the bridge operator with three blasts on the blow horn. He trolled in slow circles for twenty minutes while he waited for the bridge span to rise. The deck of the bridge overshadowed the boat, probably well above the top of the mast, but he waited for the bridge to lift anyway.

While he waited, Chad noticed what looked like graffiti on one of the concrete bridge supports. He ventured a little closer, keeping an eye on the bridge above. Carved or drawn into the concrete were many names, a few colorful suggestions, and a couple of indecipherable pictures. Near the waterline, he saw what looked like a thin, jagged line drawn with bright paint or white chalk. It branched out at the bottom like a bolt of light-ning or a crack in the concrete.

The bright blast of a horn sounded high above and the bridge deck groaned on its way up. Moe's boat passed beneath it, and Chad was on the other side. The river widened, the wind rose, and the boat struggled along in choppy water. Windsurfers and kiteboarders zipped dangerously close to his boat, their bright colors whipping by on all sides. The sailboat became a refuge in the wind for birds flying across the river. Kingfishers fought with red-breasted nuthatches for space on the spring lines. Swallows didn't bother to alight, but swooped behind the stern to gulp down flies congregating in calm pockets of air above the water behind the boat. Dry trees and scrub grew increasingly lush along the shore, covering the stone like layers of thick cloth. That evening, he pulled into the dock of a small, man-made inlet at the Port of Cascade Locks, just upstream from the Bridge of the Gods.

As the sun set, Chad walked up the hill to the tollbooth for the bridge. The attendant took two of his quarters for the toll and waved him through. There was a sign along the walkway that read The Pacific Crest Trail. This trail led hikers, and the more serious backpackers, from Mexico all the way to Canada. Through the metal grating under his feet, he could see turkey vultures passing over the deep green water. Cars hummed over the bridge, sounding low, sustained notes, somber and resonant.

On the Washington side, he held on to the railing. A white marking on one of the bridge buttresses caught his eye. It was that same bright white streak of branched lightning he'd seen on the bridge in Hood River. He'd been feeling alone so far on his journey. This strange mark brought him near in thought and spirit to other travelers and their many ongoing journeys—north and south along the Pacific Crest Trail or east and west along the river. Chad found a stone at the side of the road and scratched the shape of a sailboat next to the jagged mark, then turned away from the Washington shore and headed back to Oregon.

The next morning, Chad arrived at the top gate of the locks at Bonneville Dam. He pulled up along the river's smooth surface above the dam just as the massive gates closed, sending a barge down the next step of the Columbia River system to the swift passage just below Bonneville Dam. He watched the pilothouse of the barge sink from high above him until it disappeared below the gates as the lock slowly drained its load of water. He tied off to a transient dock along the wall near the top of the dam and waited. In time, water filled the lock again, and the gate swung open.

Chad let down the mooring bumpers from the deck and tied off to a massive floating cleat that ran up and down a track in the lock wall. He waited. He touched the wall with the flat of his palm. As the water drained, his hand slid down the wall. When dry concrete gave way to green wet, he pulled back. "Great," he said to the slick layer of green algae on his hand. Looking up at the dry portion of the wall he saw it again: a bright streak of lightning marked on the concrete. He watched it while the walls rose, and he smiled. He imagined a person tagging their way along the Columbia with this signature, sharing some of their journey with him. "Thank you, friend," he said out loud.

Finally, the doors on the other side of the lock opened, he twisted the handle of the outboard to rev the engine, and the boat spilled out into the current again.

Barry sat aboard the *Stillwater* watching local news on his small TV. They were talking about the peace marches happening around the country. It had been a few days, but they were still effusive about the protest that had taken place in Portland. They called it the biggest war protest in Portland's history. Other cities around the globe had their own reports and footage of Iraq war protests. One commentator spoke at length about what was being called the largest worldwide protest in the history of human civilization. Millions of people. Thousands in Portland alone. On the screen were the young adults Barry had seen dressed in black at the march—they were handcuffed and lying face down in the street. There was no footage of the Arabs, the elderly, or the children with painted faces. The news anchor introduced a political science professor and asked him what effect the marches in Portland and other cities would have on the decision about whether or not to go to war. The professor said they wouldn't have any real effect, since protests—even large ones—didn't work directly to change policy. A commercial came on and the station bragged about its exclusive footage.

Policy. So much for the public, Barry thought. So much for policy. The march had had an effect on him. It might change some of his policies.

Barry snapped the TV off. He despised the smug conclusions of the commentator. He feared they might be right. What real, lasting difference could a poem or a prayer or a movement make in the face of inevitable war? What good could penance or absolution be for a soldier about to kill someone else? What good was the whole Catholic machine of written prayers and holy days and rituals when it could fail you in war?

Bill finally called Bernice. He asked how the time away was going.

"It's the worst vacation I've ever had," she said.

"Yeah," he said, "we're giving vacations a bad name."

After a long silence, he told her he missed her and asked if she'd like to go out for breakfast in the morning. He wanted her to know he was going to drop the boat delivery job if that was what she wanted. They could even consider moving back on land like they'd originally agreed, or at least go out more in the evenings to places on land. He said he was planning to bring the boat down to the waterfront tonight and walk up the street to see her in the morning if she would have him.

She told him to come up as soon as he arrived, no matter how late. She would be up.

"You're probably getting more sleep at least, now that you don't have me keeping you up at nights."

"No, Bill. I'm not sleeping well at all. I've been so land sick."

Later that night, on the couch in the dark living room, Bernice realized she hadn't asked Bill about his insulin. The phone hummed its calm tone through the receiver. No answer. She hung up and tried again. Nothing. Not even the answering machine. If he'd really left, he'd have had to pull the phone cord out of the jack next to the shore power outlet at their boat slip. She dialed again and let it ring over and over, holding the phone in one hand and pulling the binoculars off the peg with the other. She watched the dark patch of river by the waterfront until her eyes hurt from the pressure of the binoculars, then hung them back on the peg where they swung and bumped the wall. She lay on the couch and listened to the phone ring, switching ears when one of them began to ache, gazing out the window toward the broken line of the river. She imagined the miles of phone lines and cords that began at the phone by her ear and ended finally at the jack by their empty boat slip, the home for their home, where her potted flowers rested along the edge of the dock.

After a while, Bernice hung up the phone, put on one of her sister's heavy coats, took the elevator down to the street, and headed downhill toward the river. Maybe it was the darkness of early morning or the black roof of the sky studded with stars or the quiet streets or maybe the thought that she would be back aboard the boat soon, but when she looked down the hill toward the river, her eyes were steady. She waited for the dizziness to spin the buildings and streetlights around her, but it never came.

Eight

Downstream from the Bonneville Dam, Chad pulled out of the main current on the Washington side and into a small inlet. He tied off at the transient dock and called it a day a little early so he could spend the night there. A small yacht club of four large powerboats was moored there too, as well as a red, two-person kayak locked to the dock with a cable. The massive, chiseled mountain of Beacon Rock rose above the river, blocking the sun. Chad filled a backpack with a water jug, several apples, a banana, and a can of sardines and jumped onto the dock. He looked up to the deck of the powerboat moored behind him to see a middle-aged woman holding a margarita glass in her hand. She scrunched her face in Chad's direction and walked around to the other side of her boat.

Chad was on his way toward shore when he stopped.

On the bow of the red kayak was a white mark: the lightning bolt. So they were here. Whoever they were. A picture filled his mind of a sporty, middle-aged couple bedecked in REI apparel from hat to socks to boots, chomping away on Cliff Bars and squeezing packs of gooey electrolyte gel into their mouths; their water bottles would be filled with expensive, berry-flavored water. Water with plenty of bioflavonoids in it. Sweetened with stevia. He realized he was judging these people and resolved to be less condescending. "Maybe next time I see one of the yacht people, I should actually wave and say hello," he thought.

The trail was steep and hard to find in some places. It wound around Beacon Rock and wove its way up. Around each corner, Chad looked for a couple who looked like they might be kayakers. "Nice lightning bolt," he would tell them. "You've kept me company on my way down the Columbia. Thank you." For the last ten minutes of the hike, it looked like he was just a few steps away from the top.

Chad whispered to himself between breaths, "Maybe at the top of Beacon Rock there will be someone who has just slipped and is hanging on a tree root, and I'll arrive just in time. Maybe there will be a gorgeous woman at the top and I'll say to her: 'Nice lightning bolt,' though she might take that the wrong way. Man, I'm thirsty. And a little dizzy. I should have brought more water. I'm talking to myself a lot. ..."

Sweat poured down his face. He took a sip of water from the one or two inches left in his jug. He hoped there was some gooey electrolyte gel waiting for him at the top. He listened. Nothing but the sound of a light breeze in the pines and a few birdcalls. Nobody was going to be up there. Just because there was an empty kayak on the river didn't mean there were kayakers climbing the rock. Why was talking with other humans taking up so much space in his head? This was a particular kind of loneliness, a longing for fellow pilgrims.

And just like that, Chad was at the top.

He saw the dog first, because it was skidding to a stop in front of him and barking. An Alaskan husky. It was surely stronger than Chad and would gnaw on his face. He covered his face and screamed. The dog stopped barking. Chad kept his hands over his face.

A female voice called out, "Ko! Down!"

Chad lowered his hands. Behind the dog there was a young woman.

"Sorry about that," she said. "He was just startled."

Chad opened his mouth and nothing came out. She raised an eyebrow. Her hair was dark. Brown or really dark blonde. No, brown. And pulled back into a ponytail. She wore a thin, gray, long-sleeved hoodie with pockets on each side and dark green canvas pants rolled up almost to her knees. She was barefoot, one hand half inside a hip pocket and the other holding a white crayon.

The dog growled.

"Ko. Sit," said the woman. The dog sat.

Chad heard himself say in a dry, raspy voice, "Do you have any electrolyte gel?"

"What?"

When Chad didn't say anything else, she picked up a pair of sandals from under a stumpy pine tree and said, "Listen, weirdo, I'm just going to step around you and head back down the trail. I'll try to keep my dog from getting at you."

"Ko?" said Chad. The dog tilted his head.

"That's right. Enjoy the view. Bye."

She stepped lightly sideways.

"Wait," said Chad. "I'm sorry. I didn't mean to surprise the dog."

"Not to worry," she said as she headed down the trail. The dog followed.

Chad held up his hand. He was still out of breath. His heart was beating in his ears.

"No, wait. I'm sorry. I just ... Are you the one who has been making the white lightning bolt markings on the things along the river?"

She stopped and turned. "The what?"

"There was a white mark on the kayak down there," he said. "I've been seeing that same mark along the river." He paused. "On things." He pointed at the crayon in her hand. "That's brilliant. Crayons would be impervious to rain."

She looked at him, her lips parted a little. "OK, weirdo. Whatever it is you're trying to say, I'm leaving now. You better not follow me."

The woman and Ko disappeared around a bend in the trail. "I'm sorry," Chad called after her. "The white marks! I just . . ."

"I've got a Glock in my pocket!" she yelled from a little ways down the trail.

"What's a Glock?" shouted Chad, and then he remembered what a Glock was.

No answer.

She didn't want him to follow her, so he paced in circles at the top of Beacon Rock for a while. He tried to remember how long it took him to get up to the top of the rock. An hour? He thought he should wait an hour so she would be all the way down, and then he wouldn't be following her.

He waited. He saw a white streak of lightning on a tall, smooth stone. The view of the river and the surrounding hills of the Columbia Gorge Scenic Area were spread before him. Green hills. Tiny trees far below. The river shimmering in the sun. He tried to breathe deeply and take in the view, but all he could think of was the woman with the Glock in her pocket—or had she said it was a rock? He tried to picture her face and couldn't. She had been ... dazzling. Gorgeous. Smart, using the white crayon. Amazing dog. The dog totally obeyed her. You could tell a lot about her, just from the dog. He wanted to be that dog's new best friend.

When he thought it must have been no later than an hour and no sooner than half, he started back down the trail. He turned each corner expecting a dog to jump at his face. He could offer his arm as a chew toy. He had another arm. He climbed down slowly, wincing when his feet scuffed stones near the edge of the trail and they slid over the edge. He pictured the woman lying in a heap, her head bleeding from rocks he'd let fall. Or Ko. Chad would get to the bottom of Beacon Rock, and she would be there, sitting beside her dead dog and saying, "You killed Ko."

In Junior High Sunday School, Chad had learned a short prayer he still used occasionally despite otherwise being partic-ularly unreligious: "God, may your blessing and protection be upon this person." The prayer began to loop unbidden through his mind. It figured. He became a person of religious faith as long as he remained cognitively unhinged.

He reached the foot of Beacon Rock half an hour later, out of breath. No one was dead at the bottom. He walked down the hill through the trees to the banks of the river. The powerboats were still there next to Moe's boat. The mast rocked slowly back and forth. To his left was a small, flat, grassy area, and on the other side of that, a couple picnic tables and several camping spots. A tent had been pitched there that he hadn't seen earlier. Out of the unzipped opening, a dog's head appeared. Ko. The woman was nowhere to be seen. Chad turned away, walked towards the dock, and climbed onto his sailboat. He made the thirty- or forty-second walk without looking toward the tent, enough time to whisper seven times, "God, may your blessing and protection be upon this person … and Ko too."

Chad sat at the table in the main cabin eating apples and bananas. For about an hour, he tried to read Zora Neal Hurston, but he could only make it through several delicious sentences before his mind wandered. He read the lines so many times he found himself reciting them without even following the words on the page. The sun was setting when he looked out the window to see her walking across the grass, wearing a fleece sweater over the gray shirt, hood pulled out. Her canvas pants were rolled down, and she had on hiking boots. Chad stood, facing away from her, as her heavy boots clomped over the dock. Dog claws clicked and pattered behind her. She didn't stop at her kayak; her footsteps continued until they stopped outside his sailboat.

"Hey," she said.

Chad climbed halfway up the steps and stood looking out of the hatch, about eye level with her. She smiled and her smile brought a stab of panic to his chest. He took a deep breath, trying not to sound like he was taking a deep breath.

"Hey," he said.

"Now that we're around other people, I just wanted to say sorry for being so rude and defensive up there." She pointed a thumb back over her shoulder. Chad looked up at Beacon Rock behind her, his eyes wide, like he hadn't seen the towering pinnacle until just now.

"I'm sorry I startled you too," he said. "I was probably not making a lot sense up there. I promise I'm really not that much of a weirdo."

It was quiet for several seconds. Ko looked up at her.

Chad climbed up onto the deck and sat on the cockpit bench facing her. "I don't mean to be impertinent, but ... that lightning bolt on your kayak?"

"Impertinent? Not a bit." She shook her head and smiled. "That mark isn't lightning. It's supposed to be a rough outline of the river. Of the Columbia."

Chad smiled and put his hand over his unshaven cheek. "So, the graffiti tag you make up and down the river is ... the river? I didn't recognize the shape."

"Yep," she said. "It's a rough outline. I'm following the river downstream."

"Me too. You want to come aboard?" He immediately wished he hadn't asked.

"Nah. Better not."

She leaned closer and looked through a window into the cabin. "This thing reeks," she said, then backed away. "Now, that there is a lot of bottles."

Chad looked through the hatch at the mess of bottles resting in the sink. "You probably wouldn't believe me if I said those belonged to the boat's previous owner, would you?"

"I might," she said. "The boat smells like a dead skunk, and so do you. But you don't smell like you've emptied those bottles anytime recently."

"Nope. I guess I've gotten used to the smell. I cleaned it out, but this thing has been abandoned for quite a while."

"You don't cook meth on this boat or anything?"

"Absolutely not. I don't cook—I mean I cook things. Boil them or fry them. Meat. Vegetables. Fish." He paused. "I'm going to stop talking now."

She smiled again.

Chad felt light-headed. He steadied his hands on the seat. He thought he might pass out if she didn't stop smiling at him like that. He looked just past her at the grass on the shore.

"Well," she said, "I don't get onto strange, stinky boats with weirdos, but if you want to join me, I was just going to make something to eat over there at one of the picnic tables."

"Yeah, I'd love to. I've got some fruit and some sardines."

"Maybe you bring the fruit. And keep the sardines here."

Chad nodded. "Right. I'm not usually the kind of person who eats sardines. But the guy who owns this boat, or used to own it, he was an Indian. Or a Native American. He had sardines on-board. And I wasn't really planning to eat them, it's just that they're there."

"Right. It sounds like there's a story in there somewhere. Go ahead and grab what you want to bring, I'll be right over here getting a few things from the kayak."

She was smiling when she said it, but Chad didn't pass out, so he stepped down into the galley and filled his arms with produce without really paying attention to what he was grabbing—when he climbed off the boat and followed her up to the picnic table, he was struggling to balance in both arms a banana, a head of lettuce, a browning apple core, a stalk of celery, a spatula, a butcher knife, a lukewarm ice pack, an almost empty bottle of dish soap, and a can of sardines.

Her name was Emma. She called her dog "Ko," which was short for "Kodiak," where Ko's forebears came from, she said. She'd visited her older brother in Alaska and brought Ko back to Oregon with her. She and Chad shared a package of lasagna that was a just-add-boiling-water-to-a-prepackaged-plastic-sack-of-dried-food-flakes kind of meal. Backpacking food. They used different spoons and took turns scooping lasagna out of the thick plastic bag. Under the picnic table, Ko sniffed at Chad's legs. Chad held his hand out toward the dog's nose, and Ko nudged it with the top of his head. Chad scratched behind his ears.

Emma peered over the strange pile of things he had set on the picnic table. He looked at them curiously and turned red. "Huh," he said matter-of-factly and, picking up the nonedible food items (including the can of sardines), he dropped them all into a garbage can a few steps away from the picnic table. He sat back down, shrugged his shoulders, and smiled. She handed him the bag of food without any indication that something a little odd had happened. This was good, Chad thought, and his smile grew to a grin.

She was twenty-five. Older than Chad by a year. They compared notes on their river journeys. She'd been kayaking the
Columbia starting from where it crossed the Oregon border,
taking her time with it through the summer and aiming to finish her staggered trip in Astoria. She worked as a nurse and was
adjusting her schedule, working seven days on and seven days
off, kayaking for a few days, resting, and then returning to work.
On again, off again, since she couldn't get enough weeks off to
make the journey in one go.

She brought a box of red wine out from a waterproof bag that
contained another large box of wine.

"Whoa," Chad said.

"Yeah, I could've probably left one of those at home."

They stood looking at the ground.

"I'll have a glass with you."

"Just one," she said.

They sipped from tin cups: a not exactly exquisite cabernet.
It was the best cup of wine Chad could remember having tasted.

He listed the white river marks he had seen since The Dalles.

"Well, that's not even half of them," she said.

After the sun set, Chad got a campfire going. They sat beside each other on the picnic bench. Ko sat under the bench, just
behind their feet, shielded from the heat of the fire. Chad told
Emma he was partly taking this trip to put closure on the marriage he'd been a terrible husband in.

"How long since you split up?" she asked, sipping and peering
over the rim of the tin cup.

"Almost five years ago," he said.

"You take your time getting over things."

"I suppose. It was a whirlwind of major and minor tragedies.
I didn't really face the death of it until after I graduated from
college and found myself four years older but not much more
mature."

"Hmm," she said. "Tell me about tragedies, and I'll tell you
why I'm on this trip."

Chad told her about their chaotic year on the sailboat and
then about the accident, and Abby's injuries. It was the first time

he'd talked to anyone about it since right after it happened. He had tears in his eyes and had to stop talking. Emma said, "Don't take this the wrong way, but I'm going to put my hand on your shoulder." Her hand was warm.

"So," she said. "Shawn was my younger brother. He drowned. He was with friends, exploring a long culvert from the foot of a waterfall to the river—it stretched all the way under the highway and the railroad tracks. Halfway through the culvert, they turned around because they started sinking into deep mud. Shawn's feet sank in so far he couldn't move them—he was up to his chin and stuck. His friends ran for help, but he just kept sinking. Help arrived, but it was too late." Emma grew quiet.

Chad said, "Wow. You seem much more stable than I would be in your place."

"I doubt it. I'm looking for closure, too. My family hasn't been handling his death very well. We haven't been able to draw close without hurting each other worse. We probably need counseling together, but that isn't likely to ever happen."

"Were you and your brother close?" asked Chad.

"He was my protector. He beat up guys at school who gave me any trouble. He was a big, tough guy, but he was also sweet. He called me 'Angel,' but he was more my guardian angel."

She picked up a stick from the fire, blew on the glowing tip and drew a gray, ashy, lightning bolt sketch of the Columbia River on a flat rock. She carved several short tributaries from the main stem and pointed with the stick at one of them. "Here, near the base of Crown Point, is the culvert where my brother died. I'll stop there, take my kayak into the tunnel." She looked up at Chad. "Too morbid? I want to see the last things my brother saw. My family doesn't like the idea. None of them have gone near that place."

Chad said, "Being morbid sounds perfectly appropriate to me."

"I wish my parents could understand my ways of mourning. They are teetotalers and I'm ... not. Anyway, I'll stop by the culvert, and I'll end this leg of the trip up the Sandy River. My car is there, in Troutdale."

She looked down at the marks she'd drawn. "Sometimes, I think this doesn't look anything like the Columbia. It looks more like a crack in the sidewalk. Or a crack in a concrete dam."

Chad thought of Moe. He held out his hand for the stick, "May I?"

He drew a small loop a little further downstream. "This is Sauvie Island," he said. "And this is the Multnomah Channel."

She rested her head on her forearm and said, "I've paddled there. The island is a great place to explore by kayak when the river's high enough."

"I work at a marina right here. When you get to that part of your journey, you should take the channel route downstream and stop by the marina on your way. I'll show you around."

She said she would think about it. She and Ko stood up, ready to call it a night. Chad said he was sorry about what had happened to her brother.

"That's what people say," she replied. "Other people say that and try too hard to make it heartfelt. But it's different to hear it from you." Boisterous laughter came from one of the yachts. Joyful yelling. Someone singing an indecipherable song.

She grinned and waved her hand in the direction of the dock. "You weirdos go sleep over there."

Chad smiled and stood up. Ko got up with him and looked from him to Emma.

She said, "Well, I guess I won't have to Glock you after all."

"Do you really have a Glock?"

She pulled the bottom of her shirt up over her hip revealing a small handgun in its holster. He held up his hands and said, "I can see there's no messing with you. But you should know that I'm wearing a special bullet-proof T-shirt."

"Don't tempt me."

Early on a Saturday while Chad was gone, Barry was reading at his desk when three boys entered the store. Each carried a fishing pole. One had a tackle box. He set the box on the ground and looked at Barry. "Can you sell me some bait?" he asked.

Barry smiled. "Absolutely. What do you need?"

"Well, Chad said you would know."

"He did, huh?"

"He said you would know what was running and where the good fishing spots were and what to use for bait. We don't know any of that stuff, and we never catch anything but the tiny little ones you have to throw back."

"Well, there isn't a run right now, but you can still have some luck in a few spots. I'll set you up with what you need."

When they were gone, Barry sat back down and listened to the quiet behind the buzzing refrigerators and the slow ceiling fan above him. The store and the dock were empty for some time.

It felt odd to be the go-to person for anything. Especially with children. When he saw children on the dock, and the adults they were becoming, he could see in them the infants and children he'd failed to bless over the years who might've been helped along a little by those blessings. Every day, Barry saw grown men and women stumble down the ramp who had never taken a sober step on the dock since he'd known them. They, too, seemed a result of his lack of faith. He knew this was a judgment upon lives he didn't know, but it weighed on him.

Lately though, as he offered what he could, he felt the stings to his conscience less. He offered blessings in his mind for children who entered the store clamoring for candy or ice cream, or for the ones over eighteen who bought cigarettes. These things Barry sold to young people made their way across the counter with his feeble prayer attached to them. They were tentative at best. He figured the lives of others were mostly none of his business, but he didn't know what else to do when he sensed a need and found the burden of a blessing resting lightly in his mind or in his hands.

In his worst, most depressed moods, he thought maybe no good could come from good, and even the intentions of a quiet prayer might bring more hurt later on when additional loss ripped through the lives of those touched by a blessing. A blessing could be swallowed up, like a drop of fresh water in the salty ocean. Light could fill that tiny bead of water for a moment, then drip, it was gone. What good were his prayers or blessings in the face of loss or longing? Somehow, it had to be sufficient to have seen the drop suspended in the air and to remember it existed for a moment, under the sun, over the water.

Early in the morning, at the shore near the foot of Beacon Rock, Emma and Chad shared an oatmeal breakfast. When they finished, she told him he would be doing her a favor if he helped her pour the unopened box of wine into the river. So they walked down to the sandy shoreline, Emma holding the box. She held it out to him.

Chad hesitated. "You want to do it instead?" he asked. "I can be the witness. Cheer you on." She nodded and poured.

Emma started humming a mournful tune. Chad recognized it: "Danny Boy." He hummed along. Her voice trailed off into a laugh. "No, shut up. We'll wake up the booze club."

The dark shape of the wine in the water slowly spread out and drifted like a shadow downstream.

"Almost gone," she said.

Chad reached out a hand. "Wait. Why don't I hold on to the rest of it, and we can share the last couple glasses after you reach your . . ."

"Tunnel of death? My closure cave?"

"I mean ... I don't have to be there."

She handed him the box. "Yeah. Hold onto it."

When they were both done packing, they stood beside each other looking out over the water. The powerboaters were awake now, grinding their blenders loudly and singing an ode to Bloody Marys. Emma looked at Chad. "Let's get out of here."

She paddled beside him for a while, going slow enough that he could keep up. Ko sat in the front seat, his body mostly hidden in the belly of their small vessel, his head resting on deck, facing the bow.

Over the sound of the diesel engine, Chad asked her to tell him about her brother. She told him about the bootleg cassette tapes he used to bring home to her. Female punk bands like the Slits, the Runaways, Patti Smith. Once, she tried to run away when her parents confiscated her Walkman and her headphones. She packed a bag and headed down the railroad tracks several blocks from the house. Her brother followed her and said he was coming too. They walked and talked for an hour until he convinced her to turn back. Shawn taught her how to punch. And how to take a punch. "Not a very hard punch," she said, "but hard enough that I cried for a second. Then I got so pissed that I gave him a black eye."

Beacon Rock passed around the bend in the river behind them and out of sight. The thin, white brushstroke of Multnomah Falls appeared above the trees. Cars hissed along on the Oregon shore. Northward, across the main current of the river, Skamania Island seemed to float on the surface like a long, many-masted ship anchored offshore. They decided to stop at this thin strip of sand and trees. Chad dropped the anchor and climbed down onto the kayak so they could paddle to shore. Ko licked Chad's face whenever it was near enough and leaned back into his arms as Chad held onto him for balance. Emma laughed as the two of them struggled—Chad to keep from falling in, and Ko to smother Chad with affection.

They landed, ate sandwiches, and walked around the sandy shore of the island three times, talking, while Ko ran up and down the shoreline in the shallow water. They sat on a large driftwood log and gazed south across the main current of the river. They thought they could maybe see movement in the white smudge of Multnomah Falls on the south shore.

Emma asked Chad why he loved sailing. He told her about learning knots with his grandfather and going to Sea Scouts. "When I was a kid, my grandparents' house was more like my real home," he said. "My grandfather lost a foot when he was a Merchant Marine. It got caught in a mooring chain and he was pulled down into the ocean. His crew rescued him but his foot had been pulled clean off at the ankle. When they eventually pulled up the anchor, there was his shoe with his foot still inside it, wedged into a link of the chain. He had a wooden foot that he could strap and unstrap to the stump of his ankle. We used to take turns hiding the foot somewhere in the house, and then he'd hop and crawl around to look for it. I always hid the foot in the same places, and he'd pretend not to know where it was. He'd hop from closet to closet, or crawl under the kitchen table hollering, 'Where is that stinky foot? I think I can smell it, now. We're getting warmer.' He could get me to laugh so hard, holding my stomach until I was gasping for air.

"Once, he took a turn and hid his foot in a spot we'd never used before. We looked everywhere. We went down to the basement, and all of a sudden he couldn't remember where he'd hidden it. He seemed confused and said he needed to sit down and think. He sat on an old wooden trunk and stared off into the distance. His face sagged into a kind of twisted frown. He'd been holding my hand, and his hand went cold and limp. I remember wondering if he was going to have a new pretend, wooden hand, like his foot. I'd never heard what a stroke was before that. Scared the crap out of me. Eventually I ran upstairs and got my grandma. We couldn't get him to even stand up, so she called 9-1-1. He had smaller strokes after that and died a few months later."

"That must've been pretty frightening," Emma said.

"For a long time, I believed he was still around. As long as the wooden foot remained hidden, it was like he was still alive—just hiding. I found the foot when I was older. He'd hidden it in the trunk in the basement. That was hard, but I still had the sense he was present in my life. Like whenever I pray—which is pretty rare—I picture him as the one listening."

They sat together watching the gray sheet of the river begin to break up in the afternoon wind. Ko galloped back to them every few minutes and searched for Chad's hands to sniff. He brushed Chad's legs with the side of his head.

Emma said, "Looks like he's smitten. You've got a big, dumb heart. Don't you, bud?"

Ko turned toward her and leaned onto her legs with his massive head. She scrubbed his neck then pushed his head away and said, "Go on! Go run yourself ragged, Ko-Ko. We've got a lot more hours of sitting to do today."

Chad watched the dog prance back toward the waterline. An osprey dove into the river and came up with a small steelhead in its talons. As the bird wheeled toward shore, the fish shook violently every couple seconds.

Emma laughed. "It looks like a cartoon, aiming ahead like that—like a flying fish."

The fish lurched and slipped from the bird's talons into the water with a loud slap. The osprey circled above the surface and then turned away, pounding its wings, aiming up toward the rock ledges high above.

They paddled the kayak back to the sailboat and resumed their journey together quietly until, all of a sudden, Emma slapped the surface of the water with her paddle. She made an exasperated growl.

"What?" asked Chad. She saw him stiffen. "What's wrong?"

"You," she said. "You're wrong. I'm supposed to be here taking this trip to remember my brother—not floating around with you and your smelly boat with that engine buzzing away, drowning out all the sounds on the river. And if I wasn't here, you'd probably actually be sailing and having the kind of trip that you should be having."

Chad's face fell. Unable to stand the sight, she dug in her paddle and sped away downstream. Over her shoulder, she yelled back at him, "And you keep sitting there, looking like you're in a freaking cologne ad or something!"

"I don't wear cologne," he said.

She continued to pull ahead.

"That sounds like a bad thing, then?" His voice had become hollow, distant.

The minutes went on, and she could hear the engine receding behind her. She turned to see the white sliver of the sailboat on the horizon and stopped paddling to let him catch up.

She was right, Chad thought. The engine was loud. He rolled down on the throttle until it sputtered to a stop. Moe had tied a mainsail to the boom, but there was no cover to protect it from sun and rain. When Chad untied the straps and hoisted the main halyard, the sail rose like an expanding accordion, with horizontal stripes worn through canvas as stiff as plastic. The breeze spilled right through it. Chad lowered the sail and rummaged through the locker under the cockpit bench on the port side. Eventually, he pulled out a small blue bag that contained a tiny storm jib. It reeked and was spotted with mildew, but it wasn't torn or cracked. Not much sail space to catch the breeze, but it would do.

He attached the ring at the peak of the sail to the forestay and pulled it up. A tiny triangle of canvas. The wind was blowing, and the sailboat actually leaned, the bow cutting through the water. Water sloshed by. He was going faster under a storm jib than he had gone with the motor.

Ten minutes later, he caught up to Emma. He loosened the jib halyard and let the sail drop to the deck. They drifted next to each other for a minute. Then Chad asked, "Should I keep going? Are we OK?"

"We," she said, seeming surprised at the word. "Yes. We are fine. I'm sorry. I've been looking for something this whole time on the river. Many things, maybe. Impossible things. Grief. An end to grief. A final conversation with him. Some dreamlike, impossible state of mind that is so vague, I am bound to be disappointed. I blamed you back there for some of it, but it's really just me. I'm sorry."

"It's easy to do that kind of thing," Chad said.

"The truth is I've already gotten used to my brother being gone, but I don't want to be used to it yet. I can't just go through the motions of grief. I intended for this trip to be one thing, but now those intentions seem artificial. Now, this trip is . . ." She trailed off. "Whatever I want it to be, I guess."

She reached out and scratched Ko with the end of her paddle. He leaned into her scratching.

Chad said, "That sounds pretty freeing. Probably exactly what your brother would want for you. I'm jealous, in a way. I used to think I was an easygoing guy and open to whatever might come. But I'm not really all that easygoing. I just know how to avoid things." Crap. Here she'd been talking, and he'd stepped right in and filled the pause with thoughts about himself. Himself and blah, blah, blah. He looked at her. She reached her paddle toward him, and he grabbed it and pulled her closer. She reached for his hand and held it.

The space between them—the air and water and the words they had spoken—seemed to drop away. Chad said, "Now that I know we are OK. I'm just—I'm really happy about that."

A gust of wind blew through her hair, pushing it up into her eyes. She hooked it behind her ear. Her cheeks flushed, reddening.

Chad looked away. He was shivering, his heart beating fast. He felt a sudden dread that now there would be no going back. Nothing was going to undo what Emma was doing to him. They couldn't undo what they had already done together. Chad recognized that he might never again be completely safe to just drift away from her. He would have to trust her. She would have to trust him. He wasn't sure she was safe trusting him. His shoulders shook. His teeth began to chatter.

Before he knew it, he heard himself saying, "We're getting close to Crown Point, where you said the tunnel was. I think you should make that part of the journey alone when you get there."

She shook her head. "I don't want to. Not now."

"I've already stolen too much from you. From your brother. You need something more right now, and I'm in the way of that."

"No, you're not." she said.

Chad shook his head and said what he knew was a terrible, hurtful, untrue thing. "We don't even know each other." He smiled when he said it. "It's been good to meet you."

"No," she said.

They drifted in silence.

Emma stood up on her seat and pointed at Chad's face. "This is stupid. You don't have to do this."

Ko whined. Chad said nothing.

"Don't you say goodbye to me, you asshole!"

"We've known each other, what, twenty-four hours?"

"OK. So I'm going to go see where my brother's life ended, and then I'm coming after you. If you're going to be stupid, then I'll one-up you. I'll be in Astoria in three weeks. You're going to meet me there, on the dock, by the maritime museum."

Chad looked downstream.

She said, "I'll just drift out to sea until you come."

"You're right," Chad said. "That is stupid. We might as well meet at the top of the Astoria column at the strike of noon three weeks from today like in a movie. Except you would probably get hit by a car or something and not show up. You have your brother waiting for you right over there." He pointed toward the shore. "Once you get back to your journey and see I'm right, you won't even think to look for me when you eventually get to Astoria."

Still standing, Emma shouted, "You're on, motherfucker!" Saliva sprayed from her mouth into the sunlight and onto Chad's face. She grabbed her paddle in both hands, pushed off against the hull of the sailboat, sat, and paddled toward the Oregon shore. Her sobs carried across the water. Ko barked. She didn't turn around again, even as she slipped from view among the grass and pylons sticking above the surface like jagged fence posts.

Halfway through the tunnel, Emma set the paddle on top of the kayak and drifted to a stop in the dark. She wiped her eyes and her nose with the edge of her shirt and sighed. She felt for the walls to either side and for the curved ceiling above. They were rough and wet with grime. It must have happened here, some-where within twenty or thirty feet of this spot. She squinted in the dark at the walls, not entirely sure what she was looking for.

Ko whined.

"I'm sorry, buddy. It's alright. We'll get going in a minute."

She felt the cool surface of the water. Were his footprints still in the mud below? Not likely. She felt for the gun in the pouch by her hip. She could fire a bullet down into the muck. But there was no need. She didn't need to climb out and feel for footprints. She didn't need to say anything. She spoke anyway. "If you know anything, you know I miss you. And you know I love you. You probably also know I've cried more about a patient I saw die in front of me than I have for you in quite a while."

The tags on Ko's collar clinked and echoed. She could see the shape of his head silhouetted against the round opening of the tunnel. He opened his mouth to breathe quick breaths, and the rich, bitter smell carried back to where she sat.

"I thought I might say goodbye to you here, but I don't feel your presence any more than I do anywhere else. I've already said goodbye a hundred times, and yet you still feel close sometimes, so goodbye just seems indulgent. Like something Mom and Dad might feel the need to say. Can I say 'goodbye' and 'let's get out of this tunnel' at the same time?" She sighed. "I already cried a few minutes ago about another guy, so I don't see that happening again here."

"Oh," she said, "don't let me forget this."

She pulled her white crayon from a pocket and drew the familiar marks on the wall in the dark.

"Goodbye, and let's get out of here."

She grabbed the paddle and pushed through the water.

"His name is Chad," she said. "He's kind of an idiot, but thoughtful too. He's got compassion. You'd like that."

She squinted as they glided out into the wind and the light. Downstream, the sailboat was nowhere in sight.

Nine

When Chad returned to Rock Creek with Moe's boat, he tied it in Moe's old spot upstream from the fuel dock. He didn't want to see or talk to anyone, so he walked quickly off the docks, climbed up the slope of the parking lot and into the broken down *Arctic Loon*, and didn't come out for two days. He wanted to think about Emma. Turn over his conversations with her in his mind and think about the things he wished he'd said. He wanted to picture her face. He wanted to imagine her with him, in a future that could really exist, where he could apologize for being an ass and make plans with her and join his life with hers.

His life. Right. His life in a crushed sailboat hull resting on stilts on dry land, pretending to be at home in a boat that wasn't a home, that wasn't a boat, that wasn't in the water, even while his body swayed and rocked, telling him that he was.

He tried to picture Emma's face and her clothes and her body, but all he could see was the face and the broken body of his ex-wife. The image of Abby beneath the mast had parked itself in his brain and wouldn't leave. He imagined for the first time in a while the many possible disabilities she was living with and the unknown damage that had come of their headlong dive into an unfamiliar life on the river. Chad wasn't sure which would be worse: living with Abby these past years and being forced to contend with the consequences of her injuries, or being denied the opportunity to do so, as he was, with Abby's life and concerns largely concealed. He knew that life could get bad. He also understood that he had been spared the weight of what he felt was his to carry.

At the end of his first day back at the office, he pulled a beer out of one of the fridges on his way out of the marina store, locked the door behind him, and joined Dory, Marge, and Jack on the fuel dock.

"Welcome back, Mopey," said Jack, after Chad sat down. "You look like shit. How was the trip?"

Chad took a couple of sips of beer. He said, "Good."

The others sat quietly, obviously expecting more.

"Good?" said Jack. He took in a breath, about to speak—Dory interrupted him.

"Jack. Can't you tell when somebody would rather not talk about something? Maybe you could tell us something about yourself instead. Like, what are some of your biggest fears in life?"

"Just one," said Jack. "Fear of stupid questions." He stood and left. Dory shrugged. Chad emptied the bottle, went back into the store, and got another beer. When he sat down again, Marge was finishing up a list of her own biggest fears.

"When Moe used to disappear for a few days. And then when he left for good, and we didn't hear anything from him for a while. That scared me. Even though we weren't together anymore." She paused and they looked at Chad, who stared down at his beer. Marge continued, "But I'm also scared of storms at night while I'm on the boat. It's impossible to sleep with the wind howling like some hungry beast and the rain pattering on the deck above you and the boat scraping off the bumpers with that horrible screeching sound. I went to a hotel in Scappoose one weekend when the rain hadn't stopped for two weeks straight."

"Honey," said Dory, "you just come right on over the next time that happens. You come and you stay until it's plumb gone, do you hear me?"

"I couldn't do that, and wake you and Mark up," said Marge.

"Let's skip to the part where you just agree, because I'm going to come get you if you don't. Promise me you will."

"Oh, alright. I promise."

"You should know that promises are very important to me," said Dory, grabbing Marge's hand across the table.

Chad said, "I love sleeping on a boat, especially when there are storms."

Dory looked at him. "Wait, you don't … Did you live on the 'Looney Bird' on the water too?"

"Yes," he said. "It was a few years ago." Chad told them about his year on the river with Abby and that it didn't end well and that there was nothing much else to say about it. No one said anything for a few seconds until Marge looked at her watch.

"I've gotta get back. I have some paint that is going to harden if I don't put it away."

After Marge left, Dory looked at Chad and said, "Look, you've obviously got something on your mind, honey. And I've obviously got to know what it is if I'm ever going to leave you alone, so you might as well just spit it out."

Chad unlocked the store again and got another beer. He grabbed a Red Dog for Dory too. Her favorite. Then he dove into it. He told her about Abby. He told her about making meals on the boat with their tiny oven and two-burner stove and the fire they started in the galley once. He told her about their long weekends anchored off Government Island. He told her about losing his wedding ring in the river, and how Abby had slowly lost interest in sailing and living in such a cramped space. "During our first Thanksgiving together on the boat," he said, "we were both sick for a week. It started out as allergies then turned into a flu, then back into allergies, and then into a cold."

"It's the mold around here," said Dory. "The river goes down and we all breathe that nasty crap in the air from the muddy shoreline. Mark gets sick after being here for a week. That's partly why he drives truck. To get the hell outta dodge for a while, just so he can breathe."

Chad continued, "Abby moved our mattress out of the forward cabin to clean underneath it. She leaned it against a wall, and a couple minutes later half a gallon of water had drained onto the floor. We couldn't believe it. It'd been covered with a plastic sheet so we didn't realize we'd been sleeping on a giant, wet sponge."

"Oh, you poor kids. I should get her phone number from you. There are some ladies who think they just can't do this life. I mean it's not for everybody, but I bet I could talk her through it."

"Dory. You're a gem. That ship, as they say, has sailed." Chad described their marriage, their drifting apart, their inability to see things the same way. "She approached the world around her pragmatically, sizing things up long before she spoke, whereas I live way too much in the moment. I'm a processer. I feel things and then figure out what I think about them. That was a pretty inefficient way of living and laboring and loving for her. She was getting pretty tired of my need to work through things. And then it all came to a head. ..."

Chad stopped. He looked at the top of the table.

Dory put her hand on Chad's forearm. "Honey, you're the gem. It's OK. What happened?"

"There was an accident," he said. "It was a car accident. And I was the one driving." Chad looked at Dory for some flicker of an expression. He wasn't used to telling flat-out lies. He was better at deceiving himself than he was at intentionally steering someone else away from the truth. No doubt she knew some wacked-out version of the real story through the currents of gossip she navigated better than just about anyone he'd ever met. But she didn't seem to know Chad was attached to this particular boating accident.

He asked about Moe, hoping to break away from the accident before he said anything really stupid. But Dory couldn't let it end without trying to convince Chad that he was obviously still in love with the girl. She tried to get him to tell her Abby's full name so she could call her and talk some sense into her. Chad told her it had been over for years, but that didn't seem to deter her.

Someone approached the hot dog stand. Chad said, "Thanks, Dory. It was good to talk with you about it. More later?"

She reached out and hugged him. "Anytime, hon. Anytime." She greeted the customer, and Chad climbed up to land, and onto the *Loon*.

When he couldn't get to sleep, he walked down to the dark, empty fuel dock and sat at one of the tables, gazing out over the water. He put a coat on to hold back the cold, but fog set in, and it got even colder. He put a life jacket on over his coat and felt his chest get warmer, though his hands were growing numb. He dozed on one of the benches, but thoughts of Abby and a dozen imagined conversations with her kept waking him. The sun finally rose and warmed him. He drove his pickup truck to Abby's parents' house. It was 7:00 a.m. He was going to wait until 8:00 a.m. and then knock on the door, but her father saw him and walked up to the truck.

Chad rolled down the window.

Abby's dad looked at him in silence. Then he smiled. His smile seemed warm and friendly enough. "Hi Chad," he said finally. "You look ready for a flash flood." Chad still had the life jacket on.

Chad asked how Abby was. Her dad told him that Abby was doing very well and that she was married now and had a child. Chad didn't ask if it was a boy or a girl. He didn't ask for her address or her phone number, either. But he did want to know whether there was any permanent damage after the accident.

"There was nerve damage. Her hand lost all its feeling. She still keeps it resting in a sweatshirt pocket or a sweater pocket while she works mostly with the other arm."

Chad teared up. "I'm so very sorry."

Her dad said you wouldn't even know it to see her, working as hard as she did with her newborn. She was happy, and there were no hard feelings. "It's all water under the bridge," he said. "So to speak." Chad winced.

He thanked Abby's father, and the older man told him to take care. Back at the marina, Chad climbed the ramps and walked the docks, checking to make sure that the younger kids were wearing their life jackets.

Barry started exercising each morning in the rowboat after his coffee. At a recent doctor visit, the physician had told him he needed to be consistent or it would just strain his body instead of helping it. The doctor suggested getting a stationary bike instead of rowing. Barry tried to picture himself on an exercise bike on the fuel dock, or on the deck of the *Stillwater*, waving at folks as they went by. It was probably too late in life for his body to be in good shape.

When he heard Chad was planning a sailing trip to Astoria and out beyond the mouth of the Columbia into blue water, Barry lingered longer on the fuel dock, helping out at the store, giving Chad some time to prepare for the trip. He brought Chad supplies, navigation advice, and questions. He helped Chad fuel up the *Great Beyond*. While they waited for the fuel tank to fill, he pulled the poem from the protest out of his pocket and handed it to Chad.

Chad was incredulous. He asked, "You read William Stafford?"

"I've read everything of his that you see on that piece of paper there."

"Oh, ho! You just wait here." Chad disappeared into the store and came back half a minute later with a book of collected poems. "Keep an eye on this while I'm gone," he said.

Chad asked Barry for recommendations about where to fish and what to use for bait, especially across the Columbia bar, since he hoped to sail a little ways out into the Pacific. Barry copied a few charts and a small tide book on the copy machine and showed Chad where to wait over at Hammond Bay until the beginning of a slack tide. Chad thanked him for the charts. He already had a chart book, but Barry was on a roll giving him things, and Chad didn't want to discourage him.

"That should give you just enough time to get out there a ways, though you may wish you hadn't bothered. You'll probably just get seasick, and then you'll be stuck out there until the slack tide." Barry glanced at the younger man and smiled. "What are you looking for out there?"

"You wouldn't believe me."

"Try me."

"Well, to tell the truth, I may not even make it that far. I'm going downstream to see about a girl."

"Oh," said Barry, trying to hide an even bigger smile.

"If I get there too late, she told me she'd drift out to sea until I arrived. It's someone I met only recently. She may not even come."

"It looks like you're already working on that seasickness." Barry pointed to the poem that trembled a little in Chad's hand. "You could give her that, maybe. Do that, and she wouldn't stand a chance."

"I don't know. She doesn't seem like the poetry type."

"Don't overthink it."

In the first days of his journey, Chad slept very little because of nausea. The lower Columbia rolled and swelled more than the river did further upstream. Even this far inland, the tide pushed against current and made the boat uneasy underfoot. As long as he could see the horizon—up on deck, or through the window in the main cabin—the dizziness wasn't too bad, but only if he looked up every ten seconds or so to orient himself. Night was the worst. His head spun violently in the darkness of the forward cabin, and he vomited three times in the first two days—first, all over the chart book, and then into his pillow that night as the wind and rain pelted the boat where it swung at anchor. The following morning, the anchor wouldn't pull out of the thick clay at the bottom of the river, so he jumped in and followed the line down to the muck at the bottom and tried to pry the blade loose with his hands. Silt-covered branches brushed across his face and arms and chest, like unseen fingers in the dark water. In the end, he had to cut the line loose just above the anchor chain and leave it down there. Back on deck, covered with a putrid gray film from head to toe, the smell and taste of the river bottom on his lips, his breakfast lurched back out into the world.

The lantern saved him. Down in the belly of the boat at night, he couldn't steady himself by keeping his eye on the horizon like he could during the day. His throat and stomach burned. His breath only came in short, scattered bursts. But the lantern was a steadying, comforting presence. If he kept the flame going, he was OK. If he watched it balancing itself in the rolling waves, he could hold his panic at bay. The yellow light swung from a hook above his bed in the forward cabin—the flame a fixed flicker of movement, his horizon, translating the river's dance.

The wind was steady at about five knots in the late afternoon when Barry cut the engine and raised the sails on the *Stillwater*, just upstream of Tomahawk Island on the Columbia. He hiked the canvas out, ran with a quiet wind upstream, and dropped in a fishhook. A minute later, he got a bite—something really big. He reeled in and lost the fish almost immediately. A minute later he got another big bite, and it stayed on for a minute, so he started the engine to maneuver and haul in whatever beast was on the other end of the line. The engine turned over, but then sputtered to a stop. He tried it again. Nothing. He was drifting away from the fish. The spool of line slowed for a moment, as if waiting for him to catch up. The fish must have been a whole hundred yards ahead of him. Several powerboats passed over the water between the fish and him, just above the line. But it didn't break.

Barry checked the fuel level. The tank was empty. He usually filled it once a year, in August, but he'd been using the boat more. The empty tank had snuck up on him. The cafe at Harbor One slid by, and then the fuel dock, then Salty's restaurant, hanging out over the river, and the airport control tower rose above the shoreline. The wind continued to carry him upstream. He reeled in just to see how far away the fish had gone, only to find the line slack all the way up to where the fish had bit through. He'd lost it again.

Barry looked to the south shore where the nearest fuel dock floated in a forest of white masts. One more try with the fishing line, then he'd fuel up. He tied on another hook and threw the line in. A bite jolted up the line almost immediately and the reel spun until he could feel the wind of its spinning.

When it finally slackened, Barry saw that whatever crazy trickster was playing with him was headed toward the north side of Government Island. He was just pissed off and curious enough about this creature to keep following it.

It took only about a minute before the line jerked and broke with a pop—a monstrous, bright-red Coho leapt out of the water fifty yards in front of the boat. It landed with a crack and was gone. Barry looked around, wondering if anyone else had seen it. There were a few other boats out but much further downstream.

He tied on a new hook, added a spinner, and dropped the line in again. That old creature was long gone by now, on the other end of the island probably. But Barry thought he might find something with a little less fight in it for dinner. With the sun sinking low in the sky, and without a running motor, he was going to have to throw down an anchor off the island now. The fuel dock would be closed by now, and he was too far upstream to make it back home before dark. Then he remembered that when Moe left the marina, he'd sailed upstream without an engine—maybe Barry could make do without one too.

A jolt of energy rushed up his arm and through his body. It was another fish on the line, pulling hard, pulling him forward, giving him more headway than the soft wind. Maybe a big dinner, then. The line slowed down. He tugged on it lightly, and the line tugged back, as if in answer. This was getting ridiculous. No, it was ridiculous two or three bites ago. This was something more than a fish playing with him.

"Alright," Barry whispered, "you win." He sat down in the cockpit and mounted the fishing rod into a pole holder. The wind and the life at the end of the fishing line pulled him slowly upstream. The I-205 Bridge loomed high above the water on the north side of Government Island; Mt. Hood appeared to hover just above it. Barry looked up at the wind vane at the top of the mast. It shifted lazily back and forth. The wind always slowed down approaching that bridge. It was only a matter of time before he would have to turn back and find a place to anchor for the night.

Cars sparkled in the sun, crossing the bridge. Soon the abutments and the bridge deck rose impossibly high above him. Any minute now, and the wind would die.

But it didn't.

The bridge came and went. Slowly, against the current at maybe half a knot, the boat passed under and kept carving through the water. The upstream end of Government Island slid past. Hours went by. The sun set behind him over the trees on the island. He looked for signs of wind in their branches. Nothing. Maybe he was too far away. He looked for signs of wind brushing the surface of the water. Only a wisp here and there, the river's surface folding like lightly wrinkled fabric. Deep into the night, the wind filled the sail above him—soundlessly, barely, but always there.

Barry pondered what he knew of air currents—warm and cold edges folding over and under each other, waves falling on waves. Heat rising, cool air falling, like lovers under the stars. What if the keel of the boat were cutting through a thin layer of cold water to release warmth further down, which rose upward and curled into his sails? What if the heat of Barry's own body were enough to push a boat through this stretch of cool, night air? Maybe heat still rising from rock walls along the shore and from the concrete of the bridge behind him had found the shape of his sail and passed its energy from stone to canvas.

Barry slept here and there, or at least rested in that hazy line between sleeping and waking. But he sat up straight when the Coho began to jump at first light, catching flies newly hatched from the mud flats at the mouth of the Sandy River where it flowed into the Columbia. The fish was impossibly fast, and it seemed to be everywhere at once. First it was behind him, then in front. He saw it rise in front of him and heard it land behind him, felt its movement through the air on one side of the boat, and then on the other. Droplets of water fell cold onto his hands and face from the fish's surging and falling. This was not possible. He was sleepy, but he knew he was awake.

Then he understood what he was seeing: not one Coho, but many. Coho beyond counting behind him and before him and all around. Droplets of water stung his hands and face from the dancing of bright-red fish. A thrill filled his chest.

As the sky lightened, the leaping fish turned south, heading up the Sandy River, answering a magnetic call; an underwater scent, a familiar, fishy nostalgia drawing them home into the foothills of the mountain on the horizon.

They were wild Coho, native to this thin ribbon of river that tumbled down rocks from springs and glaciers far away, this pulsing, boulder-strewn Sandy River that many people navigated in summertime using life rafts and inner tubes. Were there boat navigation rules for this stretch of water? Did vessels under sail yield to an inner tube? In a couple minutes he would need to turn away before he ran aground. Getting ready to say goodbye, Barry sighed. As if in response, the leaping subsided, and the Coho arced and thrust their way up the new river just under the surface.

Barry unlocked the jib sheet and held it tightly, ready to haul it in and turn back, into the wind. He told himself he would turn the tiller the next time the wind faltered or died down even slightly. The trees towered along the shore beyond the mud and sand to port and to starboard. He was definitely not sailing the Columbia anymore. He was Barry, an old fool, sailing up an unsailable river, waiting for the god of the Sandy to hold up his hand and say, "This far, and no further."

As the light grew, he began to see fishermen along the shore and to hear them hooting and cussing, some of them even cheering him on. Several followed him along the shore, snapping pictures. Barry pulled the brim of his hat down over his eyes. Eventually, their attention and their cameras turned from Barry to the churning water around the sailboat. Shimmering red flashes of light surged through swiftly flowing water. Men dropped their phones and struggled with fishing rods and tackle; a low murmur trembled through the air along both shores.

Sometimes boats drifted into dangerous circumstances. This sailing boldly into them expressed a strange intention Barry had stopped trying to understand. He was caught up with the Coho now, and he was surprised to find he didn't want to stop. Maybe this was the way his sailboat would spend its final minutes. He began to think he might soon be homeless.

The red, muscled Coho kept to the deepest channels on their journey upstream. Barry followed their example.

He pulled the jib and main sheets or let them out with each new bend in the river. Several times, the keel whispered softly over sand and stones, a soft trembling through the tiller in his hand. Once, the boat almost shuddered to a stop, but he swiveled the tiller back and forth and the ship broke free, bobbing again in deeper water.

Around another bend, Barry saw what he took to be the end: a low freeway bridge and what looked like the spilling and rushing of rapids. Barry braced for the thump of hull and stone, but the water was deeper than it appeared. The Coho were leaping and rising and falling with a level of ferocity he hadn't yet seen. The noise of their jumping and crashing was a wall of sound in front of him and behind. Fishermen up ahead were struggling with their quaking, arced poles and helping one another lift the thrashing creatures from the water with two and three pairs of hands. Barry closed his eyes and listened to it, imagining his mast crashing into the low bridge up ahead. Not a bad way to die, joining what might be the first of an ancient race of Coho returning to its native waters. What was the drowning death of one man in the face of a river reborn?

Water rose and fell all around, and soaked through Barry's clothes. His eyes remained closed. He thought of Moe and wished he could tell him about this. He could see Moe's face nodding and smiling. Tears formed in Barry's closed eyes at the thought of his friend.

Even with the waterfall of sound, he felt peace and a great fullness in his chest. There was music in the wind. A song that played in the sails and jib sheets and whatever it was that pulled him upstream. The din of traffic from the highway blended with the crashing of the water, but there was music in that, too. What he could only think of as a violent peace had taken hold of him, as if peace were not silent at all but rather a wild, roaring blessedness.

The bow pulpit sank into the dark shadow of the bridge— the forgotten fishing pole bent sharply and snapped, the line spiraling in the air above him. He leaned hard on the tiller, the wind spilled out of the sails, and the canvas shook softly in the breeze. For the first time in what seemed like days, the *Stillwater* drifted back downstream, carried in the current. Barry dropped to the floor of the cockpit among the tangle of lines, utterly spent. The sound of rushing water dissipated. Barry drew in deep, painful breaths and let the river take him wherever it would.

A few hours later, the attendant at the fuel station threw Barry a line as he eased in alongside the dock and lowered the main sail. It was risky, pulling up to the dock at the mercy of the wind, but without diesel in the tank, his options were limited. Another boat was parked at the pumps—a speedboat—but Barry left plenty of room, pulling the sailboat up to the dock nice and easy, spilling the wind out of the canvas, and coming to a smooth stop. The attendant yelled sharply as the *Stillwater* approached. What the hell was he doing, crazy old man, pulling in under sail, right behind another boat that he could have plowed right into? The attendant handed Barry the fuel hose and stood back, arms folded, glaring. There were several teenagers on the speedboat— they were glaring too.

While Barry filled the tank, the attendant said he'd heard that some idiot was out there sailing up the Sandy River and that there were some seriously exaggerated fishing stories start- ing to spread over the airwaves. "That was you, wasn't it?" he asked.

Barry told him that Coho by the thousands were practically splashing all the water out of the Sandy River.

The man shook his head and said, "It's people like you who're gonna get the government down here making up new rules until none of us can even dip our toes in the river." The gray cloth of his cap was worn at the seams. He had on a massive silver belt buckle sporting a leaping trout. He took Barry's twenty-dollar bill for the fuel, put it in his pocket, and folded his arms across his chest again. Barry waited until it became clear he wasn't going to get any change.

Barry spoke again about the Coho. About following them upstream under sail, about watching them jump red through the air right in front of him, and about the wind that had been strong enough to take a sailboat up a swift, rolling river. While Barry spoke, a shadow passed over the man's face. His mouth twisted into a Cheshire-like grin.

The teenagers in the speedboat grew quiet as Barry told about the fish. They rolled their eyes. When he got to the part about the fish bringing the water to a violent boil near the I-84 Bridge, they climbed into their speedboat and roared off downstream.

Barry turned to the gas attendant and stepped toward him. His thoughts came rushing, as if against the current. This poor, defensive soul, dooming himself and the world he inhabited to a shallow understanding of what was all around him. You had to help someone like that see the wonder they are determined not to see. Barry told him about the fish, how red they were, and the river, red as blood.

The man stood firm and shook his head and said, "You think I don't know that you ran out of fuel out there, and that's why you came in here with your fucking sails up and your fucked-up story about some ancient, extinct salmon run?" He jabbed Barry in the chest for every word as he shouted, "Get the fuck out of here."

Barry swayed back on his heels, then stepped right in his face and told him the fish were real, that they were still returning from the sea, that it was evidence of healing in the world. The attendant backed away then, toward the door of the office behind him, his smile fading. The words spilled out of Barry—words about life reborn right underneath the dock, about how everyone was in danger of missing the beauty right under their noses, about how love was just under the surface. It was in the wind that you couldn't hear or see, and you couldn't tell where it came from or where it was going, but you could put up a sail sometimes and listen for it, watch it play in the canvas and feel it pushing you along through the water. He said that love filled everything in every way, even our deepest losses and longings. Even after the guy's face went pale and he stepped inside his office and shut the door, Barry kept on talking. He turned and faced the river and talked and talked, and he reached his hands out over the water and kept on saying what there was in him to say.

Chad climbed from a transient fishing dock and walked through the old town of Astoria, up the steep slope of the hill, and when he reached the park at the top, he labored up the winding steps of the Astoria column. From the observation platform, he could see the wide mouth of the river, the glittering line of the Pacific, the towering Astoria Bridge crossing from Oregon to Washington, the docks along the southern shore, and even the small speck of the *Great Beyond* moored to a long pier where the edge of town overlapped the gray, rolling mix of salt water and fresh water. Chad made this climb from the river to the highest point on the peninsula three times, once per day for three days in a row, and spent hours waiting, looking, watching, squinting into the wind, dreaming waking dreams that had finally unraveled. He walked the streets of Astoria until seasickness and landsickness became a cavernous lovesickness.

He woke early on the second day, and, unable to sleep, he checked over the boat in anticipation of heading out to the deep, blue water. Chad checked to make sure his VHF radio would work if he had an actual emergency, or if he found a red kayak upside down in the choppy water. The radio registered only static, so he opened it up. All the wiring connections were good. There was a little corrosion, but electricity was getting through fine. Something was wrong with the wiring inside the mast or with the antenna on top. He'd need to check it.

He pulled himself up the mast with the assistance of a fisherman who was mending nets at the end of the dock. At the top, he saw a strange sight: a penny bolted faceup to the top of the masthead. The year read 1947. The birthday of the original owner, maybe, or the date the boat was launched?

At the very top of the antenna, a dead spider clung to the small bead of aluminum, the highest point on the whole boat. The dry husk of its body trembled in the wind. Chad talked to it while he respliced the frayed antenna wires, wondering out loud how tight a grip the spider must have had when it was alive. He asked if it had hidden the penny for safekeeping. Clouds rolled in on the wind. A drop of rain landed on the copper Lincoln head. The spider skin clung to the peak with its dry, transparent legs. Chad wound a long strip of black electrical tape around the wires and hollered to the fisherman for help easing himself down. The rain hit with a vengeance just as his feet touched the deck. The fisherman waved and ran off, and Chad climbed into the cabin and listened to the water rattle on the deck above.

By midmorning, the rain clouds had passed, and Chad started his climb for the day. He searched monuments, walls, and every board and foot of the dock, looking for Emma's whitecrayon mark scratched onto a surface somewhere. A few times, he thought he saw it, a flash of brightness on rock or wood or steel—a stab in his chest—but it always ended up being unintended, indecipherable scratches or sun-bleached twigs or bird shit.

During his three days in Astoria, he walked six times by the house where the movie *The Goonies* was filmed. He drank three milkshakes. He went into a bookstore on the main drag in town, picked up a copy of *Wuthering Heights*, put it back on the shelf, picked up a copy of a paperback romance with a picture on the cover of a woman with large bosoms and a Fabio-like man, also with large bosoms, and paid the man at the counter. He went into a dive bar, sat in a corner booth, and started reading and sighing. When the waitress came over, Chad told her to bring him a pint of whatever beer they had on tap that tasted like piss. She said all their stuff on tap tasted good, so he said to bring him whatever was her least favorite. She brought him a glass of something that tasted like skunky apples, then backed away.

At the end of three days, Chad was still on the first chapter of the romance novel. He tossed it onto the bunk in the forward cabin and climbed up into the cockpit. Romance was not to be had. Even from a romance novel. It was time to go. Without even

starting the engine, he dropped the mooring lines on deck and
let the current take him away with the outgoing tide, out to sea.

Late one night, Marge walked down the dock from the laundry
room holding a hamper full of clean clothes. She stopped for a
moment at the slip where Moe's boat had moored to see if she
could discover new thoughts about him, or glean some warm
sense of his presence still lingering. The boat was gone—Chad
had it out on the river—but she stood at the end of the slip anyway, gazing down at the water and then at her feet and then beyond her feet at a greenish strip of color between the planks,
something illuminated by the small light mounted six inches
above the dock. She bent down near the edge and felt a smooth,
box-shaped object held there by a length of stiff, frayed twine.
It must've been fairly old because the moistened twine gave way
with a yank. She pulled it out from under the dock and examined
it. It was a small Tupperware container. The plastic lid cracked
when she opened it. On top was a plastic bag with a note inside
and underneath the note was another bag. Marge opened the
note. It was signed at the bottom with Moe's full name, Morgan
Molalla, and dated May of 2000. The note read:

> To the person who finds this, it is yours. I relinquish all ownership of
> any of it. It was a gift I received from the Creator, and now it is the
> Creator's gift to you. May it not burden you, and if it does, may it find
> its way to another soul in their time of need. Many blessings to you,
> weary traveler.
>
> Moe

Inside layers of Ziploc and plastic bags Marge found a thick
stack of bills. She flipped through them; they were old $10,000
bills. Moe had always claimed to have won the lottery.

That crazy dope!

This gesture was outrageous, even for him. Though she knew
he must've meant it sincerely, his note would never hold up legally. She couldn't possibly keep this money.

She could spread the cash around, maybe. Many of the older tenants at the marina were there because they couldn't afford even the tiniest rooms in a retirement community. For some of them, this was as close as they would get to traveling to an exotic place in their golden years. Some would need assisted living accommodations soon. Not that you would be able to talk most of them into it. The moorage rates here were low, and some old folks had inherited their boats or rundown floating homes; they barely had enough to feed themselves and pay for medication after paying their monthly moorage and buying booze. The only way out of the marina for them was the inevitable ambulance ride at some unknown, rapidly approaching date. Jack would die on the water, no doubt. Barry too. Dory would probably run on fumes until she was a hundred and fifty years old. There were a couple of others that would have nothing to do with anyone and were wasting away in unkempt floating structures.

A couple of boats from out of town were temporarily moored close by—their windows were dark. One of their automatic bilge pumps came on and water sloshed out of a spout in the hull. She could smell the brackish scent of salt water.

Marge looked down at the money again. Such fragile paper. If even a small flame touched one of the bills, it would all be gone in less than a minute. Yet you could use these fragile bills to open doors to a lifetime of beauty and grace. There were places and creative endeavors that existed behind exclusive doors barred to most people. "Fling the doors open, she thought." Moe would have liked that.

The wind rustled over several of the bills. Marge closed the Tupperware and nestled it into her laundry, all whites. White shirts, white socks, white underwear, white sweat pants, and at least a million dollars in cash. "What else do I need?"

She looked up and down the dock and started walking. She knew with certainty now where she would go, and what she would do when she got there.

Ten

Jack drifted in and out of sleep where he sat on the porch of his one-room floating home. Barely awake, he reached for the half-empty can in the armrest of the camping chair, took a sip of stale, warm beer, then threw it over the deck rail into the current before drifting again into a kind of sleep. Images floated through his mind of objects he had thrown or dropped into the river over the years. He saw them flying from his hands and hanging in the air above the surface for their final exhilarating moments of life in the world above. He watched them land and float along on the water while gravity poured them down and underneath the rim of the world: reading glasses, an alarm clock, propeller, engagement ring, TV, seized-up outboard engine, burnt pot roast, dog shit, chewed-up copy of Moby Dick, revolver, Bible, telephone, frying pan, dead light bulb, lamp shade, lamp stand, wristwatch. Jack saw his own body flying in an arc through the air over the water—saw himself as a boy tossed from his father's arms off the back of a large boat, his hair and clothes aflame.

When he was still young, Jack had found a gas can and was dropping fuel-soaked rags into the river, lighting matches, and tossing them at the floating bundles when it happened: flames rippled over his clothes. Rather than rolling him over the deck to put out the fire, his father cursed and scooped him up, tossing him over the side, through the air, into the cool water. Jack pushed back up through the surface, gasping. He saw his father's stern face looking down just before it turned away, and then he saw the life preserver spinning in the air above him.

His dad always said he preferred to accomplish at least two things every time he acted. He boasted later that he'd accomplished two things when he threw his son in the water: he saved Jack from burning to death and helped him learn to swim.

By the time Chad had pulled away from the plume of fresh water at the mouth of the Columbia and entered the rolling swells of blue water, the edited and reedited scenes in his mind became actual hallucinations: phantom islands passed by and tiny boats with long wakes of white foam and Emma's kayak, a red speck in the distance. Was she out here? Waiting? She was a bold one, but floating out here on the swells with Ko? That would be insane. The Coast Guard would show up for that. He squinted when he saw what looked like a red and brown dragon beating its wings and landing on a rock in the distance. He knew these objects weren't really there, even though his eyes saw them, and he could feel their weight in the water before him—sense the wind shifting to accommodate their presence. There was so much to attend to when sailing alone—more alone than he had ever felt. So many lines to work with only two hands. So many dangers to anticipate.

For two days and one night, he sailed up and down the Pacific coast in the deep, rolling water, following the compass needle north to the tip of Long Beach, and then south, always into the wind, always keeping one eye on the shoreline and the other on the chart book. He felt like a victim of his own obsessive attention to the depth soundings in the book and its symbols of impending disaster.

On his first day at sea, he'd been sailing too close to shore, trying to get as much distance out of a tack as he could when his keel had slammed into something hard under the surface. He spent the next few days focusing his mind's eye on what he could not see, swerving to avoid unseen dangers—rocks, logs, and shipwrecks all ominously labeled and just waiting to punch a hole through the bottom of his sailboat to make a real, live dead man out of him.

He tried to hide the chart book down in the main cabin, but it never stayed down there for long.

Bernice smiled to herself as she counted up the weeks since she'd started walking again. No, she should call it what it was: exercising. Walking sounded like going for a stroll and enjoying the weather. Not that she didn't enjoy the weather. Even when it rained, she'd been exercising, carrying her new golf umbrella—a big, bright orange one. Up and down the dock she went, along each row, twice a day for fifteen minutes, minding her form and rolling from heel to toe, holding her elbows up to keep them from brushing her sides and throwing off her momentum.

Today might be her last day of exercise for a while. She and Bill were leaving to deliver another boat down the coast to Los Angeles. Their longest journey so far. All of a sudden it was as if she were saying goodbye to this dock, this stroll up and down it in the wind and fresh air, these people she knew waving and smiling at her. Her chest rose and fell with a deep sense of sadness she didn't quite trust. She was going to miss her exercising was all it was. She didn't know if she'd be able to start up again when they returned home in a couple weeks.

The sun was out and the air was warm. She rounded the corner to the upper marina's laundry room, and there was Barry, curled up on the dock, clutching his chest, his laundry bin on its side—damp, smelly laundry scattered around him, some of it in the water already floating away. Bernice brought a hand to her chest and gasped.

She ran and kneeled next to him and spoke his name pleadingly, "Barry, what is it? Do you need pills? What? Your heart? What's wrong?"

Barry's face wrinkled in pain and his eyes met hers for a brief moment before he clamped them shut again. "Sorry," he said. "Sorry. I'm sorry."

Bernice stood up and yelled for help. First too softly and then several more times, louder, until someone's head popped out the door of a houseboat and another peered up through the hatch of a sailboat.

"Call nine-one-one!"

The ambulance arrived and several paramedics made their way down the boat ramp, pushing a rattling gurney along the walkway's wood floorboards. They arrived to where Bernice sat with Barry's head propped up on several flannel shirts draped across her lap.

"It's alright Barry," she whispered into his ear. "You're not alone. I'm here. It's alright."

Barry, his eyes still shut, nodded his head.

"They're here, Barry. You're going to be OK." And to the paramedics, "A heart attack, I think."

Bill appeared and ran to Bernice's side, kneeling next to the paramedic who was checking Barry's heartbeat. Another medic draped an oxygen mask over Barry's face. "Hang in there, buddy," Bill said. "We're here for you. They're gonna take care of you."

"Let's back up, please, give us some room," said one of the paramedics.

Bill stood up. Bernice still held Barry's head in her lap. She looked up to meet Bill's gaze.

"Somebody needs to go with him," she said. "He doesn't have anybody."

They lifted Barry off her lap and onto the gurney. He cried out in pain.

Bill offered to go. "You can stay here and keep packing. I'll get a ride home ... from Chad, I think. I'll go grab him. He would want to go." He remembered. "Wait. Chad's gone. On his trip."

"Bill, you ninny. We need to stay with him. We can't just leave. Don't argue with me about this. Go with him, honey. I'll follow in the car."

"I guess we could push our trip out a day, but we'll have to make up the time. ..."

"Bill. Please."

Bill watched his friend being pushed up the ramp toward the parking lot.

Bernice said, "Billy. We have to stay with him. He's ... He's our people."

Bill leaned over her and kissed the top of her head and said, "Yes. He is. I'll see you at the hospital in a little bit."

Bill jogged to catch up to the gurney as it wobbled further away. His inefficient, hopping jog wasn't really much faster than when he walked normally—Bernice smiled because she knew she loved him for it. She could smell the bitter aroma of dirty shirts and damp, sweaty socks all around her. Several people gathered near her and reached to help her up, but she crawled over the dock, gathering up Barry's socks and pants and even his underwear into her arms.

It wasn't until the sailboat swung eastward back upstream and he passed under the Astoria Bridge late in the night that Chad finally accepted Emma was not going to meet him after all; the hallucinations of red kayaks and Alaskan huskies walking on water subsided, and he began to notice things. Small things on big water: tiny flashes of light on the surface of the river reflecting in wide arcs the illuminated bridge high above; the rope in his hand, its frayed ends thin as hair; the horizon, a long, broken line of faint lights in the distance. The vast expanse of the river was made up of small, tangible parts. For most of the trip, he'd missed these things as his mind's eye edited scenes of meeting Emma, of the words they would share, of their bodies meeting and exploring one another. The current and the gravity had pulled him into a future he now understood was improbable. There would be no Hollywood beginning or ending for him and Emma.

But there could still be a life for him that found beauty in the subtle shiftings of the world around him. He looked down at the water passing by, at the flecks of light on the waves, at the jib sheets in his hand, and he spoke out loud, saying hello to one thing after another. Hello, rope. Hello, bowl. Hello, lantern. Hello, smell of the sea. Hello, cracked lips and the taste of salt and blood. Hello, wave after wave of folding gray water.

In the moonlight, a breeze blew over the stern, hiking the boom out over the water—it scooped him into its arms, and he ran with it until he could barely feel its breath on his way upstream. The hull sighed with relief after its long, downstream trip, heeling into the wind with lines taut and singing. Now the jib sheets hung in easy loops, warm and smooth in his hands. The smell of the sea hung in the air just below the canvas. The lantern handle creaked softly where it hung in the rigging. On the incoming tide, the water rushed upstream under the bridge, bubbling around the base. The current swirled and turned back on itself. Upstream became downstream. Here at the mouth, the river was elusive. You could no longer properly call it a river with all the other forces stirring the air above and the waters below.

The keel jittered over a bar of sand that shouldn't have been there, and he finally accepted that, given the ever-shifting contours of the riverbed, his ten-year-old chart book was actually a hazard to him. He could switch over to the copies from Barry instead, if he really needed to. With the lights of the Astoria Bridge glimmering above, he set fire to the book and dropped it, burning, into a deep, aluminum mixing bowl he used for washing his hair in the morning and peeing in at night when he was too sleepy to climb on deck to lean over the rail.

You never know what a bowl might be good for until it's one of the only containers you've got as you bob along in the current. You never know what might need containing—soup, soapy water, piss, flames, ash.

He'd hoped to start writing about his life on the water—living aboard a sailboat, Emma, the characters he had met on the dock—and yet all he'd gotten down in his notebook with its moisture-rippled pages were details about a cheap aluminum lantern, a silver mixing bowl, and getting up at night to pee. Who needs a river to write about these things?

Flames poured sideways over the lip of the bowl, away from the wind. He watched until the light had burned a patch in his vision and the rest of the world turned dark. The surface of the river continued its rhythmic folding against the side of the boat. He could hear it dance in the dark, feel it vibrating through the line in his hand.

Jack had tried to move the rocker over to the window but felt like he'd torn his spine to shreds in the process. He froze until he could summon the courage to move, then he brought a lawn chair in from the deck out back instead and sank into it. The window was already open. A couple inches. The width of a gun barrel.

Skookum sniffed at the shotgun where it leaned against the wall beside the window. Jack didn't want it out in plain view in case someone went by. Unless what came along was that sleek, red speed rig that flew by most mornings, kicking up a wake that washed over all the stringers along the marina, splashing the siding, putting strain on docking chains, pushing one house into another, stressing the saturated wood, and otherwise pissing him off with the arrogant presumption and entitlement to go as fast as a goddamn bat out of Hades.

Jack waited for him, the young guy in the red speedboat. He'd waited yesterday too, but the guy never came. Or maybe he came after Jack fell asleep in the chair. This time, he'd stay awake—to show him that he's damaging property and the fragile shoreline and the burrows and homes of animals that have dug out a life along the water. "While you roar down the river, making your passengers yell, 'Faster! Faster!'"

Last week, one of the trawlers jerked loose when the wake came rolling by. A line snapped, and the thing swung around and just about smashed Jack's house into kindling. Time to get British and start throwing cannonballs over the water. He checked the chamber on the gun again with a click. Just one shell. That was all he'd need.

Jack waited.

He hadn't bothered to leave the house in several days—not even to meet the others for coffee in the morning. There were no others. Moe. Gone. Chad was sailing off to who knows where. Bill and Bernie were nowhere to be found, probably on one of their little trips up and down the coast. And Barry. No idea if Barry was ever coming back.

Jack had gone to visit Barry in the hospital. The place smelled like bleach with something flowery attempting to cover up the bleach. They'd put several stints in Barry's heart, but he was still in bad shape. They were hoping to find him a new heart and perform a transplant sometime in the next few days. Barry wasn't up for talking much, so Jack left pretty soon after he arrived. Barry looked pathetic in his thin little gown, and Jack told him so, told him he looked like a damn Old Testament prophet or something. Barry gave Jack the keys to his boat. He said there was a notebook on board that he wanted Chad to have. Made it sound so final.

Trying to find his way out of the hospital, Jack got lost in the maze of hallways. A nurse stopped him to ask if she could help him back to his room. He turned away from her and got the hell out of there before they tried to strap him down and check him over. The houses, the boats, the marina, the whole world was coming apart. He had to do something.

Jack heard the hum of the engine before he saw the boat coming. He tipped the barrel of the gun away from the wall until it bumped heavily against his rib cage. Then, with both hands, he hoisted the gun up and anchored the stock into his shoulder. Skookum's eyes rolled in his direction, her head still resting on her paws. Jack slid the barrel through the gap in the open window and pointed it upstream.

A red shape moved over the water, white foam trailing in its wake. Jack clicked the safety off and sighted down the length of the barrel. The boat came faster. He waited, deciding to hold off until the speedboat reached a spot downstream of the marina. That way, the shot would land in the water, mostly out of sight from the dock.

The boat came on, a red blur, parallel with the lower marina now. Jack imagined the guy behind the wheel, his hair blowing back in the wind, a smile on his face, totally and completely oblivious. The face of oblivion comes with a smile, Jack thought. The engine roared. The boat moved past him at an impossible speed, and Jack placed his finger lightly over the trigger.

A flash of light downstream caught his eye. He turned to see it: a sailboat tacking toward the opposite shore, the sun shining off its white canvas. Chad's boat, maybe, on its way back from Astoria. Jack took his finger off the trigger. The red speedboat swerved to miss the sailboat, and continued downstream around the bend. Jack pulled the gun back inside and laid it to rest on the ground next to the wall. He watched the bright blur of sail in the distance. No, it wasn't Chad. Moe's boat was an old Catalina. This was something newer, glossier. When the sailboat reached the wake of the red speedboat, it rocked violently, the mast whipping like a fishing rod. Then it tacked back in Jack's direction.

Jack stepped outside. Skookum got up and followed him onto the back deck. The wake hit them then, crashing into the stringers, all the way up to the siding, pouring over the deck. Jack held onto the railing. Skookum was swept off her feet. She went down, rolled once over the deck like a small fire log and stopped just before she reached the opposite edge. Downstream, the waves pounded into the shore. The sailboat moved closer, straight for him. Jack leaned back, still holding onto the rail. At the last moment, it tacked, and the sunny face of a young man looked up. It wasn't Chad. The kid waved and shook his head, jerking his thumb back in the direction of the speedboat. As the young man wound the jib sheet around a deck cleat by his foot, he shouted, "Some idiot, huh?" Jack nodded and waved back. The boat slipped away, surprisingly fast in the breeze.

Skookum shook the water out of her fur and hopped onto the skiff. Jack looked down at her. "That's right, Skook," he said. "Smart dog. Time to fill that empty spot in the fridge. Vámanos!"

Eleven

Keith and his friends were up on land, throwing rocks into the small pools that passed for Rock Creek during the driest time of the year. Steve's cousin, Jessica, was there, and one of her friends—another girl. Nick was rambling on about how he had climbed into his parents' car the night before and driven into Portland. The girls were whispering into each other's ears and rolling their eyes; Steve stood, hunched over, balancing rocks into a stack as tall as his chest.

When Nick stopped to catch his breath, Keith blurted out, "Sometimes, late at night, I take my canoe downstream and climb aboard the *Susan K.*" Everyone grew quiet. "You have to be careful of the old man that lives in the house nearby," he said, "but if you're quiet, you can get up inside of it. I've seen *Playboy* magazines on board, and guns and ammo, and other stuff you wouldn't believe."

Everyone was looking at him. The girls had stopped smiling. Steve picked up a stone, glanced at his cousin and her friend, and spoke into the silence. "I think you're full of shit."

"What?"

"If you've been on board the *Susan K* and seen all those things, then you should go and bring something back to show us."

"Nick should be the one to show us how he drives a car around at night. He's the one that's full of shit."

"Yeah, but we know he's full of shit. It's you we're not sure about."

"Hey. Watch your fucking mouth," said Nick.

Steve placed the rock he'd been holding on top of the stack and slowly pulled his hand away. "Let's find out, shall we, Keith? You can bring us that bullshit gun you were talking about."

The girls were watching.

"OK. Whatever. But not right now in broad daylight. I'll go to-night after dark." Keith heard the sudden bravery in his own voice, the nonchalance, and spoke again just to hear it. "Yeah, whatever. I'll do it. Like it matters."

They talked it over. Steve and Jessica would sneak out after mid-night when their parents were asleep and watch from the shore to make sure Keith really did it. Nick couldn't make it; he was headed to his grandmother's that night, and Jessica's friend didn't want to do it. They parted ways but Jessica turned back. She looked at Keith. "Do you really have your own canoe that you can use any time you want?"

Keith smiled at her. "Yeah. It's not that strange, really. Have you ever read *Huckleberry Finn*?"

"No."

Keith looked at the ground. "Well. He lives on a river. He's basically me."

"I've got to go," she said, and she turned to leave.

Keith watched her go. "See you tonight," he said.

At the fuel dock, Rick was on the phone. Jack helped himself to a half rack and set a ten-dollar bill on top of the till. Back home, he thought about calling Barry to see if he wanted to share a few beers. Then he remembered Barry was in the hospital. He thought of Chad. Chad would want to know what was happen-ing with Barry. He called the marina office and Rick answered. He gave Jack Chad's cell phone number and said, "Good luck. I've been trying to call him for days." Jack dialed the number, and it went straight to voice mail. He started to speak, but then changed his mind and hung up.

He looked over at his dog, asleep under the wood stove and, spoke out loud. "Well, crap in my lap, why don't you?" he said. Skookum raised her head and looked at him. Jack brought the box of beer over to his bed and dropped it on the floor with a clang, falling onto the sagging mattress. He opened three cans of beer at once, stacked them on an end table by his bed, and started drinking.

Chad set foot on land for the first time in days at the northern tip of Sauvie Island, near the mouth of the Multnomah Channel. He anchored the boat sixty or so feet from the shore, dove into the mucky water with a line, and tied it off to a cottonwood along the shore to keep the boat from drifting. Then he walked over to the lighthouse at the tip of the muddy peninsula. Its white paint was beginning to crack and chip. He walked around it several times, looking for Emma's river mark in the dark patches of concrete where paint had flaked away. When he didn't find anything, he took a pocket knife and carved it himself into one of the smooth, dark shapes.

By the time he tied off at the nearby public dock at Sand Island just across a narrow channel from the shore near downtown St. Helens, the sun was setting. When the boat was secure, he climbed ashore and made a fire out of driftwood he'd gathered down by the waterline. He balanced a pot of water over the flames and boiled fresh coffee grounds, filtered it into a large mug, and wrote in his notebook for a couple of hours, stopping here and there to stoke the fire or add more wood or stretch his legs.

He paced with the cup of coffee from tree to tree, running his free hand over the rough bark in the dim light of the fire, searching, searching. He was impulsively looking for a white mark everywhere now. Maybe if he left his own marks on rocks and trees, she would find one. He'd just have to be patient. Or maybe she had already offered some kind of message that he'd been too preoccupied to see or decipher? By some wild chance, had she gotten his cell phone number and left a message for him? He'd kept his phone in a box labeled "In Case of Emergency" under a bench in the main cabin, reasoning that leaving it inaccessible on this trip would be good for his mind and spirit. But maybe now that his trip was almost over, he would discover her voice, captured in a phone message while he searched the river for her in vain. He might as well check, just in case. The air on Sand Island turned cold. He smothered the fire and walked back to the boat. In the forward cabin, he struck a match and reached quickly under the glass of the lamp as the match head flared to life. The flame caught the blackened tip of the wick, and its familiar golden light filled the cabin.

He found the phone and flipped it open.

The tiny LCD screen lit with a greenish glow. It took a minute, but eventually a list of missed calls appeared: three calls from Rick, or someone who'd called from the main office of the marina, one from a random area code, and one from Jack.

Did Rick not remember when he was going to be back from the trip? Or maybe they had found an empty red kayak—or Emma's body facedown in the water as it floated by the marina? Ridiculous, he thought. Something must've happened at the marina. The possibilities were endless. The store might have sunk. Maybe someone had died. He dialed the marina's main office and store phone number. Nothing. He looked at the list of calls on the tiny screen, barely visible in the dock lights suspended above him. Why Jack? If he had called, surely it was a big enough deal that he should call him back right away even as late as it was.

When Jack picked up, Chad apologized for calling so late. Jack coughed and cleared his throat. "Don't give me any of that sorry crap. You called. I was asleep. Now I'm not. I don't give a shit. I had to get up and piss anyway. Where the hell have you been? Working on your tan while the marina goes to hell over here?"

"What happened?" asked Chad.

After long pause, Jack said, "Barry had a heart attack. He's in bad shape and waiting in line for a heart transplant. They're keeping him stable, but the clock is ticking."

After filling Chad in as best he could, Jack wanted to know about his trip, so Chad told him about the wind, the current, the tides, the height of the waves at the mouth of the Columbia, and the distance between the whitecaps. He kept expecting Jack to interrupt him, but he never did. Chad told him about the things that didn't work on the boat when he needed them to, and the things that did, and about climbing the mast. He mentioned the penny mounted on the masthead, wondering if there was something to it.

"A penny? That would be some previous owner's doing. Smart guy he must've been, though a bit excessive. It's an old trick. Before insurance. Before boat registration. You hid a penny onboard somewhere in case someone stole your boat or came along and claimed it was theirs. The owner would be the guy who knew where the penny was and what date was written there under Abraham Lincoln's nose. I've got a few good stories about boat pennies I could tell you sometime. And not a shred of bullshit in any of them. That boat's truly yours now. But you probably didn't check the date when you were up there, did ya?"

"1947."

"Pretty good. There's hope for you yet. Except that now, of course, your boat could be mine, you numbskull."

"I'll have to trust you."

Jack coughed once more and said, "Well then, to make it even, I got a 1923 penny under the foot of my wood stove. I forget which foot."

"I guess that makes us even, then."

"No guessing. It either does or it doesn't."

"Even, then."

"Damn straight," he said.

Before hanging up, Jack told Chad to watch for the sandbar below Sauvie Island on his way up the channel. Said it was lined with old pilings resting below the surface. "Just get your ass back here," he said. "Rick has been trying to run things in the office on his own, and you can imagine how well that's going. We're almost out of beer and people have been settling for some of those low-carb bottles in the back of the storage room. It turns out our number one marina financier doesn't know shit about running a marina. So get going. Vámanos!" His voice got muffled in the earpiece and Chad heard: "No, Skook, not you. Shut your fucking yapper and go back to sleep."

Later that night, Chad drifted in and out of sleep as the lantern rocked and creaked above him. By this time tomorrow he could have arrived back at the marina and ridden the motorcycle to visit Barry at the hospital. Chad spoke Barry's name—and other names—as if praying for them, if a prayer could be just saying their names aloud. Barry. Emma. Jack. Bill. Bernie. Dory. Marge. Moe.

That night, Keith's father went to sleep early. He'd worked several double shifts already that week. From inside the aft cabin, Keith could hear the wind humming through the rigging overhead. The boat shifted under his feet.

He waited until he heard his father snoring and pulled a can of beer from the icebox. He took a sip and gagged. He plugged his nose, took in several gulps, and gagged again. Then he went over to the drawer in the main cabin where his father kept his socks and T-shirts and poured the rest of the can over the piles of white cloth. A laugh rose in his throat as he dropped the empty can into the trash.

He chose his own clothes carefully: black jacket, black pants, black socks, and his navy-blue shoes. He removed the white shoelaces and replaced them with black ones from his father's worn out boots. He found an old can of black shoe polish in the back of the closet and smeared some on his face. He filled in the gold snaps of his jacket with black marker to avoid reflecting any light. No flashlight. He would use his own eyes, let them adjust to the dark. When he was dressed, he sat waiting in the dark, breathing slowly, almost imperceptibly, his eyes closing and opening until he could see all the light there was in the room. He would become a shadow, stepping lightly, his hands brushing softly on all they touched. He would be there, but not there. He would leave no trace. Jessica and the others wouldn't even see him. Or even better, they might get just a glimpse and know he was there.

Keith glanced at the shoes on his feet. Bare feet would be quieter. He reached down and untied the laces.

In the hospital, Barry fell in and out of sleep. A TV in a nearby room was blaring news. News of fire and calamity. He dreamed of fire. Then he dreamed of drought. In the dream he woke up aboard the *Stillwater* with a terrible thirst. He listened for the usual sounds of water on the other side of the hull but heard nothing. When he lifted his head, he saw he was lying on the wall of the boat, inside the forward cabin. The bed hung oddly over his shoulder. The world had turned sideways. His boat lay on its side. He crawled out of the forward hatch and, with the help of the rigging, slid down the slick surface of the hull and onto the dock.

It sat firm on the ground. The river was gone. The stringers were half-sunk into the mud and pilings rose from the mire high into the air, their tops catching the light of the sun above what used to be the shoreline. Boats and houses rested in their rows. Masts crisscrossed each other down the line of the dock. No pools of water, even. Only mud.

The river. The waterline. All of it gone.

Barry recognized shapes in the mud: TVs, a bicycle, a motorcycle, a car, a gramophone, the broken hull of a boat. Then he saw bones sticking out of the pasty muck, and strangely shaped skulls. One pile of bones moved. No, it was a fish rolling in the thick clay. It shook violently and then grew still.

A horrible stench hung in the air. He could see it swirling, a mist that stung his eyes, feel it pushing him back when he tried to move down the dock. It occurred to him he might still be asleep and dreaming.

No water. No wind. He thought a tidal wave was coming, a tsunami. But so far upstream? No, the river had dried up or washed away. Where was everyone? Barry ran, pushing through the thick, foul air. His feet thumped on the wood dock. He pounded on the doors of several homes and shouted. Water and sewer lines had pulled away from the main lines above, but no water came from there either. He knocked on the door of Jack's house and rammed his shoulder into it several times until it broke open. Jack sat in his chair, his head drooped over Skookum. She was a huge, black Rottweiler, her black hair matted into muddy clots. A gash hung open in her neck, and a dark patch of dried blood stained the floor in front of the chair. A jagged knife rested at Jack's feet. Jack looked up, his face puffy and yellow, the life draining from it even as Barry watched. Tears came from Jack's eyes, the first sign of moisture Barry had seen. Barry wanted to catch the tears in the cupped palm of his hand and drink. He shook with thirst.

Jack's bloated body was a dull gray, the color of the mud outside. He ran his hand over Skookum's fur, rubbing behind her ears. His voice was thin and cracking.

"I tried to save them, but now everyone is gone. We'll be gone too. Very soon."

Barry was so thirsty. His tongue folded like dry leather. His lips cracked and split, and he longed to feel the moistness of blood dripping into his mouth. He bit at his lips. He opened his mouth wide until his lips split open. No blood came.

Then two things began to happen at once: the sound of trickling water came through the open windows from outside, and Jack reached behind the chair and pulled a shotgun out by the barrel. The trickling sound turned to pouring. Jack pointed the gun at Barry. Barry held up his hands and tried to scream, tried to tell him that the water was about to return, but no words came.

Jack spoke again, his voice barely a whisper. "I've got two rounds left, my friend. One for you. One for me. I'm so sorry." He wiped at his tears and leaned the stock into his shoulder. The water roared now, somewhere just outside. Jack sighted down the barrel at Barry.

"Goodbye, Barry," he whispered.

The house lurched, water came crashing through the windows on the upstream side, and Jack fired the gun into Barry's chest.

Barry woke in the hospital bed, unable to move. "Water," he whispered. Someone's cool hand brushed his forehead and dipped a wet sponge into his mouth. Barry tried to swallow but couldn't. He ran his tongue around in his mouth to spread the drops of water.

Keith made his way downstream, the current pushing him into the wind, the bow of the canoe slapping into white-capped waves, the wind roaring in his ears. The moon cast dark shadows on the water and dark streaks on the horizon. Twice, he turned to see Steve and Jessica's flashlights bouncing on the shore behind him as the river took him swiftly away. Twice, he lost his balance and almost tipped over. The canoe slid past the rows of dark boats and houses, then the trawlers and Jack's house, then around the back side of the marina between the dock and the shore. The sound of snoring came downwind from Jack's open window. Flashlights flickered through the trees.

Keith pulled up to the *Susan K* and tied the canoe to a ladder that hung from a transom below the large, painted letters spelling the ship's name. The moon gave the letters a soft glow. He placed both hands on the first rung.

He wanted to be unseen, a breath on the wind. His hands and feet seemed to glisten under the moon's gaze. He should have painted them too. He needed to be darker. He closed his eyes and felt the darkness descending upon him, imagining it covering him like a cloth.

Keith held onto the ladder, eyes closed.

When he opened them again, he felt he could see everything. He could see the leaves moving in the trees along the shore. He looked across to the island and could make out the leaves there too, shivering in the wind. He could see his reflection in the water against the stars and clouds above. He could see he wasn't afraid.

Upstream, the flashlights approached, dancing sporadically across the walls of the abandoned boathouses. Soon they would be on the shore across from him.

The rung of the ladder grew warm in his hands. When he climbed aboard, he might find something, or nothing—he wasn't sure which would be worse.

The flashlights approached through the trees. That asshole Steve. And Jessica with him. He could hear them rustling clumsily through the bushes.

Keith reached for the next rung and pulled himself up, scrambling toward the small stern door that led into the ship. To his surprise, the door was slightly ajar. He pushed it open and slid sideways into the dark. As he moved, he thought about his feet, how softly they pressed into the deck, and how they no longer felt cold.

He stepped into a dark hallway, his hands brushing the soft wood on either side. The wind poured through the cracked walls with its warm breath. The sound of dripping water echoed down the hall. He stepped over large gaps between the floorboards. In the first room he came to, his hands moved through cupboards and into closets and drawers, searching for what they knew they would find as if they were remembering. Then, there it was, high up on a shelf of rusted tools: the gun. It was small, made of thick plastic—a flare gun, but a gun. It rested lightly in his palm. Here it was, onboard the *Susan K*, just like he had known it would be. Just like he had told the others. He would show them.

Back down the hallway toward the stern, Keith found a ladder that both ascended to another level and ran down through a hole in the floor. He climbed. The ladder took him into the pilothouse. He passed through an opening and out onto the upper deck, holding the gun by the handle, high above his head. The moonlight glistened in the trees along the shore. Two gray faces looked up at him through the leaves. He could see their eyes. Steve grinned coldly and shook his head.

What the hell did he mean, "no"? What? Not a real enough gun?

Keith put his finger over the trigger, lowered the short barrel and aimed it at Steve's big, stupid grin. Jessica grabbed Steve by the arm. Steve looked up, shook his head once more at Keith and turned and followed her up the hill toward the parking lot.

Keith cursed and threw the gun with all his strength up and into the wind. He turned before it even hit the water and made his way back inside. Down, down, down the ladder, through the floor, and into the dark belly of the boat. The air grew thick with the smell of dust, mildew, and fuel. He could still see his hands and the dull glow of his feet. He needed to be darker. He breathed in the thick air and felt the darkness filling him, filling in the whites of his eyes, filling his arms and chest and legs down to his feet. His breath came out in a thick, black cloud.

At the bottom, the floorboards were moist and rotting. He stepped away from the ladder and waved his hands in the air before him, bumping into something just above his head. A lantern, hanging from a rafter. Moonlight came through windows along the wall beside him.

The dripping sounds he'd heard earlier grew louder, and the boat groaned and shuddered below his feet, deep and hollow. There must be yet another level below. The moonlight illuminated the room in front of him a little, enough for him to make out the edges of a table to one side and a counter to the other. He made his way forward, his hand sliding along the edge of the counter. On the countertop, his hands found silverware, knives, a can opener, a small box of matches. He remembered the lantern behind him and put the box in his pocket. He might want some light later. Maybe he could make a home of this place. The numbing smell filled his lungs and his head. He felt his way to a bench beside the small table and lay down, cradling his head in the crook of his arm.

The boat groaned in the wind. The dripping continued, a sloshing, pouring sound. Strange; it wasn't raining. He must be hearing the river under the hull. Maybe they were sinking. The river moved somewhere below him, pulling everything downstream, slowly saturating everything it touched, and washing it all away like dirt from a wound.

Keith closed his eyes. The *Susan K* held no secrets after all. It was only a rotted-out, old boat. His thoughts drifted lazily through his mind in a dizzying haze.

Whatever would come, let it come. Let the boat rot away around him. Let the current pull it to pieces. Let it dissolve, and let him sink with it to the bottom of the river. Let the whole marina, the whole world, decay and flow into the sea. Let his father and mother find his bones in the wreckage. Beyond their reach.

Keith could hear footsteps. He knew he was sleeping, but how deeply, he wasn't sure. An acrid smell filled his nose. A voice mumbled in the air around him. The dripping sound had grown louder and faster, like rain, like pouring water, sloshing and splashing. Another voice. Keith opened his eyes. More spilling and splashing. The sharp scent of gasoline or oil in the air. A beam of light passed over the room. Keith froze, his heart beating wildly. He rolled quietly from the bench and under the table, his forehead slamming into the edge of the tabletop on the way down. His head spun with pain. The wood planks of the floor were soft and cold under him. He remembered the knives in the drawer. The beam of light passed over the cupboards across from him, and two sets of feet stopped beside the table. Keith held his breath. Something heavy landed on the table. Something sloshed. Right above him, two men spoke softly. "Spooky. *Susan K* is talking to you."

"Turn off the damn flashlight, will you? You want someone to see us?"

"It reeks in here. We shouldn't be doing this. Let's just untie her, and let her drift downstream."

"No, the boat needs to have enough damage to be totaled out. If we let it drift downstream, probably nothing will happen. Someone will just tow it right back here and charge me for hauling it."

"What about drilling a small hole through the bottom? Let it slowly fill with water. That much water damage should do it."

"No, someone would see it listing to one side. Come on, we're almost done."

One of the men slid the sloshing container off the table with a scrape, and they moved away. More splashing.

"Watch your feet, dipshit. That's enough. Let's go."

"Shouldn't you write something in the captain's log? You know, like 'High winds today, three hundred knots bearing southeast, and the boat is on fire.'"

Stifled laughter. One of them made his way up the ladder. The other paused and spoke. "Goodbye to you, Sue," he said, "if you can hear me, if there's any life left in you."

Keith's heart pounded in his ears. The other voice said to shut the hell up, and the heavy shoes clanged up the ladder. Keith waited until he was sure the two men were on the level above him, then he crawled out from under the table. His feet sloshed through cool puddles on the floor. He felt his forehead and licked the blood from his fingertips. The fumes in the air made his head spin. He pressed his temples between both hands. All the light was gone. The moonlight had faded, behind a cloud maybe. Even the darkness spun around him. He stumbled into a wall and paused, leaning against it.

He had to think. He remembered the matchbox in his pocket. Maybe just a little light to see by. He pulled out a match and stepped across the moist floor, hands waving in the air, searching for the lantern. If the men were still there, it would be safer to wait. Unless there was someone else on board. Unless the guy had been talking to some woman named Sue. No, that was the name of the boat. The ceiling creaked above his head. Voices laughing. Drops of water raining down from the ceiling, splashing in front of him. No, not water, something slipperier. His heart was pounding. The room was so dark. His hands found the lantern. Maybe he should wait until he knew the men were gone. How long had it been? Creaking upstairs. Maybe he could light the lantern and keep it on low. He pulled a match from the box and shut the lid.

A bright flame fell through the air in front of him, from the top of the ladder to the floorboards below. The air around him surged, and flames poured across the wood floor from the base of the ladder. Footsteps thumped on the level above, and a door slammed shut with a bang.

Keith stumbled backwards, away from the approaching flames, and fell into an open closet full of coats and rain gear. He pulled the coats tightly around himself. The smell of mildew filled his mouth and nose. The air was thick with heat. He sank deeper into the coats, his head pounding and his lungs dry.

His hands passed over his arms and face. No burns. Just blood on his forehead. His feet were dripping. He breathed deeply but couldn't get enough air. What had he done? Had he lit the match? The flame had seemed to fall from the ceiling. What had he done? The coats pressed in around him. He had to get out of here. The men were gone now. Or maybe they would see the fire and come back and see what he had done. Maybe he should wait. Steve and Jessica would probably see the flames and go get help. No, they were long gone. He couldn't breathe. He had to get out.

The coats! Keith yanked a long, hooded raincoat from its hanger and hunched low, pulling his arms through the sleeves. He could see the orange light of the fire through the gaps in the clothes around him. His hands searched the floor for shoes. Nothing.

Still hunched low, Keith wiped at his feet with a shirt he found on the floor. It was easier to breathe down by the floor. He had to get out into the fresh air. Keith pulled the hood over his head and stepped out into the room.

The brightness blinded him for a moment, and pain ripped through his feet and up his legs as he dashed toward the base of the ladder. He climbed, his feet slipping on the metal rungs until he pulled himself up to the next floor where he dropped to his knees, removing the long coat and using it to pound out the flames that flicked from his legs. The skin of his feet screamed in pain wherever he touched them. An orange glow came through cracks in the wood floor. Keith dashed down the hall and burst out the back door, taking in fresh air with short, rapid breaths. Smoke poured out of cracks in the topside cabin and billowed past him.

His feet throbbed with pain and glistened a little in the moon-light, smoke rising from them. No, the smoke was rising from the floor of the deck. He ran toward the stern ladder. Smoke poured around him in a black cloud, filling his lungs, stinging his eyes.

Keith dropped into the canoe, untied the line, and pushed off. The windows on the stern of the *Susan K* glowed and flickered as he turned the canoe into the wind and paddled hard upstream. The trawler disappeared into a cloud of black smoke, the pop-ping sounds of the fire within her barely audible under the roar-ing of the wind.

The canoe vibrated when it hit the force of the main current, and Keith tried to backstroke in order to point the bow up-stream. The current and the wind pushed from opposite sides, holding the boat fast on its course toward the opposite shore. Keith moved to the center of the canoe to keep his balance. He dug the paddle into the water and fought to pull the boat around. His arms shook with cold. His feet throbbed in the small pool of water at the bottom of the canoe. The life jacket on the floor rubbed against them and he winced. The paddling was getting him nowhere. He was in the hands of the wind and the river. The marina receded behind him, smoke filling the air, the windows of the *Susan K* glowing with golden light.

Halfway across the channel, he saw there was no use fighting, so he paddled toward the island, cottonwood trees towered over-head along the shore. At night, his tree by the island road was hard to recognize.

By the time his canoe hit the sand, flames were pouring from the windows of the *Susan K*. Maybe the fire would stop, he thought. Maybe it would rain. Keith left the canoe in the water and rushed wildly up the steep slope of the riverbank, his arms reaching ahead, grabbing at roots and grass as he scrambled up. He found his tree and pulled himself up the rope.

The wind pressed him into the trunk. The tree swayed back and forth. He looked down across the water from his perch. The flames had spread to several other trawlers. Keith watched the fire move along the dock like a massive arm crawling upstream.

The wind carried smoke through the lower marina and up into the trees on the mainland. Light flickered on the wall and roof of Jack's house.

Jack. He could almost hear the old man still snoring. Sparks and flames swirled closer and closer to the small house. Several trees along the shore smoked and burst into flame.

The fire was not going to stop. He had to do something. He looked down at the shore for his canoe, but it was gone. He'd forgotten to tie it off. Keith shut his eyes and sobbed into the arm of the coat. His feet burned sharply with every gust of warm wind. His arms grew stiff and numb. Wind rushed by his ears. Minutes went by, or hours, he couldn't tell. He thought he heard an explosion at the marina. His tree swayed—the movement soothing despite how far he could fall before landing in the water or on the rocks along the shore.

The spires of the St. Johns Bridge glowed in the distance.

Keith didn't see the grain barge coming until he heard the horn blow—five short blasts. He opened his eyes. Piles of grain slowed to a stop below him. The beam of a spotlight illuminated the burning dock. Under the sharp gaze of the light, the color of the flames faded. He searched for Jack's house. Where was it? Lights came on in the houses along the marina.

Keith lowered his head and closed his eyes, his chest shaking with sobs. The wind held him against the trunk of the tree. With his eyes still closed, the air suddenly lit up around him, as if he were waking from a dream into the light of day. When he moved his hands away from his face, the light grew brighter, burning against his closed eyelids, filling his head with a new kind of pain. He held tightly to the tree, turned to face the island, and slowly opened his eyes. The leaves beside him glowed a brilliant white.

Don't look into the light! The thought echoed in Keith's mind. Don't look into the light! He wouldn't. He would tell his father later about how the barge's spotlight had been there, and he had turned and looked the other way.

When Jack woke, the cracked ceiling raged with an orange light. White flakes like snow danced above his head. Skookum was barking. Jack could smell the smoke. He reached his hand out for the wall and saw his wavering shadow, the shape of a man reaching up from his own funeral pyre.

He pushed himself up, swung his legs over the edge of the bed, and winced at the sharp pain in his knees, back, and neck. Light danced along the walls. The doorknob and hinges flashed blinking reflections of the flames shining through the windows. Skookum waited by the door, her tail knocking rapidly into the wall.

Someone shouted outside.

Jack looked down. He was still in his trousers. He'd been wearing the same T-shirt for two days, or three—he'd lost count. He opened the wooden door and then the screen door, shutting it quickly behind him before the dog could get through. She barked. Jack stepped into the light and the heat and saw two silhouettes against a blazing fire, a man and woman standing between the front deck of the house and the wall of flames beyond them. No, it was a boy and girl. They'd soaked their coats in water on their way to the end of the dock—steam rose from their shoulders, wisping above them like wings. It was the Millers' kid and some girl. The boy was shouting. Jack waved for them to come over.

Wind was blowing the flames away, but the heat and smoke and ash still swirled around them. Flames poured from the boats and the dock and the grass along the shore. Blue flames. Red flames. Flames too bright for color. The two kids were wet, shaking, and shuffling their feet. Jack reached for a roll of the line that hung from pegs outside his house. He shouted for the boy to go get the ax from a trunk around back. The boy disappeared. The girl turned to face the fire, warming herself. Jack pulled the slipknot and the line fell in a loose pile at his feet. The boy returned hefting the ax with two hands. Jack said, "Follow me."

They made their way toward the heat of the flames to where the stringers of the house were attached to the dock with rusted chains and turnbuckles at either corner. No time to twist the turnbuckles loose. "Go pull that power cord!" he shouted to the kid and stepped stiffly down onto the stringer, placing his feet on opposite sides of the chain. "Stand back," he said to the girl. When the boy was back on deck, Jack told him to hold on to something, lifted the ax as high as he could with both hands, and brought it down. The blade glanced off the chain and sank into the wet wood underneath. He pulled to free the blade and winced. It remained stuck.

"You goddamn old man!" He shouted, climbing stiffly back up on the deck of his home. He met the boy's gaze and nodded once toward the ax handle. The boy jumped down and wrestled the blade free, then drove it down through the chain with a loud "thwack." The corner of the house came loose from the dock with a lurch, and they began to swing away, the whole home pivoting on the one remaining chain. Jack grabbed the line where he'd let it drop and started winding it around a large cleat under the deck rail. He looked up just as the boy swung the ax down toward the second chain and missed. The handle cracked and the ax head splashed into the river.

"Well, that's just great, kid. I should have asked your girlfriend to take care of it."

"She's my cousin," he said. Sparks and ash swirled between them. The boy stared down at the chain.

"Don't just stand there! Make yourself useful. Go piss on that fire or something." Jack wound several half hitches around the deck cleat and pulled the line tight.

The girl stepped onto the stringer next to her cousin and took the ax handle from him. She slid the handle through a gap in the rusty turnbuckle and pulled the handle counterclockwise. The turnbuckle creaked and twisted.

"Atta girl!" said Jack. The boy leaned down and helped his cousin pull the handle. Jack watched the fire. "It's gonna take too long. Climb on up." They pulled the handle loose and stepped onto the deck of the houseboat. Jack told the boy to go around to the side of the house where he'd find a Danforth and a chain in a small, wooden crate. The boy shook his head and shrugged.

"Danforth, dipshit." Jack shouted. "A fucking anchor. You know, sticks in the mud at the bottom of the river? Go! Go! Go!"

The young man didn't move. He pointed at Jack with the broken ax handle. "I'm the one who came to wake you up, old man. I came to save you."

Jack stormed back into the house and came out with the shotgun. The boy looked around frantically. He jumped back over the stringer and onto the burning dock. Flames roared behind him. Jack walked brusquely to the edge of the deck where the boy had been. Standing over the chain and bracing one leg against a railing, he brought the stock to his shoulder and sighted down the barrel, aiming for the center of the taut chain. The gun exploded and the chain wrenched free.

"Get on, unless you want to swim!"

The boy jumped over the water and onto the deck, slipping and rolling onto his back. The girl reached to help him up.

They stood for a moment, watching the dock slowly recede. They were underway, the current taking them into the wind. Jack wrapped the line around the cleat several more times. Then the boy was at his side again, coughing, dropping the crate with the anchor onto the deck.

Jack asked him, "You know your knots? Can you tie a bowline?"

"Not really."

"Not really? Just say 'no' if you can't do it."

"OK, no."

"You?" he looked at the girl. She shook her head.

"Here." He fed the line through a loop in the anchor chain and handed the loose end of the line to the boy. "You feed the line through the chain. Hold both ends like this. Now, make a loop in the standing end. No, that one. No, twist the loop the other way. OK, take the free end and feed it through the loop. Now: rabbit comes out of the hole, goes around the fence, goes back into the hole and pull it tight. There you go."

The sound of the fire was fading. The flickering light grew dim and smoothed over their faces. "There's a lot of things you can go through life without, young man, but a bowline isn't one of 'em. Now you'll never forget that knot if you live to be three hundred years old, will you? Might even save your life someday."

The boy nodded and started to say something, but Jack turned and walked toward the side of the house, the gun dangling from his hand by the barrel. He spoke loudly over his shoulder. "Wait another thirty seconds and then drop that anchor in the drink. I'm going 'round back to get the skiff started. Come on over when you're done unless you want to hang here in the current playing with yourself. I'm going to check on the rest of the marina."

The boy stood up, the line still in his hands, and called after Jack. The dark night drew close in the air around them. "I'm sorry," he said.

Jack stopped but didn't turn around. "It's twenty-five seconds now, kid," he said. "You take that sorry, and that anchor, and you throw them in the damned river where they belong. Come on back when you feel the Danforth dig in." Jack opened the screen door and set the gun on the floor just inside. "No, Skook! No vámanos!" He walked toward the back of the house. "And hold on to something!" he shouted. Just before the screen creaked shut, Skookum bolted out. She stopped short when the door slammed home, stared once at the children, and followed Jack around to the back of the house.

The boy dropped the anchor into the water with a splash. The girl reached out and hugged him close. Over the surface of the river, just downstream, the bright horn of the grain barge sounded in the night air.

Jack rounded the corner of the house and stopped.

Where the skiff was usually tied to the back deck there was only dark water and small waves splashing against the stringers. The cleats were gone, likely ripped from the moist wood of the deck when the house had come loose from its moorings. Skookum skidded to a stop beside him and looked up at the old man's face.

The deck beneath Jack's feet shivered as the anchor in the water searched for a hold. He scooped up the dog and held on to a handle at the corner of the house just as the deck beneath his feet rumbled and lurched to a stop.

Everything resting against the back wall of the house skidded and fell, crashing like a roll of thunder onto the deck and sliding off into the water: his storage cabinet of tools, several deck chairs, a short stack of firewood, and an empty cooler. Around the corner of the house came the sound of another splash and a loud shout. Skookum scratched at Jack's arms and chest, squirming from his arms.

The girl floated by, mere feet from where Jack stood. Dark strips of hair or blood covered the half of her face Jack could see as she rolled and rested facedown in the water. Another shout and a splash from around the corner. In one swift movement, Jack swept the life preserver from the wall where it hung and tossed it in the direction of the girl. The boy appeared in the water, sliding by quickly in the swift current, paddling sideways toward her. "Kid can barely swim," Jack said to himself and then yelled with his hands cupped over his mouth: "Go kid! Get the ring on the way! Yell 'OK' when you get her secure and I'll pull you in!" He thought maybe the boy nodded, but it might've been his lurching sidestrokes.

He shouted again, just in case, "Put the ring over her head and under at least one of her arms!"

The lifeline unraveled smoothly, almost without a sound. The two forms in the water passed into the darkness, out of range of his hazy vision. Jack stepped back again as the line snapped taut against the stainless steel ring it was bolted to on the corner of the house. It hummed a like a long piano wire.

Jack placed both hands on the line and pulled, trying to discern the amount of weight on the other end. It was heavy. All that current. Plus the weight of both kids, hopefully. No. It must be too soon. Jack closed his eyes and let the slack out of the line slowly so as not to jostle it any more than the weight and movement of water already did.

The wind whistled over the roof and around the corner of his home. He looked downstream into the dark. He cupped one hand over an ear. Was that a voice? How long would it take? Best not to pull the line in yet. They were either secure at the other end of the line, or they weren't. Or one of them was. Or neither. If he pulled at the wrong moment, while the boy was balancing one hand on the ring or securing the girl, they could slip, and the current would take them away. They wouldn't have a chance. He would lose them. That idiot kid never should have jumped in without a line or a life jacket. Without a way back. He could barely keep his own body up in the water with that lame-ass swimming technique, and he'd have to keep the girl's head above water too.

"You idiot!" Jack yelled. About who he wasn't sure. He tried to listen over the sound of wind in his ears. Nothing. It had been several full minutes, maybe. If she was bleeding from her head, Jack couldn't wait forever.

A strong yank carried up the line. Slack. A few more yanks and then nothing. Pull it in? Something made him hesitate. Pull, thought Jack, but his arms, stiff and aching, wouldn't obey him. Another few yanks. Firm. Deliberate. A word formed in Jack's mind. The voice of a friend in a long-lost language.

No.

"No," in Morse code. He must have imagined it. He waited. More slack. Jack closed his eyes and waited. His knuckles and palms ached. He lightened his grip.

More tugs on the line and a pause.

O.

And again.

K.

OK. Jack tightened his hands around the line and pulled hard, hand over hand. He pulled and pulled, letting the line loop on the deck beside him, keeping his feet clear.

Jack's hands were getting numb, his fingers locking up. He pulled anyway. The bright white of the ring came into focus, and then a dark shape on the water. Jack pulled. The shape formed into two shapes. The two of them were there. Jack kneeled painfully and pulled in the last ten feet. Then five.

The girl's eyes were open. Wide open. In shock. Her head poked up from the center of the ring, and one arm was draped around it. The boy tried to lift her up toward the deck. Jack lowered himself onto his stomach and reached out over the water.

He grabbed the ring, pulled it into the crook of his elbow, and reached his free hand under her other arm to pull her up. She held his arms tightly until she was on deck, clinging tightly to his chest.

"OK," said Jack. "You're alright. You're gonna be OK."

He propped her against the wall and returned to the edge to help the boy up. The kids huddled in each other's arms, both of them crying.

Jack rolled onto his back, his chest rising and falling rapidly. He coughed several times.

His voice came out barely above a whisper. "You did good, kid." He lay there on his back and closed his eyes. For how long, he wasn't sure. It hurt him to breathe.

When he opened his eyes, the boy was standing above him. "You OK?"

"Yeah, kid. I'll go get the first aid kit." He paused. "But you'll need to help me up first."

The lights of St. Helens were blinking on to start the day—or off, for the same reason. Chad had given up on sleep. He couldn't keep Barry out of his mind. He climbed up on deck, loosened the mooring lines, and raised the sails as daylight increased on the eastern horizon just above the Cascades. He turned toward the mouth of the Multnomah Channel and adjusted the sails.

The channel was a thin strip of water that passed through the forests and farmlands of Sauvie Island before it met the Willamette. Without the chart book, Chad didn't know what the channel would bring. Even with Barry's charts, he wouldn't know every rock or every floating log.

He made his way around the peninsula, giving it a wide berth to avoid the sand and pylons on the downstream side of the island. From the Columbia, the Multnomah Channel looked more like a small bay. You could go right by it if you didn't know it was there. He aimed the bow for it and adjusted the sails. He passed between the two islands, pulling away from the main current of the Columbia, listening as the bow of the boat sliced through the channel's smooth surface. He glanced ahead and from shore to shore, searching again for white markings on rocks and trees or the sliver of a red boat just above the waterline. He resolved to renew the search for her after returning home, even if finding her would crush him. She could still surprise him. They might still both be searching and hoping.

An hour later, Chad passed by Coon Island, his halfway point back to the marina, and the wind started to pick up. He pulled his hood over his head and kept the shores an equal distance away.

There was a faint smell of smoke on the wind. At first he thought it must be farmers burning the fields on Sauvie Island, or burning garbage, or even fires in fireplaces. But it had been a hot, dry week, and field burning was probably prohibited. No one was likely to be heating their home, even on a cool, blustery morning like this one.

Chad squinted into the sun as it crept out from behind a cloud. There was a dark shape on the water up ahead. It was difficult to tell its size or judge his distance from it. A pylon from an old dock long gone perhaps, or maybe a buoy. He kept one hand on the tiller in case he needed to swerve. But it was bigger than a buoy. Also it had been nearer the shore a minute ago, and now it was in the center of the channel. Something afloat, then. He loosened the sail halyards to let the sails drop, and he started the engine to better control his speed as the object approached. Soon, he could make out a square deck below the upright rectangular shape. A smokestack or a pilot house.

It was Jack's skiff. Unmanned and spinning in the current. Had it come loose in the wind and drifted downstream? Was Jack laying on deck, unconscious or dead? Chad aimed the bow of the sailboat at the port side of the skiff, put the engine in neutral, and locked the tiller to keep on a straight course. It was approaching fast. He'd be passing right by the skiff in less than ten seconds.

He leaped onto the deck from the cockpit, dodged the flapping mainsail, and unlashed the cords that held his long pole with the hook at the end of it. He usually used it to push off rocks if they came too close, or to fend off other boats. As the skiff passed by his bow, he grabbed the standing rigging on the port side with his left hand and hung out over the water with the pole in his right. Hooking the deck cleat on Jack's skiff, he held on while the momentum of the sailboat and the skiff slowed. The hook at the end of the pole slipped free, causing the skiff to spin. He rushed toward the stern and reached again with the pole as the skiff spun closer. This time, the momentum of the two crafts wasn't working as hard against him, and when the hook caught the lip of the skiff's deck, it held. Chad pulled the skiff closer and used the stern line on his boat to secure it. Jumping aboard Jack's boat, he secured another couple lines and let down several small bumpers to cushion the two vessels. Jack's bow and stern lines hung in the water, the torn out dock cleats dangling from the ends.

Chad climbed back into his own cockpit, put the engine in gear, and pushed the throttle up until the engine roared. He sped upstream, pushing up a wake despite knowing the damage it could cause to the river banks, docks, and boat houses that slid by along the shore.

Chad squinted into the wind. The smell of smoke was getting stronger. He glanced to starboard every few seconds at the sound of the jostling skiff. Peering ahead, he saw more shapes on the water. He locked the tiller again and leaned over the side with the pole. Wood. A large bin. A trunk. A thermos. What the hell? They slid off the pole and drifted by. Nothing worth turning to retrieve, so he returned to the helm. More detritus floated by as the minutes wore on. Something had happened. A fire. They might still be in trouble up ahead. He was at the last couple bends in the channel before Rock Creek.

The smell of smoke materialized into a thin haze. Another large shape formed up ahead. It was a house. A floating home, drifting out in the main current. He leaned on the tiller and brought down the throttle. His boat passed the house to port. Water splashed over the front porch and the current swished around its sides—it wasn't drifting after all. Chad eyed the taut chain on deck that disappeared at an angle into the water. The familiar structure suddenly took on a recognizable shape despite its unfamiliar moorings. This was Jack's house. The front door opened, and Jack limped out, followed promptly by Skookum. Jack raised a hand into the air and waved. Chad pulled up alongside the porch and put the engine in neutral. He reached for the stern line beside him and tossed it down. Jack snatched it from the air.

"Is that Chad?" Jack shouted over the wind.

"Hey!" Chad hurried over the deck and tossed Jack the bow line. "Jack! Taking your house out for a stroll? What the hell is going on?"

Jack shook his head and smiled. "You little pissant, what took you so long? You nearly missed the whole show."

"Shit, Jack, your house is at anchor in the middle of the river."

The screen door opened again, and two young people emerged, arms around each other's shoulders. They were covered with blankets, and they too were limping.

Chad recognized the boy. "Hey, that's Steve, right?"

Jack said, "Come on, you gotta help me get these two back to the marina. You've probably gathered there was a fire on the dock. Not too bad, really. Just the lower marina. The smoke has died down some. We heard a bunch of helicopters and emergency boats upstream around the bend, but no one's bothered to come look for us yet. These two probably could use some medical attention. They're getting pretty cold."

Chad reached down and helped the two kids into the cockpit. Their clothes were damp, and they huddled close, teeth chattering. He helped them down into the cabin and said, "I'll be down in a minute to turn on the stove. Oh, and light the propane heater."

Chad leaned toward Jack and reached out his hand. Jack frowned and looked down at his feet. Then he looked up and said: "Permission to come aboard?"

Chad reached further toward Jack. "Get up here, you big dope."

It took several tries pulling—eventually Chad had to bring a wooden box out of the cockpit locker and toss it down so Jack could stand on it and Chad could pull him aboard.

Chad asked him, "Can you light the propane down in the cabin for those two? There are matches in one of the galley drawers."

Jack looked at him. "My fingers can't do shit with matches anymore."

Chad looked up and reached for the lantern where it hung from the boom between them. A small yellow flame still flickered in the wind. "Better yet, take the lantern down. You can use it to get a match going."

Jack nodded once, turned, and stepped down into the cabin.

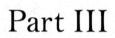

Part III

Twelve

Saturday morning, two days after the fire, Jack's house still hung
from its anchor in the current downstream from the marina. The
news helicopters and vans from Portland had come and gone,
moving on to some other local story since the possibilities in
this one seemed to have dried up. Steve and his cousin Jessica
gave several interviews and said Chad's and Jack's names on
the air, which pissed Jack off quite a bit. The newspeople tried
to approach Jack inside the marina store with cameras rolling
to get him to talk about the fire, about his history in the place,
about how he felt about everything, but Jack turned up the heat
in his vocabulary until they finally turned the cameras to Chad,
who said, "No. Sorry, but no." The familiar, made-up face of the
woman with the microphone reached into her pocket and fished
around for something.

"I'm prepared to buy a round of snacks from this marina store
for everyone here if you'd . . ."

Chad interrupted her. "Be my guest, but the answer is still no."

Jack said, "What my polite protégé here is trying to tell you is
'Go fuck yourself.'"

The woman was about to speak again but changed her mind
and left the store instead.

The news team tried to get Keith to talk about how the fire
started, but his dad said, "No cameras." Rumor had it Keith was

on the *Susan K* the night of the fire. The barge pilot found him on the island, stunned. He didn't talk, even to his father and mother, for a whole day after.

In the two days since the fire, dozens of tenants congregated at the store in the morning and late into the night, drinking coffee or beer and telling and retelling their fire stories: what had woken them up, what so-and-so had been shouting, the boxes and clothes and TVs they'd been hauling frantically onto shore, what they'd smelled in the air, what they'd told or not told the reporters. Some people spoke in hushed tones. Often, the whole crowd was quiet while they listened to one person tell their version. Often people spoke with heavy hearts or tears in their eyes. There were people there whom Jack had never seen, boat owners who lived far away and hadn't come to check on their boats for years. Everyone claimed a piece of the suddenly clear sense of solidarity in the air.

Chad quickly sold out of beverages. Dory ran two trips into Scappoose on Friday for Budweiser and Red Dog, and once more for coffee.

There was a precariousness about the place, a renewed sense of the movement of water underfoot. No one could sleep. Thoughts and tongues and homes had lost their moorings, and life dangled by a thin line anchored unseen somewhere in the mud at the bottom of the river. Each breath and each word spoken or heard was venerated and shared again and again, and words hung in the air like ripe fruit ready to be plucked and savored.

Old faces came out of hiding. Grudges were dropped or temporarily forgotten. Everyone wanted to hear what everyone else had to say too badly to let tension—or sobriety—get in the way. Folks Jack usually cared not to speak to or even look at now extended their hands toward him, clapped him on the shoulder, or passed him a cold, unopened can of beer. Jack told about what happened over and over until his voice was hoarse.

Chad was so busy in the store and on the fuel dock that he was unable to stop for long to consider whether or not he liked the sudden shift in the marina. He let it be what it was and wondered to himself what it would become as time passed.

Employees from the boatyard worked through the weekend at the still-smoldering lower marina. Rick called Tricia down to the store to give her the insurance claims he wanted her to pore over, looking for loopholes. She said she had her hands full with boat repair requests, but Rick couldn't let go of his urgency about beating insurance companies at their own game.

Finally, Tricia said, "Alright, Mr. Magoo, I'll send you the invoice for the equipment I'll purchase for your insurance investigations. A high-speed internet connection is a must, and a new laptop so I can keep up the work in the evenings and on weekends. I'll meet with a couple insurance agents—really pull the wool over their eyes by buying them lunch. I'll just bring my company credit card. Don't worry. If there's hot water out there, I'll be getting you out of it. Oh, and I wasn't going to report any overtime hours for this past week, seeing that we're all working around the clock more out of concern for this place and for each other, but I wouldn't want to leave you indebted to me. I just couldn't do that to you." She picked up her crate full of files, ignoring Rick's protestations on her way out the door. "I have to go! No time for pleasantries," she said and was gone.

Late in the morning on Saturday, the men from the boatyard used a tug to move Jack's house from where it hung at anchor. There was no room left in the lower marina for mooring the house. The downstream end was only charred remains of boats, houses, and storage units—where the main walk had been, only the stringers were left, bobbing in the water, orderly rows of thick, black nails sticking out of them like jagged bones. The Coast Guard had set up a long, yellow boom around the area to contain the spilled fuel and debris. As the tug pulled him upstream, Jack watched from the front deck of the house while demolition cranes took apart the dock. At Jack's request, the men from the boatyard made a space for his home on the upstream side, up the main walk from the fuel dock. "That way," said Jack, "I'll be able to see every last piece of bullshit that comes floating toward this place."

With the help of twice as many hands as necessary, Jack's house was secured. When he plugged his power cord into the new power meter at the end of the dock and the porch light above his front door flickered on, the small clutch of ash-covered dock workers applauded and cheered as if Jack had just dazzled them with an impossible magic trick. Jack stepped through the front door, thanked them all, and shut the door behind him. The men slowly filed away and returned to the lower marina. Jack sat down in the rocker and looked at the old walls that needed new paint and at the strange, new sights outside each window. Looking through a window that now faced the western shore, he had a good view of an abandoned osprey nest at the top of a piling fifteen or twenty feet away.

He thought about how the fire had taken everyone's attention away from Barry's departure, how no one seemed to even notice his absence. And only a few people seemed to remember that Marge had disappeared nearly a week ago and that she was still nowhere to be found. Dory had found a cryptic note in her mailbox from Marge saying she would send word when she could, but Dory seemed as confused as everyone else—if she knew more, she wasn't likely to be able to keep it to herself.

Now that he was alone and the dock had quieted down a little, Jack felt the pain in his lungs more. He tried one deep breath and had to stop and cough. He needed to get his mind busy, or he was going to start feeling sorry for himself, so he decided to check up on Barry's boat. Make sure it wasn't taking on water in Barry's absence. He stepped outside and walked over to the slip, keys in hand. They would be neighbors now if Barry ever made it back.

Jack found the spiral-bound notebook on a table in the midst of several stacks of books. He tried on a pair of reading glasses resting on top of the stack. Inside were journal entries scrawled in pencil. Jack flipped to the middle of the notebook and read. It stopped him short for a while, his eyes straining over the letters. Making his way back to his house, he opened the refrigerator—his stash of beer was about gone again.

He realized he'd brought Barry's notebook back with him and looked out his window, as if afraid someone had seen him. He could take the journal back later, he decided, after dark. He wondered if Barry was really the one who'd composed the words.

Quiet, that one.

Sitting in his rocker, Jack read the words again:

Sunday, July 27, 2003

Some things can't be fixed or healed once they are broken. Some things, or people, get hurt or broken and then just stay the way they are, just keep breathing though they don't know why anymore or what light might still be growing or fading inside them.

I have a hunch the world is darker than I could ever imagine and there is less reason for hope than I am able to see. It makes me grateful there is only so much I can see, and I am left mostly with questions. Grateful, also, that hope is not a reasonable thing. Though I have seen my share of dark- ness, I am spared perceiving much of it. And here is why I hope beyond a reasonable doubt: I think that as the darkness grows, it makes the dim lights that are left seem brighter. And the darker it gets, the brighter the light appears, until it is so luminous, eventually, even falling shadows are filled with it.

I remember one of my first masses, while I was giving the homily, rain began coming down wildly. It pelted the roof, and I spoke louder and louder to be heard above it. It was one of those moments you don't get taught how to handle in seminary, one of those unmanageable times when you have your responsibility before you, but there is no appropriate way to continue in it. The clatter on the roof went on, and I saw that something bigger than responsibility was presenting itself, and the only way to proceed was to acknowledge it. I stopped mid-sentence and looked up at the faces in the room through air still thick with incense. The congre- gation had grown very still, even the children, and the rain roared like a thunderous applause. I knew if I was going to speak again, I would either have to wait or speak louder than I ever had. I looked up to the sky, and when I finally looked back down and still didn't speak, everyone smiled as if in relief.

The pause in my homily couldn't have lasted very long, but it is all I remember of that day—one of the few things I remember of the short time after seminary and before the war. The pounding rain said what needed saying better than I could have—it knew a deeper sorrow and joy and power than I could as a young man who hadn't yet seen the horrors of war. Sometimes I still hear that rain coming down, and I think of my silence there behind the lectern as an act of worship rather than one of inhibition or fear.

I don't remember what happened after the rain calmed down. I assume it must have at some point. It is one of those memories that remains with me, the rains still pounding underneath the sounds and silences of the present. Under it all, the waters are still there, pouring down.

Jack closed the notebook and stared out the window at the abandoned osprey nest. Along the shore, large rocks marked the creek where water drained from the hills above the highway. He read Barry's words again. The current pushed against the upstream side of the house, much stronger here than downstream, where the marina broke it into a confusion of swirls and countercurrents. Here, the force of the river split around Jack's back deck and moved down either side. Through the window on the upstream side, he watched where the river came around the bend in the distance. The house had been turned 180 degrees, and the window where he'd sat waiting for the red speedboat no longer faced the river or the Sauvie Island shoreline. Maybe he'd mount a No Wake Zone sign on the outside of that upstream wall tomorrow, get Marge's help to paint a skull and crossbones next to the words. That woman could paint anything. But, he remembered, Marge was gone. Somewhere. What had made her go? He needed to go into town for a haircut. Maybe the doctor.

Jack browsed a little more in the journal but stopped reading when his eyes began to ache. Chad stopped by soon after to say he'd gone to see Barry at the hospital. The nurses told him Barry had been taken to a different hospital yesterday for a heart transplant and that he was in good hands. Chad also brought news concerning Marge's boat.

"Two guys were poking around on it, and I went over there right as they were cutting her padlock off the hatch door. Turns out they were from a brokerage, and they showed me insurance papers and the boat's title and their licenses. I asked a million questions until I was sure they were legit. They said Marge had authorized them to sell her property. I asked if they could give me a contact number for her, but they wouldn't, for legal reasons. They finally leveled with me and said they didn't know where she was. They were just doing this job on the way to the next one. So, other than the cryptic note she left for Dory before Barry's heart attack, we've still got nothing to go on."

When Chad was about to leave, Jack handed him Barry's journal. "Drop this off at Barry's boat, if you could. Just set it on the table. I'll leave it up to you whether you want to take a peek in there if you feel like having your socks knocked off."

"What is it?"

"You can figure that out on your own. Boy, another writer is all we need. I don't know if I'm gonna be able to stomach you guys. Pretty soon it's gonna be like Chicken Soup for the Sailor's Soul around here."

The store was quiet later that evening when Jack stepped in and made his way over to the beer fridge. A rainstorm had moved in. The past few days, there'd been a crowd in front of the store, but now the dock was empty. Rick was at his desk talking to the boy Keith and the boy's father. Rick lowered his voice when Jack arrived, but he overheard something about an insurance claim and forms they'd need to fill out. Rick waved toward him and said, "Make it quick, Jack. I've got to finish up some business with these two, and it's fairly confidential, so . . ."

The boy's father spoke. "My answer is still going to be no. I don't care what documentation you've worked so hard on. I'm not going to sign it. This is my son's life you're talking about. He is not going to take the blame for this."

Rick smiled and spoke quietly, but Jack could still hear him. "If that continues to be the only way you're able to interpret this, you'll be dragging things out at the expense of your son. We could talk it through without needing to involve mediation. The most the boy will have to do is a dozen or so hours of community service, and it would basically drop there."

Keith's father rubbed his face in his hands and wondered out loud if odd jobs around the marina would qualify as community service so that he wouldn't have to take even more vacation time off work to shuttle Keith around town.

"Hold on, hold on." Rick interrupted him. "Jack. You almost done over there?"

Jack paced toward the desk in slow, even steps. He pulled up a chair, sat next to Keith, and folded his hands on his lap.

"What are you doing?" Rick asked.

"You wanted a mediator. I'm your mediator."

The boy sat wide-eyed, gazing from his dad's face, to Jack's, and then back to his dad. He sat on a wooden stool, his bandaged feet dangling just above the ground, his life jacket moving faintly as he breathed.

Rick propped his elbows on the armrests of his chair and chuckled. "Jack, this really isn't any of your business."

"Like hell it isn't. I'm not just counsel tonight, Rick. I'm also a witness. You think I don't know what was going on down there at the end of the marina? I've seen that Robinson guy on his *Susan K* and he ain't been fixing it up for sale. Everybody knew that guy was gonna try and sink his own boat. In fact, I saw him down there the night of the fire, in case you hadn't heard. Saw him running off down the dock before the fire started to spread. Why do you think nobody can get hold of Robinson now?"

Keith's dad looked from Jack to Rick. "Well, now, isn't that interesting?"

Rick said, "Listen, guys. There is no mystery about what happened or how it happened. Keith was clear about that. He confessed to lighting a match before the fire started, isn't that right, young man?"

Keith looked at the floor. "Yeah. But there were other guys there on the boat too."

Rick sat up straight. "What? What guys? You mean your friends?"

"No, not my friends. There were two guys. I tried to light a match after they left."

His dad put a hand on his shoulder. "We went over this. Did you try to light it, or did you really do it?"

"I don't know. I think I did. I'm really trying to be honest about it."

Jack asked Keith, "Where did you get the matches? Did you bring them on board with you?"

Rick glared. "Are you trying to steer the boy's account?"

"Come on, Rick. Let him answer."

"In a drawer on the boat," Keith said. "On the *Susan K.*"

"Do you still have the matches?" asked Jack.

"I think I do. They're probably still in my coat pocket. Yeah, they're right here."

"Let me see those," said Rick, reaching across his desk.

The boy's dad said, "No thanks. I think we'll just take a look at them ourselves. Keith. Show us what you did when you tried to light the match."

The matches were old and brittle. They broke into pieces when Keith tried to strike one on the soft side of the box.

Rick stood. He said, "This is not the way this is going to go …"

Keith's father lifted his son into his arms and carried him toward the door. "We're done talking about this, Rick. I'll let you confer with your counsel here, and we'll see you around the docks. Goodnight."

When they were alone, Rick wadded up one of the forms and threw it at Jack, who batted it out of the air and laughed.

"What the hell, Jack? What a fucking mess. It'll take years to clear this thing up in courts. You think that Robinson guy is going to confess what he did and take the hit? We all know what happened. It's just paperwork we're dealing with here."

"Paperwork? What about that kid who'd have to grow up innocent without ever knowing it? And what about Robinson collecting money for setting fire to his own fucking rig? I guess the truth doesn't matter around here even when it's staring you in the face."

"What's this about truth? There's only paperwork in this business. And what the hell do you care? Don't you have better things to do than to waltz in here like a damn Kojak? It doesn't suit you, Jack. What are you, one hundred years old now? How much longer am I going to have to put up with you?"

Jack stood, picked up his box of beer, and turned stiffly toward the door.

"Come on, Ricardo, you know you're not getting rid of me. Goodnight. Go ahead and put this half rack on my tab."

"What tab? Oh, hell. That one is on me. But maybe you should ease up on the beer. You don't look too good."

"I'll take it under advisement."

Rick shook his head. "Yeah. See you tomorrow."

Thirteen

Barry's new heart had been donated by a man in his early twenties who'd driven into a telephone pole. Barry's body seemed to be accepting the new organ without too many issues. He could shake his head "yes" and "no," so when Chad came to visit him, their conversation was a little less one-sided. Chad didn't say anything about the journal, but he did sit for a while and read aloud from his William Stafford collection until he saw that Barry was sleeping.

On his way out of the hospital, Chad's cell phone rang. The phone reception was terrible, but Chad could just make out a female voice before the call cut out. She said: "Hey weirdo," and then the line went dead. Chad held out his phone and a scream ripped from his mouth. A man approaching from the parking lot asked if he was alright. Still looking at the phone, Chad said, "Sorry. That was a happy scream. A very happy scream." He tried to call the number back. Busy. Three more tries. Busy. Then his phone rang.

Emma was calling him from the payphone on the dock at Rock Creek Marina. Someone named Dory had given her Chad's number. Emma said, "I asked an elderly curmudgeon sitting here on the dock about you. At first he wasn't going to tell me anything, not even his name. He looks terrible, very sallow, so told him I wanted to check his vital signs."

"Oh boy," said Chad. "If that was Jack, it probably didn't go over very well."

"Well, he thought he could scare me off with a few big-boy words."

Chad could hear Dory's voice in the background shout, "That's right, she's talking to Chad about you, you crap-head! You almost ruined everything!"

Emma said, "Don't worry, I told him to get bent. I said I'd dial nine-one-one for him if he didn't let me listen to his heart and lungs. His dog was nice to me though."

"Stay right there," said Chad. "I'll be there in less than an hour. Dory can show you where my boat is. Wait there for me. Please don't go anywhere."

Chad hopped on his motorcycle and broke half-a-dozen laws of the road speeding back. Dory showed Emma where the *Great Beyond* was moored, and Emma found the hatch unlocked. She searched the bookshelves on board, found a conspicuous paperback romance, pulled it off the shelf, and sat reading outside on one of the cockpit benches. Finally, she heard feet pounding down the dock.

Emma set the book on the bench and hopped down as Chad rounded the corner of the boat slip and reached out for her. She took him in in her arms and whispered, "I'm sorry I didn't meet you. Very sorry."

Chad held her tightly and closed his eyes. "You came here. You waited. How long have you been here?"

"Not as long as you probably waited for me. I had a great time reading one of your romance novels."

"You probably got further into it than I did. I hope it's alright that I'm still hugging you." He went to take a step backward, but she had her hands locked behind his back, and he stumbled forward into her embrace.

"Whoa, sorry," he said. "You're strong."

"I want you to hug me, weirdo. And I want you to kiss me too, before I beat you to it."

They pressed close, their bodies already warm. He leaned forward to kiss her, missed, tried again, and their lips met.

In the distance, a loud cackling voice sounded over the dock. "Woohooo!"

Their faces parted and they opened their eyes. "That would be Dory," he said.

"I can already recognize her voice," she said.

"You didn't show up in Astoria … Or did you follow me and see how utterly devastated I was?"

"I'm sorry," she said. "I was almost there. I really was. But Ko got hurt."

"Oh no." Chad's face darkened.

"He's OK. He fell on a rocky shore on our way down the river and broke his leg. Then I tried to carry him up to the highway and twisted my own leg. It took us hours to get to help. But I'm so sorry I wasn't there."

There were tears in Chad's eyes. He wanted her to see that there were tears in his eyes, so he kissed her again, wetting her cheek.

She whispered, "And I'm sorry I called you a motherfucker."

"No one has ever called me a motherfucker before," he said. "It was kind of sweet, actually, that you cared that much."

"Too much," she said.

"Me too. I got scared. I was an ass."

"I scare people."

"No. Not you. I was so out of my mind scared of what was happening—scared I'd do something stupid."

"You did do something stupid," she said. "You said goodbye."

"I'm done saying goodbye to you."

"You better be, motherfucker."

Keith stepped out of the aft cabin and shielded his eyes from the sun beating through the windows and the open hatch. The clock hanging from the bulkhead told him it was 11:00 a.m.

He knocked on the forward cabin door. No answer. "Dad?" He opened the door. The room was empty. He looked up through the transparent hatch in the forward cabin just as a tangle of lines snaked to the deck above. Ducking reflexively, he walked through the main cabin, up the steps into the cockpit, and looked up as another line fell and pooled at his feet.

"Hey down there, watch out!" His dad slid a large hunting blade into a sheath on his leg. Keith picked up the frayed end of a line.

"Dad? What's going on?"

"Good morning, sleepyhead. If you're hungry, I made bacon and some pancakes. The eggs are probably too cold by now. It's all in the icebox."

"Why are you slicing the lines up there?"

"Just the really tangled lines is all. It's not worth fighting them. I've connected some new lines. In fact, if you aren't going to eat, you could start grinding away at the main halyard winch. I'll feed the new line through the center of the mast down to you. What do you think?"

Keith looked down at the frayed, balled-up lines on the deck and said, "Isn't it a waste of line? You could have soaked these in a bucket of soapy water and loosened them up."

His dad didn't respond.

"Want me to go get Chad? Chad knows sailboats. He knows knots."

Keith looked back up the mast at his dad to see if he was still listening.

His dad said, "It kind of sounds like you know what you're talking about. No, we got this. And we just had to give up on that old line. It's all dried up and hardened. It'll be quicker to let it go and start with fresh new rope that won't chafe and wear out the skin on our hands."

Keith rolled the line between his fingers. His dad was right. Some of it was cracking.

They spent the next hour feeding new line through the blocks and fairleads and through the eyelets in the mainsail. Keith ran the new rope back and forth through blocks to loosen it up. He filled a couple of large, black garbage bags with the old, knotted stuff.

Around lunchtime, Keith sat down in the main cabin and ate cold pancakes in a pool of thick maple syrup. He could no longer make out the scent of bacon through the earthy smell of his dad's fresh coffee. It smelled almost as good as bacon.

His dad was cleaning tools in the galley sink. "Hey, I wanted to ask you something," his dad said. "I've got a plan."

"Am I going to like it?"

"You'll probably make me drag you out of bed, but you'll have a blast with it once we get going." His dad looked intently at his own hands, as if searching for an elusive papercut. "We won't get the boat seaworthy today, but next Saturday I'm going to take you benchmark hunting. I'd like to start doing that Saturday mornings: take the boat out to a new destination and hunt down a benchmark."

"Benchmarks? What are those?" Keith watched his father, who was still gazing at his hands.

"Survey markers. Little solid metal disks with labels and co-ordinates on them. They're mounted on rocks, structures, and monuments. Sometimes they're driven into the ground on long poles. They can get covered up over the years. Some have been missing for decades, and the government could actually use help finding them."

"You'll probably make me wear a life jacket the whole time."

"I'll think about that. But I'm going to do this, and I'm taking our home with us, so you have to come along. You'll have to work, though. Help me sail. Learn to read maps. And if we find any, each of us gets a twenty-dollar bill for every benchmark we track down. To make it like searching for treasure. And so maybe you'll pretend to enjoy it." He looked at Keith, his face wrinkled in worry. Keith struggled to speak. He didn't want his dad to run all his Saturdays. He didn't want his dad to think he pretended to like things. He didn't want him to pay him money to do something fun. And he didn't want to hurt his feelings.

"I won't pretend," Keith said. "I'm in. Ten dollars each is probably enough, though. You don't have to pay me a whole twenty."

"It's a deal."

After Keith finished his lunch, he carried the bags of old line over his shoulder to the dumpsters down the dock, passing Chad along the way.

"Hey, Keith," he said. "Good to see you out and about. Looks like they finally removed those bandages from your feet."

Keith shifted the garbage bags to his other shoulder and looked at his sandaled feet. "Yeah. They're a lot cooler now. And not so itchy."

"I bet. Hey, I saw your dad climbing the mast earlier. You guys alright? Can I swing by and help him work on anything? You guys want help?"

"Nah. Thanks. We're good. He's got me."

The second time Emma met Jack, she held out her hand, and, recognizing it, he recoiled and squinted up at her face. "Oh no, not you!"

Emma smiled and pulled her hand back to hook it around Chad's elbow.

Jack said, "Watch out for this one, Chadwick. Did you know she's a certified nurse? She tried to needle a string through my nostrils to see if I was dead the last time she came slinking around here."

"I bet she didn't," said Chad. "And I bet you were trying real hard not to be a big baby in front of a beautiful young lady."

"If you were anyone else..." But Jack's threat turned into a series of coughs. When he recovered, he said, "OK, ma'am, give it to me straight: does this guy stand a chance? Because I better not hear that you're stringing him along just so you can get a listen to my lungs."

Emma did get a listen to his lungs, and she checked his vitals. "Your lungs sound like a couple of soggy punching bags," she told him.

In the end, the only way Jack agreed to get treatment was for Emma to sign up as his hospice nurse. Jack's health declined quickly after the fire, and they moved a hospital bed aboard his floating home. Skookum rarely left his side.

Fourteen

When a next-day-air package addressed to Chad arrived at Rock Creek Marina, he opened it to find a handwritten note and a football-shaped object shrink-wrapped inside a thick layer of wax paper and tape. He read the note first and was transfixed. Barry tried to get his attention for a good ten seconds before finally resting a hand on Chad's shoulder, startling him.

"You're not going to believe it," Chad said. "You got your knife? Open this."

"What the hell is it?" Barry asked. He picked up the heavy object, and his face softened. He opened the serrated blade connected to his keychain and ran it slowly over the top of the wrapping.

"Careful," said Chad.

"I'm nothing if not careful. Is this your first loaf?"

"Yeah. She stopped baking before I got here."

"Then you smell it first," said Barry, grinning.

Chad pried apart the paper a little, held it up to his face, and breathed in, his eyes rolling back in his head.

"Don't touch it with your nose!" Barry said in an intense whisper.

Chad carefully peeled the rest of the thick paper away and a slip of cardstock, a small label, fell to the counter. Barry picked it up. In the center of a purple background, elegant, fluid text read, "Loaves of Abundance."

"What does the letter say?" asked Barry, giddier than Chad had ever seen him.

"I'll read it to you, but first . . ." Chad came around the counter, headed for the door, "I'll be right back."

"Chad. You've had me just about convinced you're not a complete space cadet, and then you do this kind of thing."

Chad stepped onto Jack's floating home and startled Ko and Skookum from sleep. Both dogs leapt to their feet and barked in unison. Halfway through their lunges in his direction their snarls turned to joyful whines. Skookum returned to Jack's bed. Ko pranced and licked. Jack continued to snore.

"Heel." They didn't heel. "OK, I love you too. Now get out of the way."

Emma wasn't inside, so he went around back and thrust the letter toward her where she sat in a deck chair. "Hey Emma. How are you? I missed you. Read this."

"Keep it down. Jack's asleep," she said.

Chad kissed her on the forehead and handed her the letter. She read it out loud:

Dear Chad,

Greetings. It feels like years since I've seen you or any of the others at Rock Creek. Tell everyone I miss them all!

I tracked down a sourdough starter that matches the old one pretty closely. This is the first of many loaves I hope to send to you all there. See also the form I included to connect you, Chad, to the trust fund I created to help pay for in-home or onboard caregiving for some of the older folks there at the marina. You're the only one I can trust to distribute it fairly. Don't mention it's from me. In case someone else runs across the paperwork in the coming months, the fund is set up on behalf of the "Moe" estate.

The world is warming up, and you can clearly see the waters rising here in Venice. One of the friends I've made is helping to find ways of lifting some of the smaller structures, and they are building up others to be higher, but most of this place as it has existed will be gone in a matter of years. You don't have long. Come visit. Plan to stay as long as you want. There's plenty of bread. There is an abundance of every-thing here, except for time. As declining, dying things go, this place is one not to miss. Send word. I hope to see familiar faces soon.

Affectionately,

Mar

"Wow. That's pretty unreal. So, I notice you didn't bring along any bread with you," said Emma with a sly grin.

Chad smiled. "I'll bring you a slice."

"Forget it," said Emma. "You'll probably wait too long and it'll be gone. I'll walk you back to the store. I need to get up and move anyway."

Chad helped her to her feet and kissed her on the lips and put his arm around her. "I've missed you. How's Jack doing?"

"Don't get me started. His stomach hurts. His ass hurts. He wants the keys to his boat. He called me a 'wench.' I told him that sounded like flirting, and he'd better cut it out, or I would smear ground beef all over his face and lock him in the bedroom with Ko."

"You've got his number. You're amazing," said Chad, and he held her face between his hands and kissed her again.

"Feed me bread," she said.

"It does have whole grains and seeds in it. Not your favorite..."

Emma leaned toward Chad and whispered softly into his ear. "Feed me bread, motherfucker."

"I love the way you put things. Let's go. We'll bring Jack a piece. Give it to him if he plays nice." The door squeaked loudly when he opened it. "You can come too, Ko." Both dogs stepped out, and the door swung closed behind them.

Chad and Emma were about to step down onto the dock when they heard a soft whimper behind them. Skookum hesitated, a few steps back, looking from the house to Chad and back to the house again. Chad held out a hand and said, "Come on, Skook!

Vámanos!" Skookum skittered toward them and fell into step beside Ko as they walked down the dock.

They held their small wedding on Barry's boat. Chad's parents both flew in, and Emma's entire family was there, crowded onto the dock all around. The end of the slip sank down just about level with the surface of the water under the weight of all the people. Barry married them, not so much in his capacity as a priest but as a captain on his own boat.

It wasn't long after that Barry officiated Jack's funeral.

Emma was still getting authorization and paperwork set up for her private caregiving service when Jack died late in the night. She entered the house in the morning, and he was gone—the small, bony, black dog stretched across his blanketed legs whimpering softly.

The following Sunday morning, Barry stood facing the people who'd gathered on the fuel dock. He waited a moment before speaking. Steam rose from coffee mugs and curled in slow, wavering arcs among familiar faces. Water sloshed quietly below his feet. A rumbling diesel engine echoed far upstream. A heron's wings beat loudly, and Barry saw the massive bird soaring away between the masts and pylons.

He spoke louder than most of the people gathered had ever heard him speak, with a tone and cadence that caught their attention.

"I thought it would be good to mark this occasion with a moment of silence. But then I realized silence wasn't really Jack's way of being in this place. Or any place." A few people laughed softly. "He asserted himself into whatever pockets of silence he determined needed to be filled with something: a story, maybe, or a barbed hook of words or a hurtful insult that may have convinced you he didn't care. But of course he cared. You could do worse than to stop and remember the worst thing Jack ever said to you. Jack was a floodwater. When he was near, you might do well to put a life jacket on. At the same time, it feels true to say that as long as Jack was present here, the river was better off. The Mighty Columbia was going to be OK. Now, with him gone, you can only hope. It's going to take a lot of people, and a lot of work, to pick up the slack he left behind. So while silence wasn't Jack's way, maybe we could still pause for a moment anyway and listen. A moment of silence here, where Jack lived most of his life, is never really going to be all that quiet."

Epilogue

The last time Chad saw Jack out of doors was early one morning, several months after the fire. When Chad climbed out the hatch of Moe's boat with a French press filled with coffee and stepped over to Jack's front porch, the old man was already sitting outside in sweatpants and a thick jacket. His eyes were closed. Skookum lay beside him, and beside her was a green oxygen tank. Jack opened his eyes when Chad adjusted the breathing tube under his nose.

"Hey there," Chad said. "I brought some coffee. You up for some?"

"Yeah, I feel too shitty to say no, even to what you call coffee."

Chad went inside and came out with a mug for him. Jack held it but didn't drink. He watched Chad, his eyes moving slowly and sleepily.

Chad drew in a breath, but then he hesitated.

"Spit it out," said Jack.

"I'm thinking about turning the *Arctic Loon* up there into a kind of playground for the kids here at Rock Creek. It's practically a big toy boat, already. I could just make the hole in the hull bigger and put in a ladder, file down any sharp edges. I've got some other ideas about play structures. Maybe it will help to give kids a safe option other than hanging out in life jackets on the dock all day."

Jack sat up and sipped at the coffee. "I knew there had to be at least one good idea rolling around in your brain."

"Also, Emma and I are getting hitched. Now that Barry is back. We need an ordained priest to marry us, right?" Chad took a sip of coffee. "To be honest, it scares me to death. All of it. Living on the water. Committing to this life with someone again."

Jack huffed.

When he didn't say anything else, Chad asked, "What do you think, Jack? You alright with us being around all the time, living so close by?"

Jack looked at him, sat up even straighter, and said: "I thought you were done looking for the world to give you permission to do the shit you'd already made up your mind to do. And don't talk to me about 'commitment is hard.' All you ever do is commit to everything around you with all your heart and soul. Kind of makes some of us feel like shit, actually. Try committing to dying sometime. Now that's a warm bowl of turds. London bridges. Knock me down."

Chad laughed. "I don't know what the hell that means, but it's bat-shit funny." Before he realized what he was doing, words spilled out of him, "I might as well tell you. You know that stupid kid who knocked his mast down running his sailboat into the railroad bridge a few years ago?" Chad paused for a few seconds and pointed his finger at his own chest.

Jack smiled. "You think I didn't know that? You fucked that one up pretty good, didn't you?"

"I did," said Chad, "but there are certain details about what happened that've been exaggerated. Like about me abandoning ship." Jack didn't say anything, so Chad continued. "The girl who got hurt. She and I were married. She usually stayed in the cabin while I worked the deck. Nobody should be sailing by themselves at night with the wind gusting that hard. Especially on the Willamette." He stared into his coffee.

Jack sat forward in his chair. Skookum, on the floor at their feet, had been quiet until now. She lifted her head and looked back and forth between the two of them.

Jack looked at Chad and said, "Why don't you tell me what happened?"

Acknowledgments

I am very grateful to the many friends, proofreaders, editors, and skeptics who have offered their guidance and perspective in the shaping of this novel, especially Michael Demkowicz, Joseph Van Buskirk, Rachel Zasadni, Aaron Scotthorn, and Fritz Lidtke. Heartfelt thanks to professors Daphne Read, Greg Hollingshead, Ellen Bielowski, and Paul Hjartarson at the University of Alberta for their input and encouragement during the initial drafts of this manuscript. Thank you, Daphne, for helping me to limit my excessive use of the word "pile" as a metaphor. There is still much work to be done.

I am extremely thankful to everyone at Ooligan Press for their passion and dedication. I have been inspired by their masterful editing, designing, illustrating, proofreading, marketing, whip-cracking, and up-with-me-putting during the development of this book. I'm especially grateful to Jacoba Lawson for her leadership and careful attention. She is an artist on so many levels.

For their guidance, inspiration, and influence, I want to thank Shelley Reece, Tony Wolk, Kim Stafford, Robin Cody, Tim Kelley, Susan Reese, Joe Pope, Eric Costa, Vince Wannassay, Elizabeth Woody, Ed Edmo, Gina Geary, Norm Wilkins, Skookum, David Robinson, Brooke Jacobson, Katya Amato, Joshua Coles, David James Duncan, Kele Goodwin, Batman, coffee, all the employees over at Forty Five Wines, M&M's, seltzer water, and the greatest Cowboy of them all.

Love and thanks to my family for their patience and generosity. I would say that I am deeply indebted to you all, but you have set me free with your love and grace.

Thanks to the US Coast Guard for their help that one time. ... Well, OK, two times.

OOLIGAN PRESS is a student-run publishing house rooted in the rich literary culture of the Pacific Northwest. Founded in 2001 as part of Portland State University's Department of English, Ooligan is dedicated to the art and craft of publishing. Students pursuing master's degrees in book publishing staff the press in an apprenticeship program under the guidance of a core faculty of publishing professionals.

Project Manager
Jacoba Lawson

Project Team
Maeko Bradshaw
Brendan Brown
Bridget Carrick
Mackenzie Deater
J. Whitney Edmunds
Grace Evans
Emily HagenBurger
Alyssa Hanchar
John Leavitt
Hilary Louth
Elizabeth Nunes
Riley Pittenger
Amylia Ryan
Stephanie Sandmeyer
Nicholas Shea
Julia Skillin
Thomas Spoelhof
Amanda Taylor
Katey Trnka

Acquisitions
Bess Palares
Molly Hunt
Emily Einolander
Jacoba Lawson

Editing
J. Whitney Edmunds
Jacoba Lawson
Nicholas Shea

Copyediting
J. Whitney Edmunds
Jacoba Lawson
Lisa Hein
Gloria Mulvihill
Elizabeth Nunes
Nicholas Shea

XML Coding
Jessica Clark
Jessica DeBolt
Alyssa Hanchar
Lisa Hein
Hope Levy
Hilary Louth
Alyssa Schaffer

Proofreading
J. Whitney Edmunds
TJ Carter
Alyssa Hanchar
Lisa Hein
Hilary Louth
Amylia Ryan
Alyssa Schaffer

Design
Leigh Thomas
Alyssa Hanchar
Jacoba Lawson
Andrea McDonald
Riley Pittenger

Digital
Emily Einolander

Marketing
Jordana Beh

Social Media
Elizabeth Nunes

CPSIA information can be obtained
at www.ICGtesting.com
Printed in the USA
BVOW03s0802180417

481286BV00002BA/2/P

9 781932 010923